# Her happiness turned to terror

When she reached her hotel suite, Tracy could hear the phone ringing inside. She smiled. Shane was probably calling to invite himself up again. She quickly unlocked the door and, by the light spilling in from the hallway, managed to locate the phone.

She picked up the receiver. "It's getting late, Shane," she began. "I think—"

Suddenly Tracy realized she was talking to a dial tone and started to replace the receiver. But then she froze.

Someone else was in the room. She could *feel* it.

Before she could turn on the nearby lamp, a blanket was thrown over her head and she was spun around. Tracy stumbled blindly across the floor, screaming....

## ABOUT THE AUTHOR

Fran Earley, who comes from a newspaper family, had her first article printed at age eighteen and since then has been nominated twice for the Pulitzer Prize in journalism. Now living in Houston with her family, she previously lived and worked in Denver. *Moving Target* is her third book for Intrigue.

## Books by Fran Earley

HARLEQUIN INTRIGUE
52–CANDIDATE FOR MURDER
69–RANSOM IN JADE

# Moving Target
## Fran Earley

## *Harlequin Books*

TORONTO • NEW YORK • LONDON
AMSTERDAM • PARIS • SYDNEY • HAMBURG
STOCKHOLM • ATHENS • TOKYO • MILAN

Harlequin Intrigue edition published October 1987

ISBN 0-373-22076-6

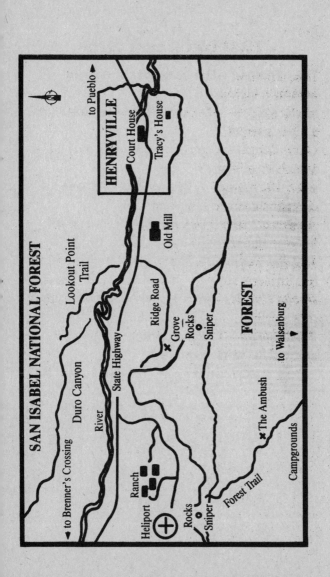

# CAST OF CHARACTERS

*Tracy Hannon*—Her peaceful sheriff's job became a nightmare

*Shane Keegan*—His business decision made him a killer's target

*Oliver Brock*—A consummate politician and associate of Shane's

*Evan MacManus*—The president of Shane's company had a volatile temper

*Alphonse "Alfy" Deschamps*—He was loyal, but also dangerous

*Martina Tatarescu*—She was Alfy's girlfrend, but formerly close to Shane

*Bubba Crowley*—Was Tracy's ambitious deputy trustworthy?

*The Ragman*—The professional hit man enjoyed his work very much

# Chapter One

The client peered through frost-glazed goggles at the man sharing the ski-lift seat. The man was bundled up in a parka, multiple layers of woolens, heavy gloves, ski mask and muffler, but still appeared cold and miserable. "Butcher, baker, candlestick maker," the client muttered self-consciously, although sure no one else was within earshot. The next chair in the lift was twenty feet below them and empty. The client was nervous, all the more so for having to recite this inane bit of doggerel. But the friend of a friend who'd set up this meeting had insisted on the code words. The Ragman was a professional, as much a professional in his field as a doctor or lawyer, and thus could dictate the terms. The client had no choice; he needed The Ragman.

"Everyone dies sooner or later," The Ragman said through lips that were blue-white in one hole of his knitted ski mask.

How true, the client thought. "The financial arrangements are satisfactory?"

"For now."

The client turned away to gaze at the blanket of virgin snow on the mountainside. He knew that The Ragman was wondering how he could milk this arrangement for even more than the agreed-on ten thousand dollars. Well, The

Ragman—what a stupid sobriquet!—was sadly mistaken. Never again would they meet in person. Subsequent contacts would be by phone, the fewer the better. Neither would ever be able to identify the other.

"You know what has to be done?" the client asked.

"More or less. Dimitri said you would furnish the details."

"Of course." This was the difficult part. It had been one thing to make the decision to contact the middleman named Dimitri, but another to spell everything out for a hired assassin. Once that was done, there could be no turning back. The client thought of the ten thousand dollars already paid to Dimitri through a Bahamian bank. The money could be written off as a bad investment, buried in any one of a dozen corporate slush funds. The client could break off the arrangement before it went any further, and no one would be the wiser. No one but the client, the middleman—and The Ragman, of course.

"I am waiting," The Ragman prompted. The Ragman's teeth were chattering in the unaccustomed cold of the mountainside.

"Very well," the client said, finally convinced there was no other way. "This is what I want you to do...."

The Ragman listened without comment.

"Do you see any problems?" the client asked.

"There always are problems," The Ragman said. "Tell me, what sort of law enforcement will I have to deal with?"

The client smiled. "You need not worry. The sheriff is a young woman who is no match for you...."

TRACY HANNON sat astride her horse, one long leg hooked loosely around the pommel of her saddle, and watched in quiet fascination as the runner sprinted along the ridge a quarter mile away. She sensed a poetry to his movement—a gruff, taut poetry of restlessness and determination that proclaimed a special kind of presence. She'd seen him every morning for two weeks as she rode down the rock-strewn trail from Lookout Point. He'd appear at the east end of the ridge at precisely 7:10, his breath a snorting mist of ice crystals against the swirling buttermilk of the November sky. Thirty seconds later, he'd vanish amid the clutter of boulders and scrub oak at the west end of the ridge.

This morning, when Tracy had driven out of town to take Festus for his daily exercise, she had brought along binoculars. A second after the runner came into view, she had the glasses focused on him, and she liked what she saw: a husky, barrel-chested man with powerful, thick-muscled legs and slender hips. He was wearing cut-off jeans and a gray sweatshirt whose hood was drawn into a puckered oval that left only the merest suggestion of a cleanly chiseled, frost-reddened face. Tracy could barely make out tight lips curled ever so slightly in an unwavering half smile. She guessed he was forty, give or take a year. If he were younger, he'd run more slowly, pacing himself. And if he were older, he'd surely have better sense than to come out so early on a raw morning, braving frostbite and the aches and pains of middle age.

Holding the binoculars to her eyes with one leather-gloved hand, Tracy tugged up the shearling collar of her tan suede jacket to ward off the icy breeze. The movement made her lose focus, and by the time she had the glasses trained on the runner again, he was almost at the end of the ridge and had become a blurred silhouette against the bleak sun.

He had to be one of the Denver crowd that had taken over the Donnelly ranch on Gunbarrel Road, bringing with them their black-and-gold helicopters, truckloads of equipment and cadres of highly paid gofers who drifted

into town on Saturday night, drank beer at the Kachina
Inn and fed quarters into the jukebox so they could listen
to the Willie Nelson and Marty Robbins records.

Somehow, though, this man was different. Tracy hadn't
seen him at the Kachina, Henryville's nearest thing to a
singles bar. From afar, he didn't seem the type that went
for fancy embroidered shirts or designer jeans or three-
hundred-dollar, hand-tooled boots. He looked as if he'd
outfitted himself at a war-surplus store that was going out
of business, what with the sweatshirt, frayed cutoffs and
heavy, ankle-high boondockers he wore.

Tracy's Appaloosa shifted about and bobbed its head
down in search of an untrampled clump of grass that might
have survived the early winter. "Easy, Festus," she said,
locking her right leg more securely around the pommel, as
she leaned forward to stroke his black-and-white spotted
neck. "You'll get breakfast back at the barn—okay?"

Festus shifted again, then raised his head and froze, ears
perked, listening.

"All right." Tracy swung her right leg up and over his
reddish-brown mane and thrust her booted foot into the
stirrup. "It's time to get to the office anyway."

She slipped the binoculars into her saddlebag and was
about to touch her spurs to the Appaloosa's spotted flanks
when the sharp crack of a shot echoed across the valley.
She glanced up at the ridge just in time to see the runner
pitch forward.

*Oh, damn!* she thought. *Those deer hunters are at it
again!* She grabbed for the walkie-talkie clipped to her belt
and raised it to her lips. "K double A six-oh-six," she said
crisply. "Any car in the vicinity of the ridge road..."

A jumble of static, then, "What's up, little lady?"

Bubba Crowley was the only deputy on duty. The undersheriff had quit to take a better-paying job in Colorado Springs, one deputy was sick, another had been on

duty all night and had gone off an hour before, and a third was up in the hills, hunting. Bubba Crowley didn't much care for Tracy Hannon, and the feeling was mutual. Tracy had inherited him along with the job and had tried to work with him, but it hadn't been easy. Happily, their relationship would soon be coming to an end.

"Go ahead, little lady. I'm all ears."

Tracy gritted her teeth. She hated being called "little lady," and Crowley knew it. "Your location, Unit Three?" She made no attempt to keep the irritation out of her voice.

"Just pulling up to the Kachina for my morning coffee. Whatcha need?"

"Get over to the ridge road and check out a shooting. This may be an ambulance call. I don't know for sure."

Without waiting for an acknowledgment, Tracy hooked the radio to her belt and pointed the Appaloosa down the trail, toward the creek that ran alongside the highway. She kept a light grip on the reins, letting Festus pick his way carefully through the rocks. The horse slid on braced legs the last few yards to the edge of the creek, then quickly splashed across the cold, clear water and clambered up the opposite bank onto the highway.

As Tracy reined in and listened for any traffic that might be coming from around the bend a hundred yards downstream, she heard two more shots and then, a heartbeat later, still another. All the undeveloped land immediately adjacent to Henryville had signs posted that warned against hunting, and yet every fall caravans of people armed to the teeth would home in on San Isabel County and turn it into a drunken shooting gallery. There wasn't a highway marker in the county that had escaped being peppered with bullet holes.

In a rural, south-central Colorado county with a heritage of rugged individualism, Tracy was a rarity. She detested firearms. A .38-caliber Smith & Wesson revolver had come with the job, and her patrol car was equipped with a 12-gauge riot gun. A locked rack holding a half dozen carbines was bolted to one wall of her office. The revolver had remained hidden away for the past three years, and the padlocks that secured the riot gun and the office rack had yet to be disturbed. Tracy Hannon was convinced that violence generated violence and that guns provided far too many quick, irreversible solutions to life's problems.

She eased off on the reins as the Appaloosa lurched up the embankment on the south side of the highway. On the slope at the base of the ridge, she spurred the horse into a gallop, pointing him toward the spot where she'd seen the runner go down. Once she'd crested the ridge, she reined in hard and swung out of the saddle—just as a fifth shot was fired. The slug whistled by only inches from the wide brim of her flat-crowned Stetson, and then came a sharp, cracking sound that reverberated through the brush-crusted rocks.

Tracy slapped the riderless horse on the rump, sending Festus bolting down the slope as she dived for cover on the low side of the ridge road. She hoped she was out of sight of whoever was doing the shooting. She snatched up her walkie-talkie. "K double A six-oh-six to Unit Three! Where are you, Crowley?"

No answer.

"K double A six-oh-six to Unit Three," she repeated, urgently now.

Still no answer.

She couldn't stay where she was; she had to find the runner and see if he was hurt. Ahead, a hundred yards to her right, the ridge road disappeared into a grove. Could the runner have sought safety in the trees? He was nowhere in sight.

Tracy rolled away from the side of the road and back onto the slope facing the highway, being careful not to present a target for the rifleman. When she was well below the crest, she rose to a crouch and began working her way toward the trees. *You're out of your cotton-pickin' mind!* she chided herself. *You could have had your doctorate in secondary education by now and been well on your way to tenure at some school that appreciated you. But no, not you, Tracy Wells Hannon. You wanted to live in a small town with clear air, crystal streams, friendly people. Ha!*

She tried to contact Crowley again. "K double A six-oh-six to Unit Three."

No reply. Not even static.

Clipping the radio to her belt, she continued inching her way west toward a rock formation that flanked the south side of the ridge road just outside the grove. She was no sooner across the road, putting the rocks between her and the source of the shots, than she was slammed to the ground by a flying tackle from behind. As she sprawled face-down in the dirt, powerful hands seized her wrists and pinned them effortlessly against the small of her back. Then one of the hands patted roughly at her hips and waist and along the contours of her denim-sheathed legs, even poking around inside the tops of her cowboy boots.

Sputtering and squirming, Tracy tried to break free but couldn't budge. Her attacker was much too strong. She felt a tug at her waist as the radio was yanked from its belt clip. Abruptly her wrists were freed and the weight came off her back.

"Just who the hell are you?" a gruff voice demanded.

Tracy scrambled to her feet and turned to face the runner, who stood glowering at her, arms folded across his chest. The hood of his sweatshirt was down, and the face she was seeing close up for the first time was harshly handsome, almost squarish in shape under a tousled mop of sandy-gray hair. His heavy-browed eyes were an all-seeing steel blue; his chin was an obstinate chunk of granite. His nose, upturned and ever so slightly bent, looked as if it had been broken and not reset properly. As stern and forbidding as he appeared, there was still that enigmatic half smile on his lips.

"I happen to be the sheriff of San Isabel County," Tracy replied, dusting off her jeans and jacket briskly with her hat.

"You bet. And I'm King Kong."

"You act just like it!" she retorted, her dark green eyes flashing. "I risk my neck to help you, and you climb all over me as if I were the World Trade Center! Give me back my radio!"

The man looked quizzically at the walkie-talkie, then shrugged and handed it to her. "You're really the sheriff?"

Tracy ignored the question and raised the transmitter to her lips. "K double A six-oh-six to Unit Three!"

Nothing.

"Let me have a look." He lifted the walkie-talkie out of her hand, popped open the rear panel and examined the insides. He twisted two thin wires together, and the radio came to life with a crackle of static. Deftly reassembling the unit, he handed it back. "Somebody did a lousy job of soldering. Better get it into the shop—*sheriff*."

Tracy suppressed a smile. It was the way he said "sheriff": almost grudgingly on the one hand, yet good-naturedly on the other. She suspected he hadn't quite made up his mind whether he wanted to accept the modern woman.

She tried the radio again. "K double A six-oh-six to Unit Three."

**Bubba** Crowley responded almost immediately. "Where you been, little lady? I been trying to raise you for five minutes."

"My radio's acting up, Unit Three. What's your location?"

"Fifty, sixty yards behind the old mill—as far as you can get without being a mountain goat."

"Find anything?"

"Just a bunch of beer cans somebody's been using for target practice. The shooter must've hightailed it out of here when he seen me coming, little lady. How's the alleged victim?"

Tracy looked at the runner. He had an ugly scrape on one bare knee but otherwise seemed unscathed. "Are you all right? When I saw you go down, I was sure you'd been shot."

The man frowned. "My old Marine Corps training. At the first sound of an incoming round, hit the deck—fast."

"Words to live by." Tracy laughed, bringing the walkie-talkie to her lips. "Everything seems to be all right here, Crowley. Go on back to the Kachina and get your coffee."

"Ten-four, little lady. Just yell if you need me again to do a man's work for you."

Tracy wasn't aware she had let her annoyance show. She must have made some sort of face, because the runner was grinning openly. "What bugs you more, sheriff—being called little lady or having some dimwitted deputy come across like John Wayne doing his Rooster Cogburn number?"

Tracy smiled. "Six of one, half a dozen of another. There are a lot of women in law enforcement these days, but the idea is still a novelty in San Isabel County. All of the good old boys don't live in the Deep South, you know.

There are plenty of them here in the Mountain West. Bubba Crowley is one of them.''

"And you hate his guts."

"I don't *hate* anybody. Let's just say that Bubba isn't one of my favorite human beings."

"Then why don't you dump him?"

"I have my reasons. Let's just say that he has political connections."

The runner cocked his head toward the grove. "Come on.''

Tracy hesitated briefly, then trailed after him.

"How'd you happen to become sheriff?" he asked over his shoulder, noting in amusement that she was hanging back as if a bit leery of him.

"It's a long story. You wouldn't find it very interesting. Where are we going?"

"Just up ahead into the trees. You mentioned coffee and I started slavering like one of Pavlov's dogs. How do you know I wouldn't find the story interesting?"

"You just wouldn't." Tracy stopped walking. "I have to get to work."

The man turned and came back to where she was standing. "Come on," he said, his tone softening. "I may growl a little now and then, but I don't bite."

He led her to a clearing in which an old, well-cared-for, green M.G. TD was parked. Zipping open the tonneau cover, he brought out a nickel-plated thermos. "You like your coffee black or with cream and sugar?" he inquired.

"My!" Tracy exclaimed dryly, bending down and unfastening her spurs. She buckled them together and slung the spliced strap over one shoulder. "You don't seem like a man who'd permit any choices. I'm surprised. You seem—"

"I seem what?" he prompted, pouring steaming black coffee into the cup that served as the top of the thermos.

He handed the cup to her, then took a sip from the thermos.

"Much too authoritarian," she blurted out, deciding that if she offended him it was just too bad; he had it coming.

"You don't even know me, sheriff. Do you think snap judgments are fair?"

Tracy lowered her eyes. "Perhaps not," she admitted reluctantly. "All I really do know about you is that a few minutes ago someone was trying to kill you."

He reached down onto the passenger seat and brought up a packet of thin, dark, crooked cigars. He tore off the cellophane wrapper, stuffed it into a side pocket of his cutoffs, and jammed one of the cigars between his teeth. He flipped the open packet back onto the front seat. "The name's Shane Keegan," he said, chewing on the cigar, "and you're—"

"Tracy Hannon. *Mrs.* Tracy Hannon." Why did she feel compelled to stress the courtesy title? Did she really think she needed that extra edge as a defense mechanism of some sort?

With an exaggerated scowl, Shane took the cigar out of his mouth and eyed it defiantly before crumpling it and shoving it into the same pocket that now held the discarded wrapper. "I'm trying to quit, but I'm not having much luck. Give me a swift kick you know where if I light up in the next ten minutes."

"I don't go around kicking people."

"Even as a friendly favor, Mrs. Hannon?"

Tracy laughed and sipped her coffee. It was strong and bitter and tasted of chicory. "You're staying out at the Donnelly place?"

"The *old* Donnelly place. TransWorld Systems bought it last spring, as you probably heard. The company's made a few additions, and it has some long-range plans for the place.''

"What sort of plans?"

"Sort of a conference center and think tank. The company figures on bringing in a lot of high-priced talent to come up with ideas for saving the world."

"You sound a bit doubtful, Mr. Keegan."

"I'm not at all sure the world wants to be saved."

Tracy set her cup on the hood of the sports car. The coffee wasn't the only thing that was bitter, she decided. Was Shane Keegan down on life, was he a disgruntled employee, or was he just in a bad mood—and not merely because of the shooting? "What do you do for TransWorld, Mr. Keegan?"

He retrieved the packet of cigars from the car, then fished a crumpled book of matches from a pocket of his cutoffs. "This and that," he said, lighting a cigar. "Call me Shane, huh?"

Tracy pointed reproachfully at the cigar. "Your ten minutes aren't up. Do you still want me to kick you?"

He grimaced as he inspected the smoldering cigar. "Thanks," he said, pinching off the lighted tip and shoving the rest of the cigar into a pocket. "Smoking is a vile habit, Mrs. Hannon. If I could quit, I could easily knock five minutes off my time for a five-mile run."

"'Mrs. Hannon' sounds a bit formal for the surroundings. Make it Tracy. Tell me, why don't you quit?"

He threw up his hands in mock frustration. "Every man's entitled to a few vices, Tracy. The secret is to control them, not let them control you." He paused, and she sensed that he wanted to steer the conversation in other directions. "If you're the sheriff, what does your husband do? Keep house and baby-sit?"

"My husband is dead. And we didn't have any children."

Shane seemed genuinely embarrassed. "Sorry, I wasn't trying to be flip. I just have a knack for saying the wrong thing."

Tracy picked up her cup and took another sip. The coffee hadn't improved with age. "He was killed three years ago in a traffic accident south of Denver, on Monument Hill. He'd just been reelected sheriff, and the county commissioners appointed me to fill the vacancy. Sympathy, I guess. That sort of thing happens a lot in these little counties where everybody knows everybody else." She paused. "At any rate, my term is up January first, so I'm looking at another career change."

"Any previous experience in law enforcement?"

"I taught school for a few years. Would you say that qualifies me?"

"Depends on the kids. I see you don't carry a gun."

Tracy felt her cheeks flush as she remembered how Shane had patted her down after tackling her. It had been a *very* thorough search. "Do you do security work for TransWorld?"

"Why do you ask?"

"Just curious."

His wry half smile wavered, and Tracy sensed he was on guard. But instead of pursuing the matter, he raised his thermos in salute and gulped down the rest of the coffee. "Horrible stuff!" he growled. "The ranch cook is a Cajun who came to us from an offshore rig in the Gulf. He thinks chicory is ambrosia."

Tracy quickly pitched out the rest of her coffee and handed back the cup. As he took it from her, his fingers touched hers and lingered. "Sorry I roughed you up," he said, the harshness fading from his voice. "I had no idea who you were. With that short hair of yours and the cowboy outfit, I didn't even know you were a woman until I grabbed you." He winked at her. "Nicest surprise I've had all morning."

"Never mind the sweet talk. I'd like to know if you have any idea why someone would want to kill you."

Shane took away his hand. "You heard your deputy. Some yo-yo was shooting at beer cans."

"My deputy is a dimwit, and you said so yourself," Tracy reminded him. "I asked you a question and I want an answer."

He began to screw the empty cup onto the thermos. "Is this an official investigation, sheriff?"

Tracy stood her ground. "If you want it that way, yes."

There was a twinkle in his eyes as Shane glanced at her. "It's like this. I've just gotten acquainted with the best-looking cop in the Rockies, and every red-blooded man for miles around wants to blow me away." He grinned openly. "I saw you galloping up the hill on Old Paint. Want help rounding him up?"

"I'm sure Festus has found his way home by now."

Reaching across the top of the car, Shane pulled back the tonneau cover. After checking under the dash and around the seats, he made a slow circuit of the M.G., finishing with a look under the hood. Satisfied that everything was in order, he held open the passenger door. "Hop in and I'll run you into town. We've both got work to do."

FROM HIS WOODEN STOOL at the end of the bar, Shane Keegan could look out through the steam-streaked front window of the Kachina Inn and see the fluorescent lights flicker on in the basement of the courthouse a half block away. Interesting woman, he thought. She was sharp, she had guts—and she was good-looking. What the hell was she doing in this backwoods town? He'd have to find out, because he'd long since learned to accept nothing at face value. There was a pay phone in back by the rest rooms. He'd make a couple of calls—better here than from the ranch—and start the ball rolling. By noon, he'd know her life story.

"What'll it be, friend?" A plump, middle-aged man wearing a soiled white apron had come out from the kitchen and was standing behind the bar, rubbing his hands together and scrutinizing Shane through sleepy eyes.

"Coffee," Shane said. He'd already had his two cups, and he didn't want another. But he did want to make those calls, and Deputy Crowley—the only other customer in the Kachina—was at the far end of the bar, not six feet from where the pay phone hung on the cheaply paneled wall. And the Kachina was the only place open so early in the morning. He'd have to wait for Crowley to leave.

The man in the soiled white apron shifted a toothpick from one side of his mouth to the other. "The cook ain't showed up yet, but I can scare up bacon and eggs if you want breakfast."

Shane could smell grease burning in the kitchen. "Scare" was probably the right choice of words. "Just coffee."

The man shrugged. "Suit yourself." He filled a chipped mug from the pot behind him, then thumped down the mug in front of Shane and shambled off to pass the time of day with Bubba Crowley.

Shane turned his attention back to the courthouse. He saw a slender figure move past one of the basement windows, but he couldn't tell if it was the sheriff.

The basic statistics he'd pass along when he made his phone call wouldn't do her justice, he thought. *Tracy Hannon, age about thirty, five-feet-eight or -nine, weight about one hundred and thirty, dark brown hair, green eyes, fair complexion, no visible scars.* The usual rap-sheet stuff; cold, matter-of-fact, unfeeling. Too bad there was no room on the sheet for the features that stuck out in his mind: the slender nose and long, dark eyelashes; the soft, full slash of lips that put an engaging crinkle in her cheeks when she laughed; the healthy glow of her skin and the sparkle in eyes that posed unspoken questions.

"You shoulda heard Her Highness on that radio!" Crowley was cackling through a mouthful of chocolate doughnut. "I tell you, Willy, she was scared spitless. 'Unit Three! Unit Three!' she kept hollering. 'You gotta come help me, Bubba. I can't handle this by my lonesome!'"

Shane reached into his pocket for a cigar.

"So'd you go bail her out?" Willy asked.

The deputy stuffed another chocolate doughnut into his mouth. "A waste of time," he grumbled as he chewed. "The dizzy broad thought somebody was shooting at somebody else, but it weren't nothing like that." He swallowed and reached for his coffee mug. "The bakery in Pueblo send you up any strawberry doughnuts this morning?"

"Nah, just chocolate, plain and powdered sugar."

"Gimme a couple of the powdered sugar, Willy. I tell you, San Isabel County's going to be a lot better off when she hauls her butt out of here. She don't belong."

*How true,* Shane thought as he lit his cigar. He glanced up at the big, round, railroad-style clock on the wall above the bar. It was almost eight-thirty, and he had things to do. Maybe he ought to try to cut short the visit between Bubba Crowley and Willy. He turned on his stool and put on his stupid look. "Say, deputy, was anybody hurt in that accident?"

Crowley stared at him blankly. "What accident was that?"

"Out east by the county line," Shane lied. "I saw it when I was driving in from Pueblo. It looked like a couple of trucks went off the road and into the creekbed."

Crowley slid off his bar stool and brushed some crumbs from the front of his khaki shirt. "Hell's fire, why didn't you report it when you first came in, mister?"

Shane looked surprised. "You mean you didn't know about it?"

"Damn!" Crowley muttered, marching out of the café.

Willy gathered up the deputy's leavings and glanced at Shane. "You sure you don't want no breakfast? We got fresh doughnuts."

Shane dropped a dollar bill on the counter and headed for the phone. "I never eat when I'm working," he said.

LIKE THE COUNTY IT SERVED, the sheriff's department had fallen on hard times. It was headquartered in three courthouse basement rooms and had an adjacent holding cell. Once the office had been located in the two-story county jail across the street, but that crumbling old hulk had been closed by order of a judge shocked by its shortcomings. The county could barely meet its payroll, much less afford a new jail.

Progress had bypassed San Isabel County. The silver mines hadn't been worked in years; the terrain was too rocky and the forage too sparse for extensive livestock operations. Tourists who wandered into the county seat seldom stayed longer than it took to buy a couple of six-packs of beer. The hunters came by the hundreds in the fall, but they brought their own supplies, and there was little cash investment in the local economy. Further chopping away at the tax base was the fact that almost ninety percent of the land was national forest.

Two young to be historic and too mustily old to attract visitors, San Isabel County skimped where it could. On those rare occasions when Tracy's office came up with a culprit who deserved time behind bars, arrangements were made to use the Pueblo County jail forty miles to the east.

And on the even more infrequent occasions when serious crime reared its head, the Colorado Bureau of Investigation sent in agents. Like many rural law enforcement officers, Tracy was rankled when she had to call in outside help, but she recognized her limitations. She felt sorry for Vince Emmerling, the lanky, rawboned retired rancher who a few weeks earlier had been elected to succeed her on January first. The county commissioners were already talking about another cutback in her staff. Vince's job would be safe—there was no way the commissioners could eliminate an elective office mandated by the state constitution—but it wouldn't be easy. If the budget wouldn't stretch, something had to give. She hoped Vince would have the good sense to fire Bubba Crowley—something she'd never been able to screw up the courage to do.

*It's time for me to get out, too,* Tracy thought as she bent over the washbasin and scrubbed off the smudge of dirt she'd found on her cheek when she arrived at the office. She supposed she'd gotten the smudge when Shane Keegan had tackled her. Shane…what a strange man. He certainly didn't belong with those people who'd taken over the Donnelly place. He wasn't someone one would expect to find in a think tank. In Tracy's mind, "think tank" conjured up images of scholarly old codgers puffing on pipes and sitting around evaluating esoteric concepts.

*That's silly!* she rebuked herself, staring defiantly at the face she saw in the mirror over the washbasin. She hadn't put herself through four years of college and two years of graduate school to learn to think in stereotypes. Shane could be anything—a professional athlete, a university president, an insurance salesman—anything at all.

Burned out after only two years of teaching at a junior high school in east Los Angeles, Tracy had come to Henryville to start over. She'd wanted to find a small town where the seasons changed and the air was pure and where youngsters hadn't yet discovered glue-sniffing and switch-blade knives. Les Hannon had been the undersheriff, one of the world's nice guys. A dozen dates and they had married, and for seven months it had been a comfortable relationship.

After having been elected sheriff, Les had been killed and Tracy had taken over for him. Just like that. She hadn't really wanted the job, but she'd been ready for a change from teaching, so she'd accepted the county commissioners' offer. And now she was restless again.

She went out into her office and sat down at her desk. *Get to work,* she told herself. *You've got a criminal case on your hands—your first real criminal case in months. Investigate.*

She picked up the phone, rang the Pueblo County Sheriff's Department and asked the undersheriff to run an FBI records check on Shane Keegan. The request would carry more clout coming from a larger department than hers.

"No problem, Tracy," the Pueblo undersheriff assured her. "I'll have somebody put it on the computer right away. How soon do you need the information?"

"Yesterday," Tracy said.

"IT WENT as planned," The Ragman said after they had gone through their prearranged telephone code exchange. "I do not know why you chose to have it done this way, but that is your business."

"No problems?" the client asked. The Ragman's well-being was the least of his concerns. But The Ragman could have slipped up, could have left a trail leading authorities to some unpleasant conclusions. The client could not have that.

The Ragman laughed. "The only inconvenience was that woman sheriff. She appeared out of nowhere, and I had to discourage her with a few well-placed rounds."

"Did you hurt her?"

"Of course not! I was not paid to do so." The Ragman's tone suggested he would have been only too happy to have put a bullet between the woman's eyes if such had been his instructions.

"You were not seen by anyone?"

"I was not seen. A fat pig of a deputy sheriff came within ten feet of me, but he did not realize it." Pause. "I could easily have slit his throat."

"I did not hire you to create a bloodbath," the client said sternly. "I hired you to carry out specific instructions. At no time are you to exceed those instructions. Do you understand?"

The Ragman seemed hurt by this little lecture. "I *always* carry out instructions. Now, will you require anything further?"

"Possibly. I shall let you know. How can I reach you?"

"Just the way you did before."

"Are you going to be in Colorado for a while?"

Again The Ragman laughed. "One never knows."

TRACY WAS JUST ABOUT to leave the office for the day when her friend in Pueblo called back. "Shane Keegan's on file in Washington—and that's all I can tell you. There's a flag on his jacket, and you're going to have to come up with a pretty good reason to get the bureau to let you know what's in it."

"I think they're trying to tell me something," Tracy said.

"They sure are. They're trying to tell you that Keegan's none of your business."

## Chapter Two

It had turned colder overnight. The pointer on the round thermometer on the front porch was quivering just above zero when Tracy stepped outside, and there was a stiff breeze whistling out of Duro Canyon on the west side of town, pushing the windchill factor into the twenty-below range.

Doing a fast about-face, Tracy went back inside, ran upstairs to her second-floor bedroom and rummaged through the closet until she found her new fur-lined suede boots and heavy mittens. She toyed with the idea of digging out her thermal underwear but decided against it. She'd be in the office most of the day, and long johns were horribly uncomfortable when she was cooped up in a stuffy room. Besides, they felt unfeminine.

"Freeze your tail off!" she muttered as she clumped back downstairs. "Any woman who wears a bikini under her jeans on a day like this can't be accused of playing with a full deck!"

She turned and took another last look around. The gas stove was off; the thermostat was turned down to sixty; the breakfast dishes were washed and stacked upside-down to dry on the rubber mat beside the sink. Last looks never took long. Hers was a tiny house, no more than ten paces wide and Victorian quaint. With its white gingerbread and bright purple clapboard siding, it would have been quite chic in Aspen or Crested Butte, but here in Henryville it was simply old and worn out, like the town itself. The house had two small bedrooms and a connecting bath upstairs, and a kitchen, dining room and sitting room downstairs. Tracy had furnished it with secondhand bits and pieces that only the most charitable visitor would describe as antiques. She'd put the place up for sale when she'd married Les, but there hadn't been any takers. After Les died, she'd managed to get rid of their six-hundred-and-forty-acre ranch north of town to a real-estate speculator from Colorado Springs at a price that barely paid off the mortgage. She'd moved back into her own house, thinking she'd feel more at home there. She didn't.

Stepping outside onto the porch, Tracy locked the front door and turned up her fleecy collar. The pointer on the thermometer had settled down to a solid zero, and she knew it probably would dip another four or five degrees before the sun poked over the hills in forty-five minutes or so.

It was too cold to take Festus out for his morning exercise, she decided as she walked to the brown-and-white Ford patrol car parked in front of the house.

*So what am I doing up at this ungodly hour?* Tracy asked herself as she unlocked the Ford and slid onto the cold seat. She already knew the answer. *I want to see him again.*

The car's engine chugged reluctantly to life, and she let it warm up for a few minutes. As she waited, she picked up the microphone dangling from the dashboard. "K double A six-oh-six to Unit Two."

"Unit Two."

"All quiet, Phil?"

"A real graveyard, Tracy." Unit Two yawned. "A couple of drunk drivers around midnight out on Burnt Mill

Road—fearless hunters, naturally. I gave 'em a warning, then followed 'em to their camp and tucked 'em in for the night. Other than that, zip. Hey, it's just six. Aren't you up and at 'em kind of early?''

"Kind of. Why don't you call it a night, Phil? I'll be in service until Crowley checks in. I can handle any calls.''

"You twisted my arm, Tracy.''

"Ten-four.''

She drove through the still-darkened downtown Henryville, passed the courthouse and turned onto the highway that paralleled the ridge road. Ahead, to her right, was the Forest Service trail to Lookout Point, and beyond that was the Keating Ranch, where she boarded Festus. To her left was a gravel lane leading to the ridge road. She turned into the gravel lane, dropped into low gear and climbed to the ridge road, her rear tires spitting pebbles up under the wheel wells of the Ford. Atop the ridge, she set the brake and shut off the headlights.

It took a minute for her eyes to become accustomed to the predawn darkness. Gradually she could make out the jagged outline of the rock formation that served as the south wall of the valley. The shots had come from over there. Somebody shooting at beer cans, Crowley had said. He probably was right.

Switching on her high beams and activating the rooftop red-and-blue emergency flashers for good measure, she headed toward the rock formation, zigzagging slowly between the boulders. When the Ford was abreast of the rocks, she turned on her spotlight and played its white beacon across the terrain.

A young doe that had been picking her way through the scrub oak froze momentarily, wide eyes staring hypnotically at the source of the light, and then scampered out of sight. That was it: a deer, rocks, scrub oak, blackness. Nothing more. Not a single would-be assassin.

"What would you do if you found one?" Tracy asked herself aloud, suddenly needing to hear the sound of a voice. "Scratch his eyes out?" She touched the dark walnut stock of the riot gun mounted in the metal scabbard bolted to the floor. The key to the padlock was on her key ring. All she had to do was...

"No!" she said firmly. She was willing to carry the riot gun in the car for appearance's sake, but that was all. Under no circumstances could she imagine herself using the weapon. Perhaps the county needed a sheriff who wasn't afraid of guns or what they could do.

Switching off the rooftop flashers, Tracy slowly drove back to the ridge road and headed for the grove where she'd had coffee with Shane the day before. She turned off the headlights but left the engine running to keep the battery charged. Even with the heater on, it was chilly inside the car.

*You're shameless,* she told herself. *You have no business up here. No crime has been committed—none you can prove. Besides, if anyone was planning to take another shot at Shane, there's not much you could do to stop it. You just want to see him again, talk to him. He's different, and because he's different he's exciting. You need some excitement for a change. Admit it.*

Maybe Shane wouldn't come this morning. It was bitterly cold, and wasn't it supposed to be bad for the lungs to run in this kind of weather? Maybe he wasn't even out at the Donnelly ranch any longer; people flew in and out of there in those black-and-gold helicopters all the time. Maybe the shooting had persuaded him to do his running elsewhere.

Gradually the eastern sky lightened, the star-speckled blackness of the night giving away to gray and the gray to an orangish red streaked with horizontal swatches of yellow.

Tracy was just about to pull out of the grove when she saw the lights of a car at the mouth of Duro Canyon. The car was traveling fast, but it wasn't light enough out for her to discern the car's shape. Then the vehicle slowed and turned into the gravel lane, and she found herself smiling. No more maybes.

A minute later the little M.G. pulled alongside the patrol car and stopped. Despite the bone-numbing cold, Shane still had the top off. He'd made some concessions to the weather, though, Tracy noticed as she watched him get out and zip up the tonneau cover. He was wearing a black ski parka over his sweatshirt, and he'd put on gray sweatpants.

Without a word or a wave to acknowledge her presence, Shane stripped off the parka and sweatpants and draped them over the hood of the M.G. He hurried through a set of stretching exercises and then set out for his run, dressed exactly as he'd been dressed the day before.

He was insane! Tracy thought. She was sitting in a closed sedan with the heater working its heart out, and she was still freezing. He was prancing around with next to nothing on and presumably enjoying it!

She checked her watch. 6:45. She'd give him until 7:10. He always came back along the ridge at 7:10. He'd started at 6:45 and he ran five miles. Good time! Could he do it again this morning? She knew she was looking for an excuse to stick around.

The minutes dragged by. Just before seven, Bubba called in to say he'd be at the Kachina. "Okay by you, little lady?"

"Ten-four," Tracy acknowledged brusquely.

Seven-oh-five.

*Hannon, why don't you go on into the office and do some paperwork?* No good. She'd done it all yesterday. She'd even helped the county court clerk prepare her January jury lists, which had been an utter waste of time because the only defendant whose case was docketed for trial had moved away, and the county wasn't about to go to the expense of extraditing him from New Mexico to face charges of altering the brands on three scrawny calves.

Seven-ten.

It had been twenty-four hours since she'd heard the shots from across the road on the Lookout Point trail. Would there be shots again today? Would there be *anything* today?

Then she saw Shane coming in at a dead run, his legs pounding like pistons, his arms swinging loosely at his sides. He didn't slow up until he was within the grove, and then he headed straight for the M.G. He unzipped the tonneau cover, groped inside and brought out his thermos and a packet of crooked little cigars. Walking around behind the patrol car, he stepped up to the passenger side and tapped on the window, the rounded black stone of his heavy gold class ring making clicking noises.

Tracy reached across and pulled up the lock button.

Shane opened the door and stuck his head inside the patrol car. "Want some company, sheriff?"

She shrugged. "Actually, I'm just waiting out the morning rush hour. However, if you'd care to join me..."

"Cute," he muttered. He climbed inside and slammed the door. Placing his cigars on the dashboard, he poured her a cup of coffee from the thermos. He handed the cup to her, then put both hands around the thermos, held it under his nose and inhaled deeply. "Ah!" he sighed just before he took a sip. He promptly made a face. "Lousy stuff, but it gets the eyes open."

"I should think a five-mile run would do that."

Shane gulped down some more coffee. "Not true. I run out of sheer desperation, to keep my body functioning the way it was designed to function. The truth is, I find that running dulls the brain. Maybe the muscles are protesting too much as I totter onto the threshold of middle age, and I've conditioned myself to let the brain idle when I run so it can't signal to me how much I hurt. Interesting theory, huh? Anyway, I need my first shot of coffee to get one thought following another in some sort of logical sequence. I don't become unqualifiedly civil—'' he took another sip ''—until I've had my second.''

"And after your third?"

Shane drained his thermos, set it on the dashboard and reached for his cigars. "I allow myself only two a day. Any more than that, I revert to my normal, unbearable state."

"Your poor wife." It wasn't really a humorous quip. As soon as she'd said it, Tracy was sure Shane would recognize it for what it was—a question, pure and simple.

There was a flash of bitterness in his eyes. "Don't worry about her. She took a hike a long time ago. I almost repeated the mistake a few years later, but in a rare flash of good sense I backed out." He withdrew a cigar from the packet and rolled it between his fingers. "You mind if I light up?"

"I thought you were trying to quit."

"In time."

"All right, but open your window a crack. It gets stuffy in here."

Shane tossed the unlighted cigar onto the dashboard and grinned, displaying strong, white teeth. "I can take a hint."

*Can you?* she wondered. *Can you really?* "You think marriage is a mistake, Shane?" Oh, Lord, what was she saying? She was just making conversation, but it sounded as though she were trying to get her hooks into him. What must he think of her?

"I didn't say that, Tracy."

"I . . . I must have misunderstood."

"I said, indirectly, I'd made one mistake and I almost made a second. I didn't say marriage itself is a mistake. All I'm saying is that it's not for me."

"Why?"

Shane reached for the cigar he'd removed from the packet and jammed it between his teeth. "For starters, I'm restless, grouchy and cold-hearted."

Tracy stole a quick glance at him to see if he was teasing her. "Restless I can believe. Grouchy? I suppose everyone gets irritable at times. But you don't strike me as cold-hearted."

"Oh, but I am!" Shane said almost proudly, shoving back the hood of his sweatshirt. "Just ask my ex-wife." He struck a match and stared at it until the flame went out, its dying fire licking at the unflinching tips of a stubby thumb and forefinger. "I'm also aloof, too demanding, over-bearing and unforgiving."

The corners of his lips were turned up in the half smile Tracy had always seen since she began studying him through her binoculars. She sensed the half smile was a mask he wore to avoid revealing emotion. Only the thin lines at the outside corners of his eyes hinted at the bitterness within. "There's an old saying among lawyers," she said. " 'He who represents himself has a fool for a client.' You could say the same for the person who psychoanalyzes himself. He'll always make things worse."

"Hang out a shingle, sheriff. You'll have the world beating a path to your door." He paused, and the half smile melted into a genuine grin. "See, I told you I was a grouch. Drink up. Time to hit the road."

"Busy day ahead?"

"Yeah. I've got a super-mean boss who's a bear cat if I don't show up on time. No living with him, in fact."

Tracy opened her door and dumped her coffee onto the frozen ground. She closed the door and handed him the cup. "I wouldn't want to be the cause of your losing your job, Shane."

He capped the thermos and screwed on the cup. "Not likely, but I do have to keep the man happy." He started to get out of the car, then turned back. "Thanks for coming out. We'll do it again sometime." As if on impulse, he leaned across quickly and kissed her on the cheek.

Surprised, Tracy turned to face him and his lips brushed hers, fleetingly, then returned, warm and soft, tasting of coffee. She started to protest, but his mouth closed on hers, silencing her. It was a searching kind of kiss, gentle and yet strangely insistent, and she tried halfheartedly to push him away, thinking, *You're still trying to prove something, aren't you? But to whom, Shane Keegan? To whom?*

As his arms encircled her shoulders, she groped out at the dashboard and flipped a toggle switch. The bitterly cold morning air was filled with the insistent wail of a siren.

Shane drew back. "I'll go quietly, officer," he said meekly, raising his hands to the level of his head.

Tracy straightened up in her seat. "This isn't the time or the place," she said primly. That was hardly the right thing to say! she thought. It sounded as if there *was* a right time and a right place. It was almost an open invitation for him to try again.

"It is if both of us want it to be, sheriff."

Tracy took a deep breath and let it out slowly in an almost wistful sigh. "You've just said the magic word—sheriff. I'm supposed to be a model of decorum. Sheriffs don't go around making out in the front seat of patrol cars."

"How about the back seat, then?"

She laughed. "Shut up, or I'll slap the cuffs on you."

"Whatever you say, sheriff." He picked up his thermos and opened the door. "Same time, same place tomorrow?"

"I've got to go to Denver on business."

Shane's bushy gray eyebrows rose. "Oh? I'll be flying up myself about noon. Want to share the ride?"

"I said *business*, Shane. The U.S. Attorney's Office is holding a seminar to bring us yokels up to date on Supreme Court decisions. I'll have to pay my own way, but I still plan to go."

He stared at her incredulously. "You mean San Isabel County won't spring for your expenses?"

"The county can barely afford to buy gasoline for our patrol cars. Anyway, I don't mind. I have to get out of here every once in a while or I'll go crazy. Besides, I've got to start looking for another job."

Shane appeared thoughtful. "I know the personnel people at TransWorld. They might have something for you, Tracy."

She studied his face. He seemed genuinely interested in being helpful. "Like what?"

"I don't know—training, maybe. The combination of teaching and law enforcement gives you unique credentials. It might be worth your while to talk to Trans-World."

"Forgive my naïveté, but just what does the company do?"

Shane shrugged. "Lots of things. Electronics, communications, some very specialized security work."

"What sort of security work?"

"The personnel people can explain it if you're interested."

Tracy was *very* interested. It might be just the sort of challenge she was looking for, she decided. "I'll think about it and we'll talk later. Take care, Shane."

"You, too, Tracy."

She watched as he walked slowly around the M.G., dropped to his hands and knees to look and feel under each of the wheel wells, then unlatched and opened the hood. She rolled down her window. "Problems?"

"Preventive maintenance," he said, not looking at her.

He took his time inspecting the engine. When he was satisfied, he closed the hood, unzipped the tonneau cover and climbed into the driver's seat, but only after checking under the seats and dashboard. He let the engine warm up for a few minutes, then pulled out of the grove with a casual wave.

Tracy noticed that he'd left his cigars on her dashboard. Had he been as disconcerted by that unplanned bit of grappling as she had? There was a mutual attraction there all right, but it was more than physical. Just being with him, talking to him, hearing him talk, made her feel alive.

She remembered that he'd been careful to inspect his car before driving off the day before. He was afraid of something, she thought. No, not afraid—cautious. He wouldn't admit it, but he must suspect someone had been shooting at him intentionally, and that someone could have tampered with his car.

A chilling thought occurred to her. She'd been parked alongside the M.G. Surely Shane knew that she wouldn't allow anyone to touch his car—unless he had doubts about her. She sat straight up. The arrogance of the man!

Tracy snatched up the microphone. "K double A six-oh-six to Unit Three."

No answer. Bubba was probably still at the Kachina. Damn it! She wanted to talk to him, get him to show her exactly the ground he'd searched. Together, maybe they could turn up something.

After trying two more times to raise Bubba on the radio, she gave up, slammed the gearshift into low and roared out of the grove.

As she came abreast of the rock formation from which the shots had been fired, she stopped the car. How thoroughly *had* Bubba investigated? He was hardly the world's greatest detective—but then neither was she. San Isabel County wasn't really the place for that sort of on-the-job training. Still, it wouldn't hurt to take a look around.

Glancing out across the highway, she lined up a fix on the Lookout Point trail where she'd been positioned when the shooting started. After she got her bearings, she backed the car to the spot where Shane had thrown himself to the ground. She took her 35 mm Pentax from the glove compartment, got out of the car and slung the camera strap over her shoulder. She took another sight on the rock formation and began walking toward it in a straight line, checking the ground on either side of her. Bits of paper and other debris fluttered across her path, and she thought dark thoughts about litterbugs. The No Dumping signs posted around Henryville had as much impact as the No Hunting signs, and most of them were riddled with bullet holes, too.

Thirty yards up the windswept slope, midway between the road and the rock formations, Tracy found three bullet-riddled beer cans. Were these the cans Bubba had seen? Probably—but they were rusty, even around the bullet holes. Metal was slow to rust in the dry air of the mountains. The cans had been there for months, even years. So had the bullet holes.

She uncased her camera, cupping one hand over the opening in the camera body as she switched to the 150 mm lens she carried in a black case taped to the strap. The camera was hers, and she wanted to protect it from the stinging grit blown by the wind. She knew the commissioners wouldn't sit still for a repair bill.

She took several shots of the cans, the slope and the rock formation itself. Standard procedure at a crime scene, she told herself. She should have thought of doing this the day before. She didn't have the faintest idea what the photos might prove. It wasn't even a crime scene, at least not officially.

Putting the lens cap back on her camera, she started walking again, glancing about even more carefully now. And then she was at the base of the rock formation. It was a tilted slab of fractured granite towering a hundred feet above her head, and here and there on its rough gray-and-beige face was a series of ledges, from some of which clumps of brush sprouted. The thickly wooded terrain behind the formation was Forest Service land, crisscrossed with hiking trails. If someone had taken a sniper's position in the rocks, he or she would have had to have gotten to it from above. For the first fifteen feet or so of its rise, the granite was too sheer to permit a climb without special equipment—and there was no sign of pitons marring the lower sections of the rock face.

Tracy worked her way around the formation, scrabbling up the ever-steeper mountainside until she was on a level with the granite top. Clinging to bits of brush for support, she edged across the rocks and looked down. She immediately wished she hadn't because it was an almost straight drop down. She hated heights almost as much as she hated guns. As a child, she'd taken an arm-breaking tumble from a tree and she'd had a fear of falling ever since.

Tracy had just about made up her mind to traverse the formation and then head down when she saw a yellow rope snaking along a crevice that ran perpendicular to the up-thrusting slab. A section of the rope was no more than six feet away from her.

Inching forward, testing each bit of scrub oak for strength before trusting it to support her weight, she made her way to the rope and examined it. The rope was expensive Dacron, unfrayed and unweathered. Tracy pulled at it gingerly, then gave it a tug. Getting both hands securely around the line, she began climbing, planting the crepe soles of her boots carefully to avoid slipping on the loose shale above the rock formation.

Ten feet up, where the ground leveled off, she saw that one end of the rope was fastened to the eye of a gleaming steel piton driven into a spur of the main formation. The newness of the rope and the shininess of the piton indicated both had been placed there quite recently.

Looping the rope around each of her mittened hands, she began lowering herself down the face of the rock formation, the soft toes of her boots providing scant purchase as she tried to get some semblance of footing. As an experiment, she turned her toes outward and pressed her insteps against the rocks. Clumsy, but it took some weight off her aching hands.

She came to a ledge thirty feet down from the top, the rest of the rope coiled neatly at her feet. Easing herself into a sitting position behind a parapet of loose rock, she let go of the rope, heaved a sigh of relief and glanced around. There were two large-caliber shell casings on the floor of the ledge, hardly the ammunition someone would use to plink away at beer cans. Besides, why would a person buy expensive mountaineering equipment and risk his neck to climb down here unless he had something far more serious in mind?

Gathering up the casings, Tracy dropped them into her jacket pocket. As she did so, one of them slipped out of her hand, fell to the ledge and rolled into a niche at the base of the parapet. She pulled off her right-hand mitten and tried to retrieve it with her bare fingers, but the niche was too small.

There was a clump of brush just below and to the right of the ledge. One hand clinging tightly to the rope, she leaned out to break off a twig to use in prying up the casing. She could see a tiny square of paper lodged in the brambly tangle. Stretching, she managed to retrieve the paper between thumb and forefinger.

It was a photo of Shane, the type that might have been made for an identification card. Refusing to speculate on the implications of her discovery, Tracy slipped the photo into her shirt pocket, leaned over the ledge and broke off a twig, then quickly recovered the shell casing that had lodged in the niche.

After a last glance around, she made her way up the rock formation, doubling the rope around her slender waist for safety's sake. The ascent was easier than the trip down. She could pick out footholds along the way and make sure her insteps were anchored before pulling herself up another few inches.

It took her almost ten minutes to reach the piton to which the rope was attached. She rested there briefly, then gathered up the rope and moved out along the slope in search of a gentler angle for her descent, giving the formation a wide berth.

Her ankles ached from the banging they'd taken against the rocks. She glanced down at the fur-lined, rust-colored boots she'd purchased in Colorado Springs only three weeks before. They were badly scuffed and scarred along the insteps. She'd have to buy a new pair.

As she inspected her boots, something caught her eye. On the ground by her right foot was a half-smoked cigar. She picked it up and carried it to the car. Shane had left his packet of cigars on the dashboard. She shook one out, unwrapped it and compared it with the cigar she'd just found. They were identical.

Shane had some explaining to do.

FROM A RIDGE across the highway, just above Lookout Point trail, The Ragman watched through high-powered binoculars. He'd come up against hick sheriffs before, and no sweat. But this one made him nervous. She was too inquisitive for her own good. She'd already found the rope he'd left in his haste, and she might try to trace it. He glanced down at the front of his parka. She'd found something else, too. Even with the binoculars, he could not make out exactly what it was, but the possibilities bothered him. He knew he should have come back earlier to get the rope and check out the area, but every time he'd driven by, somebody had been working at the old mill and he didn't want to arouse suspicion.

There was *one* thing he could do. He levered a fresh round into the chamber of his rifle and propped the dull blue barrel atop one of the rocks that shielded him from sight. A single shot. That was all it would take. A single shot between the shoulder blades. The woman would be dead before she hit the ground.

Women! Why didn't they stay at home, away from a man's world, and content themselves with doing the things they were supposed to do? Women were supposed to keep house for a man, provide physical companionship, have his babies and do whatever else the man wanted them to do. They were not supposed to tramp around mountainsides, playing detective.

The crosshairs of The Ragman's rifle scope steadied on the sheriff's back. "Bang," he said aloud, without touching the trigger. "Keep that up, woman, and you are dead, dead, dead."

He lowered the rifle. He would wait for a while. The Ragman did not like to kill without being paid for it. He would get word to the client that the sheriff was nosing around. The client would pay. He would have to pay.

Then, and only then, would The Ragman kill Tracy Hannon.

THE DONNELLY RANCH COVERED two sections of land, twelve hundred and eighty acres abutting one of the most primitive areas of the San Isabel National Forest. It was the oldest homestead in the county and had been owned by the same family since long before Colorado had attained statehood in 1876. The ranch had been a cattle operation, providing little more than subsistence income for generations of Donnellys.

Several months before TransWorld Systems had bought the ranch, there'd been rumors that a syndicate of investors from Houston might take over the property and build a ski resort, but the Forest Service had refused to grant the necessary permits. Besides, consultants who had done a feasibility study cautioned that the property might be too isolated to attract investors. And the ranch was, indeed, isolated. There was no convenient access from the national forest on the south, from across the river to the west, or from the canyon on the north, where the state highway served as one boundary line for the property. The only overland route into the ranch was the gravel road that forked off the canyon highway and came in from the east.

It was at the end of that road, in front of an ominously high barbed-wire-topped, chain-link fence, that Tracy waited for the guard to open the gate. Before her car had even come to a stop, the guard—a husky young man wearing khakis, a black ski parka and a black watch cap, and carrying a short-barreled shotgun—was leaning into the cab of his black-and-gold Chevrolet Blazer, speaking into a microphone. Finally he put down the microphone and strolled to the gate. "Something I can do for you, ma'am?"

Tracy got out of her car. "I want to see Mr. Keegan."

"Do you have an appointment?"

Tracy could feel her annoyance grow into open anger. "No, I don't have an appointment."

"Please state your business."

Tracy drew herself up to her full five-eight and glared at the guard. "I want to see Mr. Keegan, and I want to see him now!"

"Your name, ma'am?"

"Hannon. Sheriff Hannon." Tracy dug out a leather case and opened it so he could see her starred badge pinned to one side, her ID card behind a plastic window on the other side.

After examining her credentials without a flicker of expression, the guard walked back to the Blazer, opened the door and picked up the microphone. Tracy could hear a crackle of static but couldn't make out what was being said.

The guard returned to the gate. "He isn't available."

"Tell him to make himself available."

"I can't help you, sheriff."

"Open this gate!"

"Do you have a warrant?"

Tracy fumed. "I can damn well get one, mister!"

The young man's expression still hadn't changed. It remained an utter blank. For some reason he reminded Tracy of the still soldiers she'd seen manning the little sentry boxes outside Buckingham Palace. He was wholly unruffled by her outburst. "Do as you see fit, ma'am, but I'll try to save you some time. Be sure it's a federal warrant, duly executed by a U.S. magistrate and—"

"You're out of your mind! This is San Isabel County, and the local courts have jurisdiction!"

The guard shook his head slowly. "Check with the U.S. Attorney's Office in Denver. You'll find this property is classified as a federal reservation for certain purposes, including service of legal process. Have a nice day, sheriff." He turned and walked back to the Blazer.

"Just a minute, mister! Just who is this Shane Keegan?"

The guard looked at her over his shoulder. "Don't you know?"

"If I knew, I wouldn't ask!"

Still no expression. "I'm sorry, sheriff, but I'm not at liberty to answer your question."

"Yo-yo!" Tracy grumbled as she marched to her car. She picked up the microphone, switched to the State Patrol frequency and requested an ownership check on the M.G. that Shane drove. Then she sat back and waited, glaring at the guard.

The State Patrol dispatcher got back to her in less than two minutes. The M.G. was listed to TransWorld Systems, with corporate offices on Seventeenth Street in Denver.

"Ten-four." Tracy sighed and signed off.

TRACY WAS OUT OF THE OFFICE most of the afternoon. First she had to testify at a reckless-driving trial. Then a Pueblo law firm sent over writs of foreclosure and repossession that had to be served. Tracy, who disliked being part of someone's misery, was very much out of sorts when she returned to the courthouse.

Bubba Crowley was coming up the basement steps as she started down. He leered knowingly at her in passing. "Way to go, little lady!" he chortled. "I always figured you had something working on the side."

Tracy started to ask him what he meant, but didn't want to give him the pleasure of having her at a disadvantage. There was no need to ask anyway. The answer was on her desk: a dozen outrageously expensive long-stemmed red roses in a slender sterling-silver vase. Where had they come from? she wondered. There wasn't a florist within fifty miles.

Shane Keegan. She didn't even have to look at the card attached to the vase. It had to be from Shane.

The card read:

Sheriff:
Pick you up at seven. Dress warm and skip dinner.
—The Grump.

P.S. Sorry about the hassle at the ranch.

## Chapter Three

"Sweets for the sweet," Shane said amiably, thrusting an elaborately wrapped, five-pound box of Godiva chocolates at her as she opened the front door. "Try one, sheriff. It'll take the edge off your appetite until we get where we're going."

"The sheriff loathes sweets," Tracy told him, trying to maintain the sharp edge of sternness she'd been working on ever since her frustrating experience at the ranch. It wasn't easy. Shane could be so damnably disarming when he chose to be. "Candy puts on pounds, and I'm trying to get back down to a size twelve." She stepped aside for him and placed the chocolates on the hall table. "I'd be a size twenty if I pigged out on those."

Shane came into the foyer and shrugged out of his tan, melton stadium coat. He was wearing a heavy, blue wool sweater, a white turtleneck, jeans and scuffed brown loafers. "So feed them to your prisoners at the county jail."

"There aren't any prisoners at the jail, Mr. Know-It-All. San Isabel County is a peace-loving place, and what we do when we get troublemakers is tar and feather them, haul them on a rail to the county line and let somebody else deal with them."

"You consider me a troublemaker?" he asked, moving in so close she could smell the woodsy fragrance of his after-shave.

Tracy felt her resolve waver. "Yes."

"Why?"

"Because you come down here and get yourself shot at and—"

"Getting shot at wasn't my idea."

"—then you try to interfere with an official investigation. That's why."

"A bum rap, Tracy. I didn't interfere."

"The hell you didn't! You even apologized for it—for what you called the 'hassle'—in that note you sent with the roses. Now sit down. You and I are going to have a serious talk."

"Later. Grab your coat. It's a bit brisk tonight."

"We talk first."

"Suit yourself." Shane spun around a ladderback chair that was just inside the door of the sitting room and dropped down into it, his legs straddling the back of the chair. He looked up at her. "You've got the floor, sheriff. Talk."

Tracy folded her arms across her chest and tried her best to look severe. "Someone *did* shoot at you on the ridge road."

"No kidding?"

"I mean *intentionally*. The person knew exactly who you were." She stepped across the hall into the dining room and returned with the identification photo she'd found. "So there'd be no mistake, the shooter had this to go by." She handed the photo to him.

Shane glanced at it impassively, shrugged and slipped it into a rear pocket of his jeans.

"That's evidence, Mr. Keegan," Tracy said crisply, holding out her right hand, palm up. "Give it back."

Shane made no move to comply. "Evidence of what?"

"Attempted murder, damn it! There's probably a hired assassin roaming around and—"

Shane shook his head. "You're a bright woman, Tracy, but you're jumping to conclusions. Just what makes you think it was a hired assassin?"

"It's obvious! If the shooter was someone who knew you by sight, he wouldn't need a photo to identify you!"

"You can take that a step further. Maybe he—or she—just wanted us to think that. Then again maybe your dim-witted deputy was right. Someone could have been shooting away at tin cans, and I happened to get in the line of fire. The photo could have fluttered in on the breeze. The possibilities are limitless."

Tracy went back into the dining room and collected the box into which she'd put the shell casings. She showed them to him. "I'll grant you I don't know much about guns, but I have friends who do. They tell me that you don't shoot at tin cans with thirty-ought-six target loads. This is the kind of ammunition the experts use."

Shane's steel-blue eyes displayed only mild interest as he glanced at the two gleaming brass cylinders. "Where'd you find them?"

Tracy looked at him triumphantly. It was time to chip away at another of his little secrets. "The same place you did."

"Oh?"

Shane's blasé attitude infuriated Tracy. She wanted him to react strongly so she could use that reaction as a yardstick. The man could be as utterly wooden-faced as an old-time drugstore Indian, and she didn't have a clue as to how to deal with him. If she knew how he reacted to the indisputable, she'd be better prepared to tell when he was evading the truth. "You left a calling card—one of those nasty little cigars of yours. I had someone compare it with those in the packet you left in my car. He said the cigars were handmade, probably in Cuba.''

"Veracruz,'' Shane corrected her. "It's against the law to import cigars from Cuba, and I'm nothing if not law-abiding.'' He grinned. "Let me amend my earlier statement. You're not just bright, you're *very* bright—even if you do tend to jump to conclusions. Now grab your coat.''

"We haven't finished our talk yet.''

"Sure we have. Incidentally, that's a charming outfit.''

"Don't try to change the subject, Mr. Keegan.''

He got to his feet and put the ladderback chair against the wall. "I wouldn't dream of it. And knock off the mister, huh? Shane will do nicely.''

As she slipped into her loden coat, Tracy glanced quickly into the oak-framed mirror mounted on the opposite wall of the tiny foyer. The open-collar green wool shirt went well with the muted green-and-gray plaid of her pleated skirt, and the single strand of pearls around her neck helped soften the effect. The outfit didn't look bad at all. Not trendy, of course, but nice. Still, who in Henryville would ever notice such things?

THEY DIDN'T SPEND THE EVENING in Henryville. Tracy asked Shane where they were headed, and he merely shrugged and replied, "Neutral territory. Leave your badge and billy club at home.''

"I never carry a billy club," she said as she got into the open M.G. She glanced up apprehensively at the icy blackness of the nighttime sky. "Don't you think it might be nice to put up the top?''

"It's a beautiful night. There are a million stars just waiting to be admired. Who needs a top?''

"Anybody in his right mind, that's who!''

Shane chuckled and began his customary inspection of the sports car. "I'd be happy to, but I'm afraid this little job doesn't have a top. The metal frame got in the way of equipment I was installing, so I removed it altogether." He checked under the hood, then got behind the wheel and started the engine. "Tell me, why don't you carry a gun?"

"I don't like guns. Never have."

"Maybe you've never really needed one. You might feel differently if you had."

Tracy burrowed down into her seat. Even through her heavy loden coat, the stiff leather was icy cold against her back and bottom. "I really don't think so. Guns are for people who can't cope otherwise. I manage by using common sense."

Shane revved up the engine and checked the instrument panel. "Try relying on common sense when you have to handle a bandit who comes charging out of a bank with a sackful of money in one hand and a sawed-off shotgun in the other, or maybe some dopehead who wants to carve his initials all over you."

"We haven't had an armed robbery in ten years, and they tell me the State Patrol picked up the perpetrator in a matter of minutes without a shot being fired. There isn't all that much worth stealing in this county. As for dopers, all we get are college kids who go camping in the forest and like to mellow out on some grass. They don't bother anybody and we don't bother them."

"That hardly seems like a very professional attitude toward law enforcement."

"I don't delude myself, Shane. I'm *not* very professional. I try to be practical—period." She glanced across at him. "I don't suppose this car has a heater?"

"Sure it does." He reached to the dash and adjusted the controls. "How's this?"

Tracy peeled off one of her fur-lined leather gloves and felt around at her feet. There was an anemic whisper of air that was only marginally warmer than the bitter cold of the night. "Super," she groused, drawing on her glove and thrusting her hands into her pockets. This man was utterly mad. Nice, but mad.

Shane swung out onto the street, poked through Henryville at a legal twenty-five miles per hour, and then, at the city limits, tromped on the gas. The M.G. leaped forward with a burst of energy that pressed Tracy against the back of her seat. She saw the speedometer needle pass the sixty miles per hour mark, then keep going. In the dull glow of the dash lights, Shane's face shone with almost childlike delight.

She leaned forward toward him and shouted to make herself heard above the roar of the wind. "I don't suppose I can ask you to slow down?"

"Sure! Just let me run a couple of tests first."

Tracy forced herself to stop looking at the speedometer when the needle reached eighty-five and the windstream was numbing her face. She also tried to forget that, as the sheriff, she was sworn to uphold the laws of the State of Colorado and the County of San Isabel.

For the rest of the trip, conversation was all but impossible. Once, she was vaguely aware that Shane was yelling at her, and she raised the section of mouton headband that protected her left ear and leaned toward him. "Come again?"

"I said, you don't look a thing like a sheriff!"

"I don't feel like a sheriff! I feel like a block of ice!" Lowering the headband securely into place, Tracy unsnapped her purse and brought out the yellow-and-green striped woolen legwarmers she'd impulsively stuffed into her purse before leaving the house. As soon as she'd seen the M.G. parked at the curb, she had a hunch she might need the extra protection. Ignoring Shane's bemused glances, she bent forward in her seat and worked her right foot into one of the tubes, easing it over the high heel of her leather boot and sliding it up her leg until the bottom of the legwarmer was almost to the top of the boot. She tugged the top of the woolen tube up under the hem of her skirt, smoothed it out, then repeated the operation on the other leg. Settling back in her seat, she drew her peg-buttoned loden coat more tightly around her and thrust her gloved hands into her pockets.

"That better?" Shane shouted.

Tracy stared at him, taking a minute to work out the content of the question that had been lost to the relentless howl of the wind. She cupped her hands to her mouth. "No!" she replied at the top of her lungs. "The colors clash, and I *still* feel like a block of ice!"

"Fear not, Sheriff! No one will even notice. You've got style—not to mention a great pair of legs."

"Gee, thanks..."

They came out of the foothills and onto the prairie west of Pueblo. She heard a buzzing sound, and Shane immediately eased up on the accelerator and let the M.G. coast to a fifty mile per hour crawl. The buzzer came from some sort of radar detector, Tracy decided. A minute later they passed a battered pickup truck with broken taillights. The pickup was slowly rattling eastward, hauling a load of firewood. Shane flicked on his turn signal and passed the truck.

"That wasn't a patrol car!" Tracy yelled.

"Nope!" Shane shouted, glancing at an indicator on the dashboard. "There isn't another vehicle for seven point eight miles. The nearest patrol car is sixteen point three miles ahead, and moving due east."

Ignoring the frigid blast of the wind, Tracy straightened up in her seat and studied the indicator Shane was reading. All she could see was a display of computer-style digital readouts and symbols that kept changing. "Are you serious?"

"Sure. I like to know what's ahead, and that little gizmo tells me." He took his right hand from the wheel and patted her legwarmer-encased knee. "Simmer down, sheriff. I always drop back to the legal limit whenever I get within two klicks of another vehicle."

"What's a 'klick'?"

"Sorry. A klick is military slang for a kilometer. Two klicks would be a mile and a quarter. Getting a ticket doesn't bother me. I just don't want to see anyone get hurt."

"How about frozen to death?" Tracy demanded, snuggling down into her coat once again.

Ten minutes later they entered Pueblo from the west and Shane eased off to a respectable thirty-five miles per hour. To Tracy, the sudden drop in the windchill factor made the air seem almost balmy. Patting down the stray wisps of dark brown hair that had blown free of her headband, she straightened up in her seat and looked around as Shane angled onto a side street and headed through a neighborhood of well-kept, 1920s-style bungalows. "Mind telling me where we're going?"

"A place I know. You like prosciutto and banana peppers?"

She laughed. "I adore prosciutto, but it's fattening."

"You could stand to put on a few pounds. What do you weigh—one hundred twenty-five, one hundred and thirty?"

"Don't I wish! I got on the scales yesterday and I was up to almost one hundred and forty-five—and you bring chocolates and tempt me with prosciutto! Thin is in this year, Shane. Besides, if I put on any more weight I'll have to go out and buy a whole new wardrobe."

Shane gave her a twinkling-eyed side glance. "You'd look great without any wardrobe at all."

"Lecher! I may not carry a gun or a billy club, but I never venture out without my Mace." She dug into her purse, brought out her key ring and dangled a leather-cased canister in front of his face. The canister was only slightly larger than a lipstick.

"Heavens, sheriff!" Shane exclaimed in a tone of amused cynicism. "Did you ever have to use that?"

"Once. A burglary suspect we picked up on a warrant from Greeley freaked out in the office and started smashing up the furniture. I gave him a whiff of Mace before Crowley started shooting. I didn't want to do it, but it was the lesser evil."

Shane shook his head slowly, and when he spoke again he was the wise old professor patiently lecturing a student. "You made a mistake, sheriff. You had to move in close to use that little tear-gas gizmo. Take my word for it, you *never* want to get close to someone who's violent. Things have a way of happening. Your prisoner can deck you with a wild punch, come up with a gun or a knife at a range that can't miss, or any number of things."

"I certainly didn't want him shot!" Tracy protested.

"There are other non-lethal methods you could have used."

"Oh? You talk like an expert."

Shane chuckled. "Sheriff, the only thing I'm an expert at is staying out of trouble."

"Do you want to stay out of trouble with me?"

"By all means."

"Then stop calling me sheriff."

"All right—Tracy."

In the Bessemer district, a few blocks from the huge steel mill that for years had been the economic heartbeat of the town, Shane swung into a street running parallel to Interstate 25, made another turn and abruptly pulled up in front of an old-time tavern with green-enameled windows. From

the street they could hear a jukebox thumping out a lively
polka.

"This is Gus's," Shane announced. "It has the best
Dutch lunch and draft beer this side of Palermo. What's
more, it serves some of the greatest people I know—people who aren't afraid of working with their hands."

Tracy glanced at him questioningly as he came around
to open the door on her side of the car. "You come here
often?"

"Not often enough. And maybe that's what makes
Gus's so special. My job takes me to a lot of places that
leave me feeling dirty. Whenever I have the chance, I like
to come here to rub shoulders with ordinary people and
forget about all the phonies and wheeler-dealers I have to
contend with."

The tavern was doing a brisk business. Most of the pa-
trons were older men, many of them wearing work clothes
and engaged in animated conversations with their companions. Waving cordially to the white-shirted bartender
behind the oak counter that ran the length of one wall,
Shane led Tracy to one of the few vacant tables—a high-
backed wooden booth in the rear. Tracy started to slide
into the bench seat facing the front of the tavern, but
Shane gently guided her to the opposite seat and sat down
across from her.

She smiled. "You know, I think you've got the old
gunfighter instinct: never sit with your back to the door,
and so forth." She paused. "You used to be a police officer, didn't you?"

He held up two fingers for the bartender to see, then
drew a circle in the air with his hands. Turning to Tracy, he
made a face. "Can you really picture me pounding a
beat?"

"You were in law enforcement of *some* kind."

"What makes you say that?"

"Some of the things you've let slip—and that business about finding the shell casings. You were doing some detective work on your own, weren't you?"

"Every man likes to play Sherlock Holmes once in a while."

"Sherlock Holmes wouldn't have left a telltale cigar at the scene of the crime."

"Sherlock smoked a pipe."

"Damn it, you know what I mean!" It seemed hot in the tavern after the frigid ride over from Henryville, and the change in temperature was making her irritable. Slipping out of her coat and pulling off her headband, Tracy rested her elbows on the worn red linoleum tabletop and planted her chin on her interlaced fingers. "Who's trying to kill you, Shane?" she asked, lowering her voice.

Before he could respond, a waitress arrived with two huge schooners of beer and a giant platter heaped high with thin slices of Italian ham, salami and mozzarella cheese, a pile of long, yellow peppers, and a stack of hard-crusted bread slices. Shane promptly dug in and built a mammoth sandwich, took a bite and washed it down with a gurgle of beer. "Truthfully?" he asked, wiping his lips with a paper napkin.

"Truthfully."

"No one." As he spoke, he held up a hand to silence her protest. "I mean it. If the shooter wanted me dead, I'd be dead. I picked up one of those shell casings myself yesterday morning and had it analyzed. As you remarked, the shooter was a pro who knew exactly what he was doing. He could have knocked the eyelashes off a gnat with any one of his shots. *The point is, Tracy, he didn't.* He had a perfect target, a clear field of fire and first-rate equipment, but still he missed. He didn't want to kill me. He wanted to scare me."

"Did he succeed?"

"Yes and no."

"What's that supposed to mean?"

"It means exactly that—yes and no. I've been shot at before, Tracy, and I'll probably be shot at again. I don't like it—never have—but I've learned to live with it. I won't dig a hole and crawl in just because somebody's sore at me."

"He shot at me, too, Shane."

"I know. He saw you come charging up that slope like Teddy Roosevelt at San Juan Hill, and he was telling you to duck so he could get the hell out of there without being followed."

Tracy shuddered at the memory of that harrowing experience. "What about the photograph?"

"My guess is that it was a plant—something to throw me off, make me think an outsider was called in for a hit."

Tracy stared hard at him. "That suggests there are people *inside* TWS who'd be capable of assassination. Just what do you do for the company?"

He pushed the plate of cold cuts toward her. "Have a sandwich."

"I don't want a sandwich, Shane! And I don't want to let the question pass!"

Shane reached across the table and rested his hands on hers. "Tracy . . ."

"What?" she said crossly.

"Try being a woman for a change, huh?"

"I don't have to try. I *am* a woman."

"Then act like it—for tonight, at least. I like you, Tracy. I like you a lot. It might even be fun being with you if you'd stop being sheriff for five minutes."

She glared at him. She wanted to be angry, but there was no anger in her heart. She wouldn't admit it, but she liked him, too. She liked him a lot. "Do you suppose I could have something other than beer?'' she asked, wanting to change the subject.

"Name it."

"A glass of wine, I suppose."

Shane slid out of the booth, went to the bar and chatted briefly with the bartender. He returned a few minutes later with a tulip-shaped glass in one hand and a thin, dark bottle in the other. "I'm not much of an authority on wines," he confessed as he sat down, "but Freddie assures me this is decent stuff." He filled the glass with the red vintage. "You don't strike me as one of those white wine snobs, anyway."

Tracy took a sip of the Barbaresco and savored it. It was a very dry, hearty wine, gentle yet quietly authoritative; just the wine she imagined Shane might enjoy. "How *do* I strike you?"

Shane drained his beer, pushed the mug aside and reached for hers. "You strike me as someone I'd like to know better. You sure you don't want to fly up to Denver with me tomorrow?"

She shook her head. "'Fraid not. We both have business to attend to, and I for one need a clear head. Besides, I've got to be there first thing."

"So I'll leave early."

Tracy studied him over the top of her wineglass. He *seemed* sincere enough. "Let's not rush things, Shane," she said softly.

"I won't be back at the ranch for at least a week. Hey— a bunch of us will be coming down for a board meeting, followed by a Christmas party. Would you come as my guest?"

"I'd love to, but I may be off somewhere interviewing for a job."

"There's always TransWorld. I told you I could put in a word with the personnel manager."

"I'll keep that in mind, Shane. Right now I really don't know what I want to do with my life. I guess I'm just one of those people who is always searching for something without ever quite knowing what it is."

Again he rested his hands on hers. "We're both searching for something, Tracy."

WHEN THEY CAME OUTSIDE just before eleven, the sky was blurry with a luminous white cast. "There's snow in the air," Shane observed as he opened the passenger door of the M.G. for Tracy. "Why don't we stay in Pueblo tonight and drive up to Denver first thing in the morning? It'll save us both a couple hours."

"I've got to get home," Tracy said, starting to brush past him to climb into the sports car. "I have to pack, and there are some papers I want to—"

The next thing she knew, Shane's arms were around her waist, and he was pulling her close, his cheek against hers, his breath warm on her ear. "I didn't realize you were so tall," he murmured, nuzzling at her neck.

"It's the heels," Tracy said softly. "They let me look you in the eye and know exactly when you're about to feed me a line."

"I'd never do a thing like that." His cheek moved across hers, and his lips touched lightly at one corner of her mouth.

"You wouldn't? Shane, you're—" She'd wanted to say that he was a wolf if she'd ever seen one, but his sudden, smoldering kiss made speech impossible. Her fingers pressed tightly against his shoulders, her chest so snug against his that she could feel the thumping of his heart. As his tongue began exploring the warm sweetness of her mouth, one hand went to her hips, the other to the back of her head, welding their two bodies into a trembling oneness.

They stood that way for a full five minutes, locked in each other's arms, shutting out all else . . . the coldness of the night, the red and green neon of the tavern, the sounds of traffic from the freeway, the stares of the occasional passerby.

Finally Tracy pulled free of his lips. "Home, James," she said with a sigh. "This isn't the time or the place any more than the ridge road was." She squirmed out of his embrace and took her seat in the M.G.

"Tracy, I—" Shane didn't finish his statement. He simply shook his head and closed the door, then went through his customary inspection of the car. "It's going to be a cold trip back to Henryville," he remarked as he got in and started the engine. "I wouldn't want you to come down with pneumonia."

Tracy laughed, drawing her coat more tightly around her. "Tell me about it."

"Colder than it was coming over."

Tracy turned in her seat and stared at him. He was the most appealing man she'd ever met—probably the most appealing man she'd ever meet. But why did he insist on pushing her? "What you're saying is that I'm supposed to show my gratitude because you bought me dinner." She opened her purse, took out her wallet and withdrew a twenty-dollar bill. "Here—" she slapped the bill into his hand "—for my half of this fun evening."

He wadded up the bill and tossed it back to her. "Hey, cut it out, Tracy. It so happens that I find you a very attractive woman—that's all."

"I don't like being manipulated, Shane."

He shrugged and pulled out of the parking lot and onto the street. Driving in silence, he headed for the freeway and then turned north, away from the Henryville highway.

Tracy found herself confused by her feelings. She wanted to be with Shane and, yes, wanted him to make love to her . . . wanted it more than she was willing to admit. But somehow it didn't seem right, not the way their relationship was developing. Maybe *that* was it; maybe each of them wanted to dictate the terms of the relationship—she no less than he.

As they approached the northern city limits of Pueblo, the lights of a Holiday Inn came into view. Shane swung off the freeway. He pulled up under the portico, cut the engine and turned to her. "Sure you don't want to stay here tonight?"

Tracy took a deep breath. "You're used to getting what you want, aren't you, Shane?"

"I'm used to fighting for what I want."

Tracy unbuckled her seat belt and reached for the door handle. "I'm not going to fight you, Shane."

"Good." He leaned over to kiss her, but she opened her door and slipped out of the car.

"We can't go inside together," she announced in a conspiratorial tone. "We might run into someone I know, and gossip travels fast around here. I'll wait in the bar. You go in and register, then call me and let me know what room you're in. All right?"

He touched two fingers to his forehead in salute. "I won't be long."

"Nor will I, lover," Tracy murmured, smiling wickedly.

Just outside the entrance to the bar, she stopped at the pay phone and made a call. From the hallway she could see Shane approach the front desk and register. She waited a few moments, then stepped inside the dimly lighted bar and sat down on a stool as the phone behind the bar rang. The bartender picked up the receiver, listened, then looked around at the scattering of late-hour customers. "Somebody here name of Tracy?" he called out.

"Right here." Tracy leaned across and took the receiver. "Hi!" she said cheerfully.

"Two-twenty," Shane said.

"What a beautiful number." She sighed. "Plump up the pillows and I'll be along shortly."

"Promise?"

"Cross my heart and hope to die." Tracy hung up and headed for the lobby. Glancing outside, she saw the taxicab she'd ordered to take her to the state patrol headquarters in Pueblo. She pushed open the lobby door, called out to the driver to wait for her, then hurried to the pay phone she'd used a few minutes earlier. She dialed the number of the Holiday Inn.

"I'd like to leave a message for Mr. Keegan in Room Two-twenty," she informed the switchboard. "No—don't connect me, just take the message. Tell him he can't win them all. No, no name. He'll know who it's from."

THE RAGMAN was not at all pleased as he sat in the dark by the window, running his fingers across the noose he'd fashioned. Dacron climbing rope wasn't suitable for his purpose. It would allow him to do the job, but without his customary finesse. And his image had been built on finesse.

He had been in Tracy Hannon's house ever since she'd left with Keegan. He had found the rope and the box of shells in the dining room, in plain sight. Using a handkerchief, he had carefully wiped each of the brass casings and replaced them in the box. He didn't want to take a chance on any usable fingerprints being found on the shells. But he hadn't been able to find the *other* bit of evidence—the piece of paper he'd seen her retrieve from the rocks. He had decided to wait for her return. Then he would find out exactly what she knew, force her to turn over the evidence. He'd had no wish to kill her, since no one was paying him to do it, but now he supposed he must.

Without taking his eyes off the street, he began untying the hangman's noose. He would come up with another means of disposing of Tracy Hannon—something more poetic. An idea would undoubtedly occur to him when the time came.

Light snow had started to fall. The Ragman could barely make it out as it fluttered past the glow of the streetlight. It wasn't enough to matter yet. He'd give the sheriff twenty minutes more. After that, the snow would begin to cover the ground, and he would leave footprints. He stood up and unzipped his parka and wrapped the climbing rope around his waist—in case he had to get out in a hurry.

He moved silently into the kitchen and checked the back door to be certain he could open it easily and quickly if need be. When he returned to the dining room, he looked out the window again.

For the first time that evening, The Ragman swore.

Another police car was parked at the curb next to Tracy Hannon's Ford, and she was coming up the walk with a uniformed officer....

# Chapter Four

The clock-radio on the night table beside her bed had buzzed once, and without opening her eyes, Tracy had groped out groggily to tap the Snooze button. She needed another two or three hours of sleep at the very least. She'd had a hard night and faced the prospect of a hard day. She wriggled down under the covers and pulled the pillow over her head. *Go away, world. Go away and let me sleep. Please.*

The clock-radio buzzed again, more insistently this time, competing for attention with the sputtering rhythms of a stray broadcast signal. No easy listening this morning. No Neil Diamond, no Linda Ronstadt. It was too early for the Colorado Springs FM station to which she kept the radio tuned; the station hadn't even signed on yet. It was too early for anything *decent*.

Flopping over in a tangle of sheets and fluffy down quilt, Tracy reached out again and switched off the alarm. She opened her eyes and stared at the digital readout on the clock-radio. Four o'clock. Time to pack and be on her way to Denver. She wondered if she dared go back to sleep and trust her instincts to awaken her in another thirty or forty minutes. No way. Her instincts wouldn't be functioning at anywhere near normal after less than two hours of restless slumber.

Throwing back the covers, she sat up and swung her legs over the side of the bed, her bare feet recoiling as her toes touched the cold, polished-oak floor. "Damn you, Shane," she murmured sleepily. She'd dreamed about him from the moment she'd fallen into bed a little after two, after making a cup of hot cocoa for the state trooper who'd driven her home from Pueblo as a matter of professional courtesy. She'd dreamed and agonized and tossed in her sleep. Where was Shane now? Had he stayed at the motel? Had he driven back to the ranch? Had he gone on to Denver? It didn't matter, he might as well be a million miles away. Shane had wanted to make love to her, wanted to make her feel like a woman again, and she'd stood him up, been driven to the police station and hitched a ride home with the State Patrol. She had certainly shown him!

Standing up, Tracy pulled the shades down, stripped off her white flannel nightgown, then turned on the overhead light. Hurray for you, Hannon! she thought as she padded into the bathroom. You're another day older and as virtuous as ever.

She went into the shower, turned on the water full blast and stood under the hot, stinging jets, forcing herself to come wide awake and start thinking clearly. Would it have been so terribly wrong to sleep with Shane? She'd wanted it no less than he. But it hadn't been a matter of right or wrong; it had been a matter of taking control of her life for a change.

After briskly toweling herself dry, she brushed her teeth and tried to make some semblance of order out of her hair. Hair-blower, brush, comb—nothing helped. She stared hard at the frowning face in the bathroom mirror. Why did she always look as if she'd just stepped out of a wind tunnel? The frowning face stared right back at her and refused to reply.

Well, no time now...

Tracy dressed in a heavy gray Harris tweed suit and green sweater and sat down on the edge of the bed and zipped on her boots. Standing up, she checked her appearance in the mirror. Very proper and conservative; just the thing to wear to the big city on a cold, cold day. If she could line up some job interviews, maybe she'd shop around in Denver for a new outfit. Something equally proper and conservative, of course.

Angry, she unbuttoned the suit jacket and flung it onto the unmade bed. She didn't want to look proper and conservative; she wanted to look sexy and to have some man put his arms around her and say, "You're all woman, Tracy." No, not just *some* man.

She slipped contritely back into the jacket, buttoned it and added a thin gold chain necklace. Again she examined herself in the mirror. *You're exactly what circumstances have made you, and you'll just have to make the best of it.* But wouldn't it be nice sometimes to create circumstances instead of always having it the other way around?

After making the bed and tidying up the room, she quickly packed an overnight bag and went downstairs. A dozen random thoughts occurred to her. Had the garage put snow tires on her car as she'd requested? Would the county commissioners remember she'd told them she'd be out of town for the day? Would Bubba Crowley get around to serving those subpoenas she'd told him about? Would Shane...

Would Shane *what*? Would he send more expensive chocolates and more long-stemmed roses and another note of apology? Apology for what? For doing what any man might have done?

The box of Godiva chocolates was still on the hall table where she'd left it the night before. When she got back from Denver, she'd give the candy to her next-door neighbor. She flipped on the overhead light in the dining room and looked around, but failed to notice that the coil of Dacron rope was missing. Her inspection completed, she bundled up in her loden coat and blue-and-white plaid muffler and, overnight bag in hand, trudged through the snow to the patrol car, a shapeless hillock of white under the glare of the streetlamp. It took her five minutes to sweep off the snow with the broom she kept in the trunk, two minutes for the engine to fire up and another five for the transmission oil to warm sufficiently to allow her to wrestle the gearshift into low and send the car creaking reluctantly into the street.

The state highway was glazed with a treacherous layer of ice frosted with new-fallen snow, and it was slow going as Tracy negotiated the narrow, winding highway leading down out of the foothills. As she drove across the prairie west of Pueblo, the snow was lighter, and by the time she got to Colorado Springs, the road was clear. A few minutes after eight, she dropped off her overnight bag at an East Colfax Avenue motel, and headed downtown to the Federal Building.

For the rest of the day, Tracy and other representatives of Colorado's rural law enforcement agencies sat in a meeting room and listened to a succession of eager young assistant United States attorneys advise them how to do their jobs without running afoul of Supreme Court mandates. When the session resumed after midmorning coffee, the audience had dwindled from sixty-two to forty-nine. Thirteen more delegates fell by the wayside at lunch.

Tracy methodically took notes but found it difficult to concentrate. Her thoughts kept returning to Shane.

During the midafternoon break, she carried her coffee cup to a phone booth outside the cafeteria and called a

Denver *Post* reporter who'd done a feature story on her three years before when she'd taken on the job of sheriff.

"Tracy Hannon here," she began. "I don't know if you remember me, Miss Hodges, but—"

"Hannon," the voice on the other end of the line mused. "I'm afraid it doesn't register."

*Such is fame,* Tracy thought with a smile. "I'm the sheriff of San Isabel County."

"Oh, yes! Forgive me, but it's been a while. How are things in Henryville, sheriff?"

"Just fine. I need a favor, Miss Hodges. I'm in Denver today and I'm trying to track down background information about a certain individual."

The reporter's chitchat tone disappeared. "Do I smell a story?"

"Not really," Tracy said quickly. "It's all very routine. I just need to clear up some things."

"Oh." The reporter's disappointment was evident. "Just who is it you're interested in, sheriff?"

"A man named Shane Keegan. He works for a company called TransWorld Systems, headquartered here. That's all I know."

"TransWorld? *That* rings a bell. What's your interest?"

Tracy decided to stick with the truth, or at least partial truth. It was a matter of public record, anyway. "TransWorld plans to develop some property in San Isabel County. Naturally, we'd like to know a bit more about the company."

"TransWorld is a real blue-chip operation, I can tell you that much. It has the top four or five floors of one of those new skyscrapers on Seventeenth Street, just down from the Brown Palace. I don't know exactly what the company does, but I understand one of our business writers has been digging into it. I suppose I *could* ask him."

"Would you, Miss Hodges? I'd appreciate it."

"Happy to—on one condition, of course. If any sort of a story develops at your end, you'll let me know. Deal?"

"Deal. May I call you back? I'm in a meeting at the Federal Building and I'll be tied up for a while."

"I'm here till six, sheriff. I'll see what I can find out."

When Tracy returned to the meeting room, only twenty seats were occupied. An undersheriff from the Western Slope whom she'd met on business several months before had left a note inviting her to join him and some other officers for cocktails at a bar in Tabor Square where, as he explained, "serious efforts will be made to bring this here group to life."

Tracy tore up the note and dropped it into a wastebasket. She needed a good night's sleep, not a night on the town.

For the next two hours she sat in the conference room, trying her best to appear attentive but thinking dreamily of Shane. She wished she wasn't so tired. Her brain was getting fuzzy, and there was something she wanted to be sure to check out.

The reminder she needed came from an unexpected source.

"We want to thank you all for coming," the young woman at the lectern was saying. She was a willowy blonde with steel-rimmed eyeglasses dangling from a silver chain looped around her neck. "If there's ever anything we at the U.S. Attorney's Office can help you with, pick up the phone and..."

Tracy gathered up her notes and headed for the front of the room while her colleagues made a beeline for the door. Introducing herself to the attorney who'd presided at the session, Tracy got right down to business. "Would you tell me why privately owned property in my county has been designated a federal reservation without notifying local authorities?''

The attorney frowned and carefully adjusted her eyeglasses on the bridge of her nose. Sorry, she said, but she had no knowledge of the matter. She'd be happy to look into it, of course. If Tracy would care to call her in a day or so...

"I *wouldn't* care to call in a day or so," Tracy said testily. "I want to know now."

Ten minutes later she was seated in the office of the chief assistant United States attorney, getting her answer.

"It's strictly a matter of national security, Mrs. Hannon. TransWorld Systems is engaged in various aspects of classified work for federal agencies I'm not at liberty to name. Because that work is highly sensitive, it has been deemed prudent to restrict access to the company property in San Isabel County. If you'll talk to your county attorney, he'll concede there's ample legal precedent." The man swiveled about in his chair and removed a heavy, red-bound volume from the walnut credenza behind his desk. Thumbing through the book until he found what he wanted, he peered up at Tracy. "I'll be happy to cite chapter and verse from the United States Code, if you like."

Tracy made a note of the citation. "Why wasn't San Isabel County informed beforehand?"

The attorney smiled patiently. "Please try to understand, Mrs. Hannon. We have no wish to advertise the work TransWorld Systems is doing for the government. The word will get out soon enough."

Tracy decided to try a more direct approach to satisfy her curiosity. "All right, then, so much for TransWorld. What can you tell me about a man named Shane Keegan?''

The attorney slapped shut the lawbook and returned it to the credenza. "Nothing," he said curtly. "Absolutely nothing."

"You mean you don't know anything about him?"

"I mean I can tell you nothing." He stood up, went to the door and held it open for her. "It's been a pleasure meeting you, Sheriff Hannon. I hope to see you at our next seminar."

SHANE PUT DOWN the phone and reached for a cigar. So Tracy was asking questions—why shouldn't she? She was just doing the job she was paid to do, and he would have been disappointed in her if she hadn't. She probably wouldn't stop with the U.S. Attorney's Office, either. Next thing he knew, she'd be demanding some straight answers from Washington.

He struck a match, stared at it for a few seconds, then blew it out and dropped it into an ashtray. He'd really screwed up the night before, and he knew it. That business of whisking her off to the motel—the whole "Me Tarzan, you Jane" bit—didn't go over with Tracy Hannon. He should have known better.

Shane lighted another match, held it to the tip of his cigar and let the smoke escape through his teeth.

*You're an obnoxious s.o.b., Keegan,* he told himself angrily. *You don't want to be, but you are. You've been burned once too often when it comes to women, and you don't intend to get burned again. So you play the tough guy and build a wall around yourself. Only thing is, this time the wall didn't work. She still got to you. She really got to you.*

He'd wanted to go to bed with Tracy, but it was more than something physical. It made him feel good being with her, and he hadn't wanted the evening to end. He'd wanted to go to sleep with her in his arms, and he'd wanted to wake up in the morning and gaze at her face and imagine that they were off somewhere, free of all the complications of life in the real world.

Now she probably wouldn't even talk to him again. But he was going to try. He was damn well going to try.

He punched the button on the intercom. "Mrs. Hoyt?"

"Yes, sir?"

"Were you able to take care of that matter I talked to you about?" It was a foolish question, he knew. Mrs. Hoyt never overlooked anything.

"Yes, Mr. Keegan. Jerry Latimer called around and found out where the young lady would be staying, and I went out there myself. The manager was only too happy to, ah, negotiate a settlement. I gave him a check for one hundred dollars."

"Thank you." Shane leaned back in his chair and stared again at his cigar. It was his fourth of the day. He had to cut down.

He remembered how Tracy had found the cigar in the rocks where the shooter had perched. It didn't take her any time at all to put two and two together. His worried frown gave way to a grin. Word association: cigar, rocks, Tracy. It seemed that everything led back to Tracy.

He thought of the arrangements his secretary had made, and he hoped he hadn't screwed up again.

THE DESK CLERK at the motel on East Colfax wasn't the least bit apologetic when he told Tracy that a mistake had been made and that the room she'd booked had already been rented to someone else. By then it was five-thirty and already dark. It was snowing hard, rush-hour traffic was a slushy mess, and Tracy was bone tired.

"I've already paid for the room!" she protested. "If you'll check your records, you'll find I've stayed here a dozen times or more! That ought to count for something!''

''Indeed it does, Mrs. Hannon.'' The clerk smiled affably, took a twenty-dollar bill and some change from the cash drawer and handed them to her. ''The manager's so upset he told me to give you your money back and arrange for a room elsewhere.''

Tracy eyed him skeptically. ''A room *where*?''

The clerk beamed. ''What would you say to the Brown Palace?''

Tracy's mouth dropped open. As long as she could remember, the Brown Palace had been the most fashionable, and one of the most expensive, of Denver's major hotels, a redstone-faced monument to historic elegance. ''I can't afford the Brown!''

''Don't you worry about it, Mrs. Hannon. It's already taken care of. We've sent your bag over, and they're expecting you. Just think of it as our way of making it up to you.''

THE RAGMAN WAS AMUSED. Should he tell the client about this lovers' game he'd just discovered, or should he make the client pay for the information?

He'd make the client pay, of course. One did not rise to the top of his chosen profession by giving away free samples, be they snippets of information or the end product itself: death.

But for the most fortunate of circumstances—circumstances beyond his control—he would have violated that tenet last night, when he slipped into Tracy Hannon's house to kill her. If she had not arrived accompanied by a police officer, he would have gone through with it instead of beating a judicious retreat out the back door. Now, though, he was glad it had worked out the way it did. He could turn a profit yet.

He closed the door of the phone booth and dialed a number. As he waited, he reached into his coat pocket and brought out a rolled-up copy of *Time* magazine. He ripped out a page from the center of the magazine and wadded it up in his left hand. The number answered, and The Ragman asked for the client by name. He smiled as he waited. He guessed the client would be shaken up. That, too, was amusing. The Ragman enjoyed making people squirm.

"I think we should talk," he said as soon as the person came on the line.

Pause. "Who is this?"

The Ragman held the crumpled page to the mouthpiece and squeezed it. The slick paper crackled in his fist. "We seem to have a bad connection." He squeezed the wad again, brushing it against the mouthpiece this time. "Perhaps it would be better if I called you back at—" *crackle, crackle* "—seven-thirty. It is most important that we review our arrangement."

Seven-three-zero were the last digits of the telephone number at which the client had taken the earlier calls from The Ragman. "Most important" signaled that he was to be waiting by the phone at the top of the following hour.

Another pause. "Call me back." The client sounded ill.

The Ragman hung up and dropped the wad of paper on the floor. He looked at his watch. It was five-forty. The client would just have time to get to the restaurant by six and could mingle unnoticed in the cocktail crowd. Perhaps he would even have time for a drink before the phone rang. He would need it.

Twenty minutes later The Ragman and the client resumed their conversation.

"How did you get my name and office number?" the client demanded.

The Ragman stifled a yawn. It had been child's play. The middleman had told the client to designate a telephone number through which he could be contacted without fear of a tap. The middleman had passed along the number to The Ragman, and The Ragman had done some elementary footwork and found the location of the phone. It was a simple matter to hire a seedy private detective to stake out the phone stall, see who answered the call, then follow that individual and determine his identity. The Ragman hadn't felt he was violating his principles when, after receiving the private detective's report, he'd slit the latter's throat in an alley off Larimer Street. It hadn't really been a *free* hit, but a business transaction, one that had bought The Ragman peace of mind.

"I have my ways," The Ragman said. "We have problems, my friend. I should say *you* have problems."

"What sort of problems?"

The Ragman smiled. "First let us again talk money...."

THE UNIFORMED DOORMAN at the Brown Palace didn't bat an eye as he opened the driver's side door of the patrol car and helped Tracy out. He ushered her inside the plush, old-fashioned lobby with its tier-upon-tier of balconies, then touched the bill of his cap and was gone before she could even tip him. The front-desk clerk told her the registration had already been attended to, wished her a pleasant stay and signaled for a bellhop.

Her accommodations weren't a room, but a richly appointed suite consisting of a salon, bedroom, bath and wet bar. The bellhop showed Tracy around and vanished—also before she could tip him.

She was dreaming all this, Tracy thought as she tugged off her boots, tossed them aside and traced her tired, stockinged toes through the lush gold carpet. Mistakes like this didn't happen to her. Other mistakes, yes, but not nice ones.

Then she saw a slender silver vase with a dozen long-stemmed red roses on a table by the bedroom door. There was a card leaning against the bottom of the vase, and Tracy didn't have to look at the card to know whom it was from.

For a moment, a very brief moment, she was angry. The motel hadn't made a mistake. This was all Shane's doing. If he thought he could practically kidnap her from a motel where she was paying her own way and move her in here as if she were some trollop...

Suddenly she found herself leaning back on the couch, her hands over her mouth, laughing so hard her sides ached. This was the most exciting thing that had happened to her in years! Shane Keegan was something else!

Shane—Oh, Lord! The reporter with whom Tracy had spoken earlier said she'd be leaving the *Post* at six, and it was already after that. Tracy double-checked the number, then made the call.

"I'd about given up on you," Miss Hodges said peevishly.

"There was a mix-up with my motel reservations," Tracy apologized. "I had to find another room."

"Oh?" The reporter's grumpiness faded. "You're lucky you did. There's a blizzard moving in, and a lot of people are going to find themselves stranded in town tonight. Now, about your man Keegan..."

It was as if the mention of his name had been a signal, for at that very second a buzzer sounded.

"Just a minute," Tracy interrupted the woman. "I've got someone at the door." She put down the receiver and went to the door. Opening it, she found Shane standing in the hallway, boxes under each arm and a boyish grin on his face.

"Hi," he greeted her.

Tracy couldn't speak for a few seconds. He was the same Shane, but somehow different, and she didn't know quite how to talk to him. The Shane she'd known on the ridge road and on their single date in Pueblo was a maverick—brash and impetuous, unimaginable in anything dressier than jeans and knockabout sweaters. But *this* Shane who stood before her was brushed and polished, with not a strand of sandy-gray hair out of place. He looked positively dapper in a navy blue suit, pale blue, oxford-cloth buttondown shirt and pale yellow silk tie with silvery dots. There was the glitter of a gold Rolex on his wrist, the buffed glow of ebony on his tasseled slip-on shoes.

"Hi," she said cautiously.

"May I come in?"

For a fleeting moment Tracy wanted to tell him he could damn well get rid of the notion that she was a naive schoolgirl who'd simper and bow to his every whim. She had a mind of her own and a will of her own, and he'd better learn to accept that. But all she could come up with, in a stammering voice, was, "I—I'm on—on the phone."

"I can wait." He retreated across the hall, where he stacked his parcels on an upholstered bench, and sat down beside them. "Yell when you're free. I'll be here."

Tracy felt her spirits soar. "Inside," she said sternly, cocking her thumb and trying her best to suppress a smile. "If someone saw you sitting there, they'd report me to the SPCA. Do you mind telling me why the whipped-puppy routine?"

Shane rose and gathered up his packages. "I was afraid I might have come on too strong last night, so I decided to mend my ways. The meek are supposed to inherit the earth, aren't they?"

Tracy glanced appraisingly at his expensive, three-piece suit. "I don't know about inheriting the earth, Shane, but you look as if you just came into a very large bundle somewhere."

"I watch the sales," he said, almost apologetically.

She closed the door behind them. Shane deposited his packages on a chair in the salon and took her hands. "Hi, sheriff," he said, pulling her toward him until his face was inches from hers, his breath warm and soft on her forehead, the scent of his after-shave tickling her nostrils.

Without wearing heels, Tracy was three inches shorter than Shane. She tilted back her head and looked up at him. "You're repeating yourself."

"I know. Are you still sore at me?"

"Yes."

"How sore?"

"Very sore. You keep pushing me, and I don't like to be pushed. I don't like it anymore than you do."

"I'll never do it again, Tracy. Scout's honor."

"Shane, the last thing in the world I'd ever suspect you of being is a Boy Scout! You—"

She didn't finish. His lips parted and closed on hers and his hands held the back of her head, his fingers twining through her hair. She tried to pull free, tried to tell him she had a call waiting, but the tip of his tongue nudging hers was generating a magnetism too powerful to resist. She tightened her arms around his waist and pressed her chest against his, losing herself in his nearness.

The phone . . .

Reluctantly she turned her head away, the taste of him sweet and moist on her lips. "Please," she murmured, barely able to hear her own voice over the pounding of her heart. "I have someone on the phone."

"Call them back," Shane whispered, lowering his hands until they were resting suggestively on the svelte curve of her hips.

Without taking her eyes off him, Tracy backed away and snatched up the receiver. "Miss Hodges? Something's come up. Do you suppose I could get in touch with you later?"

"I was just leaving the office, sheriff," the reporter grumbled. "It's been a long day."

Shane stepped in behind Tracy, his hands now at her waist, his cheek brushing the back and sides of her neck. "Is there, ah, someplace I, ah, can call you?" Tracy asked, reaching behind her with her free hand and running her fingertips across Shane's solidly muscled shoulder.

The reporter sighed. "Well, I'm not even going to try to drive home to Evergreen for a while—not in this storm. If you want to, you can give me a jingle a little later at the Denver Press Club. I'll probably be there for a couple of hours."

"I'll do that," Tracy said quickly. "'Bye now—and thanks." She dropped the receiver into its cradle and spun about on her toes to confront Shane. "I find you extremely distracting," she scolded, thumping an accusatory fingertip against his chest.

"You're supposed to," he said, kissing her on the side of the neck, just under one ear. "It's chemistry. We interact."

"We do, do we?"

"Sure. Can't you tell?" He began working free the buttons of her wool jacket.

She deftly pushed him away and stepped back. "I'd say it's more like physics than chemistry. You know, an irresistible force meeting an immovable object."

He grinned and reached for her again. "You may have a point. I *do* find you irresistible, Tracy." His lips homed in on hers, and she turned her head, certain she would lose any argument if he kissed her one more time.

"I don't know that I care for being moved out of my motel without even being asked."

"What would you have done if I'd asked?"

Tracy thought about it. She was sure she knew the answer, but she wasn't about to admit it. "I probably would have slapped your face and told you to get lost," she lied.

Shane seemed hurt. He sat down on the couch and gazed at her. "Why?"

"Because I choose to think of myself as a very independent woman—that's why," she replied, avoiding looking at him, afraid that his eyes would see the truth she was trying so hard to conceal.

"You're the most independent woman I've ever met, Tracy."

"You've met a lot of women, I'm sure," she countered. She dropped down into a wingback chair opposite the couch and tucked her legs underneath her.

"A few," he said with a shrug.

"You must tell me about all your women sometime," she said, still afraid to look at him.

"Sometime—not now." He reached into the inside breast pocket of his suit jacket and brought out a packet of cigars. Biting off the cellophane wrapper of one, he stared at it for a few seconds, then shoved it back into the packet. "You suppose I could ask a favor?" The playful mood was gone, and he was suddenly all business.

Tracy smiled, wondering why he had become so serious. "You can ask," she said.

"I've got to go to a reception tonight in the hotel. Will you come with me?"

She hesitated. "How formal is it? I really didn't come prepared for partying."

Shane brought out the cigar he'd unwrapped, struck a match and started to light the cigar. He suddenly changed his mind, blew out the match and put the cigar aside. "Just your typical corporate-type thing. The company's trying to impress some prospects. I'd like to have you there to size up a few people."

Tracy stared curiously at him. "Shane, I really don't know a *thing* about your business. Every time I try to find out, I run into a brick wall."

He shrugged. "You know about people. That's all any business is: people. And don't tell me you have nothing to wear." He got up and collected the boxes he'd brought with him. "You might not have come prepared, but I did. Take a look."

Incredulous, Tracy slipped the red ribbon off the first and largest of the boxes and removed the lid. Inside was a dazzlingly gorgeous black silk sheath that she knew would have cost her at least a half-month's pay. She stood up and held the dress to her body, studying it in a gilt-framed mirror on the wall. With a wistful sigh, she carefully folded the dress and put it back inside the box.

"Sorry, Shane," she said softly, "but the answer is no."

He looked surprised. "Why not?"

"I already told you. I choose to think of myself as a very independent woman. Whisking me off to this hotel is one thing. I suppose I can rationalize it, if only because I want to rationalize it. I'm certainly not going to wander all over town tonight in this snow, looking for another place to stay. But this—" she glanced longingly at the box she'd just repacked "—this implies something else."

Shane struck another match, picked up his cigar and lighted it. "*What* does it imply, Tracy? That you're a kept woman?"

Tracy hesitated. "Something like that, I suppose. The dress is lovely, and I'm sure everything else in those other boxes is equally lovely. But I can't accept any of it, Shane. We hardly know each other."

"We know all we need to know. Open the other boxes."

A new wall had come between them. It was an invisible wall, but nonetheless impenetrable. "No," Tracy said firmly.

Shane drew on his cigar, held the smoke in his mouth for a moment, then let it escape slowly between his teeth. "Consider the clothes a bonus. You've got something I want, and I'm willing to pay for it. It's as simple as that, sheriff. This is strictly business."

Tracy stared at him for a full half minute, wondering if she'd heard correctly. "Business?" she echoed.

"Business," he said, nodding.

Tracy looked around for her boots, then tugged them on angrily and yanked up the side zippers. When she had finished, she started for the bedroom. "I'm going to get my bag," she announced, fighting to hold her temper in check. "I'll have the hotel send me a bill. Now get lost!"

Shane jumped to his feet and went after her. "Hey!" he protested, putting his arms around her from behind. "When I said business, I was talking about the reception—not our relationship, for God's sake, Tracy! The company wants to hire your services for a very specific and legitimate purpose. Cops everywhere engage in moonlighting."

Tracy batted his hands away and spun about to face him. "I've got a full-time job. I don't have time to moonlight."

"You could use the money, though. You're going to be out of a job in another month."

She looked at him skeptically. "Just what would I be expected to do?"

"Size up some people who'll be at the reception. We can run computer profiles and intersects until they're coming out of our ears, but all the microchips in the world still can't give us the kind of logic we need."

Tracy frowned. "Why me, Shane? Why a lame-duck county sheriff? If TWS can afford this—" with a sweep of her arms she indicated the suite "—it can afford to hire professionals."

Shane took her hands in his and squeezed them. "Two reasons, Tracy. No—*three* reasons. The first is that I trust you, and there aren't a whole lot of people in this world I can say that about. The second is that I need you. The third is that you've got the makings of a real pro. You've got a brain and you know how to use it." He grinned at her disarmingly. "The body that goes with the brain isn't so bad, either."

"Strictly business, huh?"

"The reception, yes. The rest of our relationship—no. I never mix business with pleasure."

"You've been doing it since you walked in here, you idiot!"

"No way. A few minutes ago I made a move on a very desirable woman whom I happen to like very much. Right now I'm negotiating with a law enforcement officer whose intuitiveness and deductive abilities I respect. There's a difference—a big difference, *sheriff*."

Tracy shook her head slowly. "Damn it, Shane, you should have been a lawyer. You could convince a jury of almost anything."

"As a matter of fact, I used to be a lawyer. But you're the only jury that counts now, Tracy."

"Do you mind telling me just what it is you do for TransWorld Systems? The company obviously doesn't keep a very close eye on your expense account."

He chuckled. "I have friends in the comptroller's office who let me get away with murder. How about it, sheriff? Come to the reception with me, mingle with the guests and pay particular attention to three individuals I'll point out to you. Listen to them talk—for style, not necessarily for content—and judge how they handle themselves. I want to know your impressions.''

"For what purpose, may I ask?''

"If I told you, it would prejudice your assessments. We'll talk about my reasons later. Agreed?''

Tracy thought it over. "You said TransWorld Systems wants to hire my services. What sort of fee am I expected to ask?''

"Whatever you think is fair. The clothes—'' he glanced at the boxes "—are yours to keep, of course. A bonus.''

"Very well, Shane, we'll make it a business arrangement. I'm authorized to charge thirty-five dollars plus mileage for service of subpoenas, writs and other legal papers. The mileage would come to—let's see, three hundred miles round trip at twenty cents a mile—a total of sixty dollars. Since I used an official vehicle to drive up here, I'll have to turn the mileage money over to San Isabel County. Say ninety-five dollars total.''

"Say a thousand dollars, Tracy, and TransWorld will send the county a separate check for the mileage.''

Her jaw dropped. "*You* may have friends in the comptroller's office, but I don't!''

Shane laughed. "If there's any squawk, I'll put in some overtime to make up for it.'' He stepped back, still holding Tracy's hands. "You probably want to freshen up and get changed. I'll be back for you within an hour. I've got a couple of things to take care of.''

After he had gone, Tracy looked up the number of the Denver Press Club and called Miss Hodges. She apologized for having broken off their previous conversation.

"No problem, sheriff,'' the reporter assured her in a voice that suggested she was slightly tipsy. "Where'd we leave off?''

"You were going to fill me in on Shane Keegan.''

"Oh, yes. Wait a sec—" The rustle of paper sounded, close to the phone. "Here it is. Don't let this get around, but our business-news people are doing a full takeout on TransWorld in a couple of weeks, and it sounds like quite a deal. TWS is a real success story. It started in Washington as a one-man operation, providing consulting services to the State Department. TWS would go in and analyze various countries' methods of protecting their elected leadership, then come up with ways to minimize risk of assassination and abduction. All very hush-hush, of course. The theory was that private enterprise would be more effective because, if the job were done on a government-to-government basis, it would appear Washington was meddling in the internal affairs of other countries. Anyway, as the company grew, it got into the high-tech end of things, developing all sorts of hardware for surveillance and security, along with the training of personnel to handle this sort of assignment. Now TWS is into just about every related field there is, including customized bullet-proof automobiles and production of some very sophisticated anti-tampering devices. It has something like eighteen hundred employees worldwide. The company is privately held, but our business editor has heard educated guesses that TWS is worth about two hundred million dollars."

"Where does Shane Keegan fit into all this?" Tracy asked.

"Keegan," the reporter mused. "Ah, *there's* the real story." She paused, as if consulting her notes. "Shane Mahaffey Keegan, age forty-two, a graduate of Annapolis, four years in the Marine Corps and then five with the FBI. His wife divorced him a few years after they got married, probably because he's so damn secretive about everything he does. Did I tell you? He managed to put himself through law school while he was in the Marines, which is highly unusual. Anyway, like most FBI types, he's a real nut on privacy. He won't say word one to the press. Won't even return phone calls. He owns apartments in Denver, Washington and Paris; and as far as we can find out, he lives alone and likes it. He's an electronics genius and a very unorthodox businessman—he'd rather tinker around a workshop than call the shots from a board-room. As I said, he's a real nut on personal privacy. He's going to be positively livid when he sees our story.''

Tracy winced. She'd seen Shane when he was annoyed. She didn't want to see him livid. ''What's his connection with TWS?''

''You're not listening, sheriff. Shane Mahaffey Keegan is founder, chairman of the board and the principal shareholder. He *is* TransWorld Systems.''

## Chapter Five

"Sensational!" Shane exclaimed, leaning against the entryway and watching Tracy spin about in the black silk sheath.

Tracy glanced over her shoulder at him and sighed. "I'm an impostor. You know it and I know it, and everybody I meet tonight is going to know it as well. This dress doesn't go with the apple-cheeked, outdoorsy look. It's much too elegant."

"I don't know about that. You're pretty elegant yourself."

The dress was without a doubt the most expensive she'd ever worn. It was sinfully sleek, with a plunging, ruffled neckline and side slits that did things for her legs. The whole effect was superbly muted by an overlay of black chiffon that hung in soft folds and whispered sensuously with her every movement. To go with the dress, Shane had bought a black silk evening bag and mid-heeled patent sandals that clung to her feet with a delicate network of thin black straps. He'd even remembered such items as dark hose and a black slip.

"Well, I guess everything fits all right," she admitted.

Shane seemed pained that such a question would ever occur to her. "Of course everything fits. My secretary did the shopping, and I've never known her to make a mistake."

Tracy gave him a puzzled frown. "Your secretary's never set eyes on me. How'd she know what would and wouldn't fit me?"

"She took your overnight bag with her, just to make sure. It seemed reasonable to assume she'd come up with the right sizes if she went by the clothes you brought with you."

Tracy stiffened. "I'm not sure I care for anyone prowling through my things."

"It was for a good cause," Shane said, taking out a packet of cigars. He started to open the packet, then changed his mind and returned it to an inside pocket of his coat. "I'm ahead of my quota," he said, as if anxious to change the subject. "Kick me in the shins if you see me light up before nine o'clock, huh?"

How long would it take her to know this man? she wondered. He could be brash, assertive, grumpy and distrustful, and he could be easygoing, thoughtful, fun—and everything in between. At the moment he was a schoolboy who'd ruffled teacher's feathers and wanted to make amends. It was difficult for her to remain irritated.

She came across to the entryway, put her arms around him and looked him in the eye. "Do you *really* want to quit?"

"Yes."

Without hesitation, Tracy reached inside his jacket and plucked out the cigars. She crumpled them in her fist, then held up the jumbled ball for his dismayed inspection. "Guess what? You've just quit."

Shane made a face. "Be warned, woman. Nicotine withdrawal produces some strange and terrifying symptoms."

"Such as?"

"Insatiable lust, for one thing."

Tracy laughed. "I'll hold your hand till the worst is over."

Shane pulled her close and kissed her lightly on the forehead. "Holding hands won't cut it. I crave your body." His head came lower and his parted lips touched hers.

"Whoa!" she protested, pushing him away. "You start *that* again and we'll never make it to your reception!"

"We'll probably never be missed."

"Sorry, Shane, but I was hired to do a job and I intend to earn my money. You might be the chair—"

He froze. "I might be what, Tracy?"

"Nothing."

"I might be *what*?"

Tracy decided it was ridiculous to play games. "I know who you are, Shane. It's no big secret."

He frowned. "I suppose not. It's just that after a few false starts, the two of us were beginning to hit it off pretty well. I didn't want anything to louse up the relationship."

"Like knowing you own a two-hundred-million-dollar company?"

"Where'd you hear that figure?"

"I have my sources."

"You talked to somebody at the Denver *Post*, didn't you? Well, it's none of the *Post*'s business what TWS is worth, or what we do to earn our money as long as we operate within the law. TWS isn't publicly held and never will be if I can help it. At this moment I own the company outright, and it has a book value of one hundred and thirty-seven million dollars—not two hundred million. What the *Post doesn't* know is that January first I'm turning over control to an employee stock trust for ten cents on the dollar and I'm getting out. The employees will run the show and TWS will still be privately held. Satisfied?''

Tracy planted her fists on her hips and glared furiously at him. "Don't take out your paranoia on me, Shane Mahaffey Keegan! Come to think of it, I liked you better before you told me!"

Shane winced, but the beginnings of a grin played at the corners of his mouth. He took Tracy's hands and squeezed them. "Sorry. Will you forgive me for being a boor?"

Tracy thought about it. "I don't know. You practically accused me of spying on you, but you seem to have ferreted out some rather personal details about me—including my shoe size."

"You'd rather get blisters?"

Tracy shook her head in exasperation. "You have an answer for everything, haven't you?"

"Almost everything, Tracy. There are still a few mysteries I haven't unraveled, but I'm working on them."

SHANE WAS A DIFFERENT MAN as they stepped off the elevator and strolled across the glass-enclosed skywalk to the ballroom in the hotel annex. He seemed to tighten up, putting a barrier between himself and all others with whom he might come into contact. The touch of his hand on her bare arm was cool, his manner distant. He was a man she hadn't known before, a man who'd suddenly chosen to be deliberately aloof, almost at odds with the world. She sensed she'd become a mere spectator at a performance he felt compelled to play out.

There were perhaps two hundred people in the ballroom, most of them men wearing expensively tailored suits. But there were a number of aristocratic-looking women, too, each outfitted every bit as fashionably as Tracy. As Shane and Tracy entered the room, the unintelligible babble of cocktail-party chatter became a buzz against the soulful sounds of a piano player doing enchanting things with Gershwin's "Love is Here to Stay."

Shane led her to a cluster of four men standing near a buffet table dominated by a massive, black-ice sculpture of an open-work globe girdled by three gold rings. He nodded to the men, then turned to Tracy. "Tracy, I'd like to present Evan MacManus. Evan, this is Mrs. Hannon."

MacManus smiled cordially, and Tracy got the distinct feeling he'd go out of his way to be on his best behavior with any friend of Shane's. "Delighted, Mrs. Hannon," he said vigorously, taking her right hand in both of his and pumping it warmly. Tracy suspected he was at home in this sort of crowd, being a center of attention. MacManus was in his early sixties, thin and impeccably groomed, rather patrician in his bearing. "Are you a skier by any chance?"

The outdoorsy look must have betrayed her, Tracy thought. "No," she lied, smiling. She did ski, but she'd gotten into the habit of keeping this to herself. San Isabel County took a jaundiced view of what it considered to be self-indulgent frivolities.

"Ah, then you must take up the sport," MacManus declared. "We have a place in the mountains, you know, and with all this snow we've been getting, the skiing is marvelous. If you're in town for a few days, you might like to come up and visit my wife and me."

"I'm afraid I can't make it this trip, Mr. MacManus."

"Pity. You're from—Washington, isn't it?"

Shane spoke up quickly. "Mrs. Hannon is a personal friend. She's not in the trade."

"Oh, I see." MacManus smiled indulgently. "Well, if there's anything at all I can do to make your stay here more pleasant, please call on me, Mrs. Hannon. I'm at your service."

Shane nodded again and led Tracy to another group nearby. "Tracy, I'd like to have you meet Oliver Brock.

Oliver—" he glanced at a plump, distinguished-looking man in his mid-forties who, until Shane's arrival, had held center stage among his companions "—this is Mrs. Hannon, a personal friend. Mrs. Hannon is not from Washington, nor is she in the trade."

Brock roared with laughter. "Now *that* raises more questions than it answers! Figure out a way to ditch the big guy here, Mrs. Hannon, and we'll have a drink and get acquainted."

"I'll see what I can do," Tracy said.

Shane maneuvered her through the crowd to the back of the room where a dozen or so people were gathered around a grand piano, listening to a delicate-looking, dark-complexioned man of about Shane's age improvise on "A Foggy Day." The pianist winked at Shane and kept on playing. "Nice you could make it, Shane," he murmured throatily from under a bushy, black mustache. "I was beginning to think you might have found something better to do. Seeing the classy lady you have in tow, I think I might have been right, eh?" The pianist's accent was European, Tracy noted—French, possibly, but she couldn't be sure.

Shane seemed to loosen up a bit. "This poor man's Paderewski is the infamous Alphonse Deschamps," he informed Tracy. "He's always promising me he'll practice before he sits down at the piano, but he never does. TWS can't afford to hire a couple of thugs to break his fingers for him, so we suffer along."

"Stop it!" Tracy scolded. She smiled at the man at the keyboard. "Go on playing, Mr. Deschamps. You're very talented."

The pianist's nimble, diamond-bedecked fingers flew across the keys in a dazzling series of arpeggios. "You have impeccable taste," he said, bowing his head in feigned modesty. "Your escort couldn't carry a tune in a gunnysack, so what does he know, eh? Please, call me Alfy. And I shall call you—''

"Mrs. Hannon," Shane cut in. He playfully patted the piano player on the top of his balding head. "She's spoken for, Alfy."

Alfy sighed plaintively. "Most missuses are."

"I'm a widow," Tracy said.

Alfy's hands moved up an octave on the keyboard and his music brightened. "Then there is hope yet!"

Shane looked around the room. "Don't be so sure about that. I see that Madame Tatarescu is here. She might have other ideas."

Alfy's fingers retreated to the lower octaves and his beat became heavy, almost funereal. "Tatarescu and I are no more! She has taken up with a Milanese feather merchant, and I, being a gentleman, have renounced any claim I might have had."

"I'll tell her that." Shane took Tracy's arm and guided her away from the piano. "Come on, I'll buy you a drink."

A waiter had been hovering nearby, intent on having the honor of serving the host, and Shane signaled to him. As Shane led Tracy to a semiquiet corner of the ballroom, his back to the crowd, the waiter closed in with two tall, frosty glasses of sparkling, pale red liquid. Shane handed one glass to Tracy and took the other for himself. "Campari and soda," he explained. "Just the thing when you want to keep your wits about you."

"You feel a special need to keep your wits about you among your own people?" Tracy inquired.

"Especially among my own people," Shane said ominously.

Tracy glanced around. "I take it you introduced me to those three men for some specific reason."

"Of course."

"Am I supposed to guess what they do?"

He shook his head. "Sorry. The first man, Evan MacManus, is president of TransWorld. He runs the corporate end of things. All he knows about the day-to-day operations is that they make us a lot of money, so he leaves the details to others. That keeps him free to play bridge at Cherry Hills Country Club, serve on the symphony board and read the *Wall Street Journal*. Oliver Brock is executive vice president. He's a four-term former congressman from Connecticut who handles government relations for us. He makes sure the company is always on the right side of any given equation." Shane eyed Tracy speculatively. "Let's see how sharp a detective you are. Give me a quick read on Alfy."

She looked over at the man playing the piano. "I'm guessing, but I'd say he's a colossal put-on. He's got less of an accent than he wants you to think, and with those rings and ruffled shirt cuffs and glib patter, he's trying to come across as a harmless dandy. I suspect he's anything but harmless."

Shane raised his glass in salute. "Not bad, sheriff. Alphonse Deschamps is a Belgian national who put himself through the Sorbonne by playing piano in a Montmartre café. After he graduated, he joined the French Foreign Legion and became one of its top specialists in counterinsurgency." Shane paused and stared down at his untouched drink. "He's one of the most accomplished killers I've ever met—and that's saying a good deal."

Tracy shuddered.

Shane softened his tone. "He killed so that in the end a lot more lives—innocent lives—could be spared. He's no more trigger-happy than you are, Tracy. He's a kind of soldier, a good one. And, believe it or not, a decent human being."

"Just what does he do for TransWorld Systems?"

"Alfy is vice president for plans and operations. He sees to it that assignments are carried out properly. He's in charge of project staffing, equipment, the day-to-day nitty-gritty."

Tracy took a sip of her Campari and soda. "I'm not sure I really understand just what it is you do."

"It's very simple. We operate primarily within Third World nations, where an official presence might prove embarrassing to Washington. We survey internal security, recommend changes, and then assist in implementing those changes. Our sole purpose is to maintain stability." He smiled, but it was a humorless smile tinged with a pained sort of cynicism. "That, and to make a profit."

"Did it ever occur to you, Shane, that there's such a thing as legitimate dissent? Did you ever consider that at times you might find yourself on the wrong side of what you call an 'equation'? I'm talking about hiring out to dictators who don't have the foggiest notion of human rights. You might be maintaining stability, but you could be perpetuating evil."

Shane reached into his inside breast pocket with his left hand, groped around for a moment, then brought the hand out empty. *It's a habit,* Tracy thought. *Whenever he gets nervous about something, he reaches for one of those awful little cigars.*

He set his drink down on a nearby table. "Certainly it's occurred to me, Tracy." As he spoke, a change came over him. The wrinkles around his eyes were fading, and he seemed relaxed for the first time since they'd entered the ballroom. "I've wrestled with the problem ever since I set up TransWorld ten years ago. And that's one reason I'm getting out. Too many times our people have had to play God and decide who lives and who dies. I no longer make day-to-day field decisions, but I'm ultimately responsible because I own the company. I'm just not sure I want to go on shouldering that responsibility anymore. And in this business, if you're not sure of yourself it's time to get out."

Tracy studied him. She'd formed an impression of him as a man who liked to be thought of as tough, hard-bitten, cynical. Shane Mahaffey Keegan had finally confessed what he considered weakness, but that admission of uncertainty made him seem stronger than ever in Tracy's eyes. She wanted to throw her arms around his shoulders and welcome him to the human race. "What will you do after the first of the year? What happens after you turn over the company to your employees?"

"I'm not sure. Right now I'm thinking of taking a year off to figure out the future. I've got a forty-foot ketch moored in Galveston. Maybe I'll do the Caribbean and then head down to Rio." He winked at her. "Want to come along for the ride?"

She laughed. "Some of us have to work for a living. And that reminds me. Shouldn't we circulate so that I can collect those impressions you hired me for? I take it the people you want me to observe are MacManus, Brock and Deschamps?"

Shane nodded somberly. "Plus one more—that Zsa Zsa Gabor look-alike over there, the one talking to those three people wearing turbans. Oh, great—she's headed this way."

A few moments later the blond woman threw her arms around him and planted a glossy red kiss on his lips. "Shane!" she bubbled. "You have been in this room ten whole minutes and you have not yet introduced me to your charming companion! Where are your manners?"

Shane pulled himself free. "Tracy, I'd like you to meet Martina Tatarescu. Martina, Tracy Hannon."

The blonde hugged Tracy as if she were a long-lost sister, and Tracy found herself gasping from the heady scent of exotic perfume. "My dear!" Martina cooed. "You look

stunning! That dress—who *is* your couturier? You *must*
tell me—I insist!''

Tracy gently unhanded herself and stepped back, as
Shane had done. "It's just a little something I had them
whip up for me at Goodwill." She smiled sweetly.

Martina seemed perplexed. "Goodwill?"

Shane winked at Tracy. "Goodwill is a small boutique
that caters to a very exclusive clientele. I'm sure Mrs.
Hannon would be delighted to introduce you to it."

"Oh, would you, my dear?" Martina beamed at Tracy.
"I shall be here for a few weeks, and surely we can get together. Why not tomorrow, in fact? We could have lunch."

Shane edged away. "I'll leave you ladies to work it out."

Martina touched his arm. "We must talk later, Shane.
That African contract—"

"Is it something Alfy can handle?" Shane asked, an
impatient edge to his voice.

"I do not do business with Alfy anymore! I must talk
with *you*, Shane. It is very important."

Shane sighed. "All right. Later."

Standing on the sidelines watching, Tracy realized that
Martina, like Shane, was used to having her own way.
What was her connection with TransWorld? Shane hadn't
said. Martina seemed like an almost stereotypical femme
fatale, with swept-up hair too golden to be her real color
and a complexion that must have taken hours to perfect at
a makeup table. She was devastating in a low-cut, green-
and-gold cocktail dress, and she flaunted it. And yet beneath the glitter and the glaze, there was a cold, calculat-
ing brilliance.

"He is such a magnificent man," Martina said as Shane
melted into the crowd. "What a stupid little creature his
wife was!"

"You knew his wife?"

"I know *of* her. Shane Keegan and I go back together a long, long time, almost to the beginning of TWS."

"Tell me about her," Tracy said, trying not to seem too interested.

Martina gazed at Tracy strangely. "You do not know the story?"

"We've never talked about her."

Martina bobbed her head knowingly. "It would be wholly out of character for him to do so. He does not like to discuss his failures *or* his successes, and he has had his share of both. His wife, Christy, was a—how should I say?—a preppy little thing from Long Island, terribly spoiled and all that. She and Shane were married at Annapolis the day Shane graduated, and the marriage lasted less than three years. Shane was always assigned to some desolate Marine post, and when he was not on duty he was studying law. Christy failed to understand how any man could choose not to dedicate his every waking moment to *her*. There were other women during the early years of TWS, but Erica was the only other one Shane was serious about.

"I do not suppose he told you about the time he spent in an African prison? No, I did not think so. He was falsely accused of being a CIA agent, and for five horrible months he was held prisoner in a tiny cell, beaten with bamboo sticks every morning and told he would be shot that day unless he confessed. Needless to say, Shane refused to confess to *anything*. To make a long story short, Erica was running the office in Washington—the only office the company had at the time—and when things were at their darkest for Shane, she cleaned out the company's bank accounts and ran off to Mexico with another man. Shane had to start from scratch when he returned to the United States. He could have had her brought back and sent to prison—I know *I* would have—but he never even filed a complaint against her."

"He hasn't had much luck with women, has he?" Tracy said.

Martina laughed gaily. "Having met you, I would disagree."

Tracy smiled at the compliment. "Where did you meet him?"

"I was working for the United Nations when Shane went to prison, and I made several trips to Africa to help arrange his release. We hit it off, and next thing I knew, he opened an office in Paris and asked me to manage it for him—not the field operations, mind you, but the public relations side of things." She paused. "And you, my dear—just how did *you* meet Shane?"

"You might say we just bumped into each other."

"Tell me, are you in love with him?"

Tracy was startled by the question. "I like him very much," she said guardedly.

Martina nodded approval. "It is much more comfortable to like a man as well as love him. That fellow at the piano—"

"Alphonse Deschamps? We met a few minutes ago."

"Then perhaps you can sense it. I am quite mad about him. Alfy and I have been what the gossip columnists like to call 'an item' for almost seven years, ever since he threw in with Shane. The affair is off at the moment, but who knows? In my more rational moments, I hate *Monsieur* Deschamps with a passion. He is vain and deceitful. But on those occasions when the old embers are fanned into flame—well, there can be no other man for me." She patted Tracy on the cheek. "I have been baring my soul and have not given you a chance to say two words. Tell me about yourself, please."

Tracy noticed that the guests were beginning to drift out of the reception, and she wanted to be sure she had time to observe more carefully the three men Shane had introduced to her. "Another time, Madame Tatarescu," she begged off. "There are some people I must say hello to."

"Of course. But do call me Martina, won't you? We shall have lunch tomorrow—no? Afterward, you can take me by that wonderful little boutique. What was the name? Goodwill..."

"I'm afraid that won't be possible. I have to leave Denver first thing in the morning. I've got to get back to work."

"Ah, a career woman! All the more reason for us to have lunch. Perhaps we could compare notes."

Perhaps we should, Tracy thought.

THE RAGMAN looked half-frozen as he stepped off the elevator and headed straight for Tracy's suite. His black, wool overcoat was caked with wet snow, and tiny icicles had formed on the turned-down brim of his gray hat. There was steam on the lenses of his heavy steel-rimmed spectacles.

An elderly man wearing a tuxedo passed him in the hall, nodded and observed that it wasn't a fit night for man nor beast.

"Indeed it is not," The Ragman replied pleasantly, his voice muffled by the bulk of his upturned collar.

He took a ring of skeleton keys from his overcoat pocket, inserted one into the keyhole and opened the door. After unbuttoning his overcoat to give him freedom of movement, he turned on the lights and made a quick inspection of the salon. He examined the empty box in which Tracy's dress had been packaged, and frowned, wondering how she had found time to do any shopping. Then he saw the ribbons and he smiled. Of course, the contents of the box had been a lover's gift. How charming!

There were other gift boxes in the bedroom. He ignored them and opened the overnight bag he found on a rack in the closet. He went through it, casting each item aside as soon as he had inspected it. He took down the tweed suit hanging in the closet, checked the pockets and felt the lining.

Tracy's purse was on a shelf in the closet. The Ragman examined it. It was empty.

He picked up the boots she'd left on the closet floor. He felt inside each of them. Tucked into the toe of one boot was a small case containing her sheriff's badge and ID card. In the toe of the other was a heavy key ring from which dangled a Mace canister. He smiled again. Hardly very imaginative hiding places. Where was her gun? Surely she hadn't ventured forth with a heavy revolver in that black silk evening bag he'd seen her carrying?

If she *did* have it with her, he'd have to be careful when she returned to the room.

But then he was always careful when practicing his art.

A SLIGHTLY TIPSY Evan MacManus rose unsteadily to his feet and raised his wine goblet. "To another outstanding year for TWS," he intoned, his words beginning to slur. "I've already seen the preliminary figures, and I believe it's safe to say both revenues and return on investment will set new records. The only dark spot in the picture is—" he glanced reprovingly at Shane, who was sitting across the round table, next to Tracy "—the imminent and untimely departure of our chairman. What about it, Shane? You wouldn't care to reconsider, would you? TWS needs you, you know."

Shane gave a dry little laugh. "Let me remind you, Evan, that up to a point the monster also needed Dr.

Frankenstein. But once the transplants were completed and the electrodes attached, the monster was on his own.''

Oliver Brock, seated to MacManus's right, leaned forward on his elbows. There was a wry smile on his chubby face. ''Come on now, Shane. Is that what you think you've created? A monster?''

''It's a fair analogy,'' Shane replied, pushing aside his plate and reaching for his cigars. He'd scarcely touched his prime rib, Tracy noticed; he'd seemed preoccupied with something, and his contribution to the dinner conversation had consisted of little more than an occasional nod, an ambiguous half smile or a noncommittal shrug of his powerful shoulders. ''In ten years, TWS has grown from a one-man operation to a giant that's all but impossible to manage. The company has taken on a life of its own, and it has a mind of its own. My God, it's gotten so it controls us, instead of the other way around. That's not right.''

MacManus put down his glass, his toast forgotten. ''But does that make it any more right for you to get out and wash your hands of the whole business? If, as you say, we've become a corporate rogue elephant under your control, what will we be *without* you? With all due respect, Shane, you have certain responsibilities.''

''To whom?'' Shane demanded.

''To the company, your employees, yourself. . .''

*And to the world, on which you've unleashed this thing you call a Frankenstein monster,* Tracy wanted to add. But she said nothing. This wasn't her business, it was Shane's—Shane's and that of the others at the table: MacManus, Brock, Alfy, Martina and MacManus's wife, Pamela, a thin silver-haired woman with a face and a manner frozen in time. *I'm not actually part of this. I'm just Shane's hired hand, still floating in a dreamworld, but somehow on the outside looking in. Could I* ever *be part of this?*

Dinner had been MacManus's idea. It would, he said, give them all a chance to size up prospective clients who'd been at the reception. How incongruous, Tracy thought, to be in this softly lighted bastion called the Brown Palace Club with its crisp, white linen, gleaming silver, plush velvet and batteries of superefficient waiters—to talk about Third World problems! But MacManus hadn't really wanted to discuss prospective clients. He'd really wanted to talk about Shane's decision to pull out.

Tracy believed that MacManus wanted Shane to stay on because he was the glue that held the business together. Without him, TWS would lose the magic that had made it a success, and that would mean money out of MacManus's pocket.

"I'm sure that Shane has confidence in each of you," Pamela MacManus said. "You've all proved your loyalty as well as your ability. I just know that when Evan takes over as the new chief executive officer, you'll—"

"That hasn't been decided yet," MacManus interrupted her. He was no longer slurring his words, and the glow in his eyes indicated he was irritated with his wife.

"But, dear, you said that—"

"What I said, Pamela, was that Shane was *probably* going to choose one of us to succeed him as CEO. Naturally, we'll go along with whatever decision he makes."

"It doesn't matter who takes over," Brock said, throwing up his hands. "TWS will go on doing its thing no matter who's in the hot seat. As for me, I'd just as soon stay in Washington. I'd be a fish out of water anywhere else."

Alfy snorted. "If I had known we were here for job interviews, I would have brought my résumé." He looked imploringly at Shane. "All this talk about selecting a new chairman is hard on the digestion. Have pity on my ulcers and tell us you plan to stay on."

Shane shook his head. "January first, I'm out of here."

Martina was sitting next to Alfy, who, in turn, was next to Tracy. Martina reached out across Alfy and patted Tracy's hand. "Perhaps you can talk some sense into him, my dear. I have the feeling he might listen to what you have to say."

Tracy laughed, thinking of her own uncertainty about the future. "Vocational counseling is hardly my line," she said.

"Tell us, what *is* your line, Mrs. Hannon?" Pamela asked. "Evan said you weren't in the trade."

Shane winked at Tracy. "You might say she does peace work."

Tracy made a face at the pun. "You might, but I wish you wouldn't. Actually, my—"

Shane gave an almost imperceptible shake of his head.

"—my background is in education."

"Is that a fact?" Brock asked with a good-natured leer. "Why was it that none of my teachers were as attractive as you?"

"Oliver, you obviously didn't go to the right school," Shane said. He checked his watch. "If you don't mind, I think we ought to call it a night. It's almost eleven, the storm's getting worse, and Evan and Pamela still have to drive down to Cherry Hills."

"No problem," MacManus assured him, picking up his wine goblet to resume his toast. "Our new chauffeur seems quite competent. He's from Canada and—"

"He's used to snow," Pamela cut in. "They have a lot of snow in Canada, you know."

Shane pushed back his chair and started to stand up. "Mrs. Hannon's had a long day and I'm sure she wants to get to bed." He glanced at Tracy for corroboration, but before she could reply the maître d' was standing at Shane's side, whispering in his ear.

Shane looked around the table. "If you'll excuse me, I have to take an overseas call. It's Kagera," he told Alfy, lowering his voice. "Better listen in. You know the game plan over there better than I do."

Alfy nodded and got to his feet.

Shane gave Tracy's hand a squeeze. "Why don't you go up to your room?" he suggested. "I'll swing by in a little while to say good-night."

Tracy knew that the others were watching her. All of them had been more than a little curious about her relationship with Shane. Well, she'd just keep them guessing. "I've got a long drive ahead of me tomorrow," she said without looking at Shane. "I'd better get some sleep. Perhaps we could meet for breakfast."

"Tracy... I understand. I'll call you in the morning." Signaling Alfy to follow him, he left the table.

"I'll ride up on the elevator with you," Oliver Brock informed Tracy. "We're both on the same floor."

"Oh?" She wondered how he'd known what room she was in.

"The company leases a block of suites in the hotel," Oliver said in response to her unspoken question. "I always use one of them when I come in from Washington."

"I see." Tracy pushed back her chair and rose to her feet. She smiled at the others. "It's been a very pleasant evening and I've enjoyed meeting all of you."

"The pleasure has been ours," MacManus said, hurrying around the table to give Tracy a fatherly hug. "Pamela and I will have you and Shane out to the house next time you're in town."

"That would be very nice," Pamela said, nodding agreeably.

Martina pouted at Tracy. "My dear, I thought we had a date for lunch tomorrow."

"I'm afraid I have to return to my office," Tracy said.

"But you cannot drive *anywhere* in this blizzard!"

"We'll see how the roads look in the morning." Tracy glanced at Oliver Brock. "Please, stay here. I can make it upstairs on my own."

"No problem," he said. "I'm still on Washington time, and it's one o'clock in the morning by my schedule. A growing boy needs his rest, you know." He nodded to the others and escorted Tracy out of the room.

The elevators were just outside the mezzanine entrance to the club, and as he jabbed the call button Oliver said, "How about a nightcap, Mrs. Hannon?"

Tracy shook her head. "I wouldn't be very good company. I can hardly keep my eyes open."

"Suit yourself."

The elevator came and they stepped inside. Scarcely had the doors closed than they slid open again. Oliver put one arm around Tracy and guided her out. She looked around. They were on the main floor.

"Damn!" Oliver said with a laugh. "I must have punched the wrong button. But as long as we're here, the Ship's Tavern is just a few steps away."

Annoyed, Tracy stopped in her tracks and shrugged off his arm. "I said I didn't want a drink, Mr. Brock. I'm exhausted and I want to go to my room."

"I'd like to talk to you, Tracy." The joviality was gone from his tone.

"About what?"

"Some areas of mutual interest."

"*What* areas of mutual interest?" she demanded.

Again he tried to put his arm around her, but she stepped back, onto the waiting elevator car. "Please, Mrs. Hannon. I only..."

"Good night, Mr. Brock," Tracy said as the doors closed between them.

Riding up to her floor, she felt a twinge of regret that she'd cut short the encounter with Oliver Brock. After all, Shane *had* hired her to size up his three closest associates. But she was really exhausted. She knew that any assessment she made would be flawed by sheer weariness.

As she reached her door, she could hear the phone ringing inside the suite. It had to be Shane, she decided with a smile. He probably was calling to invite himself up again. How would she fend him off *this* time? she wondered. Or did she really want to?

Tracy fished her key out of her evening bag, turned the key in the lock and opened the door. In the darkened foyer she patted at the wall in search of the light switch. Failing to find it right away, she hurried into the living room and, by the muted light spilling in from the outer hallway, managed to locate the phone.

She picked up the receiver. "It's getting late, Shane," she said. "Don't you think—" She realized she was talking to a dial tone, so she started to hang up.

And then she froze. Someone else was in the suite. She could *feel* it. An icy chill began in the back of her neck and worked its way down her spine. It was the same sort of chill she'd felt earlier in the evening when Shane had told her Alfy was a killer.

Tracy replaced the receiver on its cradle. "Shane?" She spoke his name aloud and immediately felt foolish. No, it wouldn't be Shane. He wouldn't slip up to her room this way. And his presence wouldn't produce tingles of fear. "Who's in here?" she called out, peering into the shadows on either side of the shaft of light coming from the hall.

Silence. Cold, forbidding silence.

Moving slowly, Tracy reached for the table lamp next to the phone and fumbled for the switch. Before she could turn it on, something woolly and soft was thrown over her head and shoulders. She was spun around and stumbled blindly across the floor, banging into a chair and pitching forward onto the carpet, her screams muffled behind the blanket that covered her head.

She heard the thud of fast-moving steps on the carpet, then a door slam. *He's gone,* she thought. She rolled over and pulled off the blanket. Rising slowly to her feet, she groped out in the darkness.

And then she touched something.

*Him.*

She jumped back and he grabbed her, holding her around the throat with one hand while he slapped her face once, twice, three times with the other hand. She tried to scream, but the pressure on her throat prevented her from making a sound. So she did the next best thing. She fainted.

At least she *seemed* to faint. Forcing her body to go limp, Tracy sagged to the carpet and lay on her back. Her assailant bent down to examine her, and she made a fist and struck him squarely in the nose, as hard as she could, while kicking out at his groin with her high heels. He gave a hoarse little cry and toppled backward.

Tracy moved away quickly and crawled on her hands and knees into the bedroom. She reached up and threw open the closet door, grabbing for the boot in which she'd hidden the canister of Mace.

The canister was gone.

She felt around the floor and realized she was sitting among piles of clothing. What was happening? What in God's name was happening? The man had to be a burglar. She'd come back unexpectedly while he was going through her things, and now...

The intruder lurched into the bedroom. She couldn't see him; she could only sense him. She slid on her bottom back along the carpet. She knew the man was getting closer, reaching out to her. Then her right hand touched the key ring, her fingers closing over the Mace canister. She grabbed it, flipped up the leather safety cap and pointed the container at him. And as she thumbed down the lever, she screamed as loudly as she could.

## Chapter Six

Tracy stood alone on the balcony, looking westward into the gray clouds that swirled low over the city and blotted out the mountains. The freezing mist stung her cheeks, but she felt warm and secure in Shane's black-and-gold robe. *How would I ever explain this in Henryville?* she wondered, smiling at the thought. *The prim, proper sheriff of San Isabel County isn't supposed to spend the evening at a bachelor penthouse in Denver, not even an innocent evening.*

But for that business of the burglar in her hotel room, it *had* been an innocent evening. The man had probably been as surprised as she, Tracy decided. He'd slapped her, but he hadn't really hurt her. He'd simply tossed a blanket over her head to distract her while he made his escape. Trouble was, he'd stumbled into the bedroom instead of heading for the hall door, and she'd been forced to use the Mace on him. He'd managed to get away before she could page Shane.

"I don't understand it," she'd told Shane when he hurried up to her room. "I certainly don't own anything a self-respecting jewel thief would want."

Shane hadn't been amused. "Did he take anything at all?"

"No. He just pawed through my things. I must have stumbled in on him right after he broke into the room."

"He didn't break in. He had a skeleton key." Shane had put an arm around her protectively. "Get your coat. I want you to come with me."

They'd ridden the elevator down to the mezzanine, then crossed the skywalk to the hotel annex, where the garage was located. As they'd waited for a company driver to pick them up, she'd asked, "Where are we going?"

"You're spending the night at my place."

"Are we going to go through *that* again?"

Shane had shaken his head. "I've got one bed, and I want you to crawl into it and get a good night's sleep. I'll stretch out on the couch. I won't lay a finger on you—and that's a promise."

He'd kept his promise, and now he'd gone off to shower and shave. Tracy, bundled up in his robe, his quilted gold after-ski slippers flopping loosely around her ankles, had taken her coffee to the balcony and the raw bleakness of a new day.

Her coffee was cold when he came out onto the balcony and stood behind her, his arms around her waist, the scent of his after-shave lotion pungent in the frigid air.

"So who's the fresh-air fiend now?" he teased.

"I didn't want to be in the way," Tracy said. "I know how it is first thing in the morning when you're trying to get going."

"You could never be in my way," he said, kissing her lightly on one ear and then turning her around until she was facing him. He'd changed to a blue-and-white checked shirt and khaki slacks. "You realize my promise expired at sunup, don't you?"

"Did it?" She raised up on her toes and kissed him on the chin, just under his lower lip. "I'd forgotten all about it."

"Tracy, I—" He kissed her again, on the tip of her nose, and led her back inside the apartment. "Want some more coffee?"

She could still taste the chicory in the pot he'd made. "You don't happen to have any instant, do you?"

"I think so. Help yourself."

Tracy put on a pot of water to heat and rummaged around in the kitchen until she found a jar of instant coffee. Shane perched himself on a stool at the counter that divided the kitchen and the living room. An unopened packet of cigars appeared in his hands and he began toying with it, crinkling the cellophane between his fingertips. "How about giving me a reading on the people I introduced you to last night?"

Tracy leaned over the counter and plucked the cigars away. She crumpled the package and stuffed it into the garbage disposer. "Where do you want me to begin?"

"Wherever you like." Shane sighed, his face a contorted mask of resignation as he watched the cigars vanish.

"All right, let's take MacManus. He comes across initially as an affable glad-hander, a real country-club type, very solicitous and smooth. But under that Brooks Brothers' exterior lurks a quick temper and, I suspect, an unpleasant disposition."

"Oh? Why do you say that?"

"I saw a waiter accidentally brush his arm, causing him to spill some of his drink. You had to look fast to catch it, but there was a flash of rage in his eyes, and he started to say something nasty—I could tell. But other people were around, so he didn't follow through. It was one of those looks-could-kill situations, far out of proportion to the actual incident. I get the feeling Evan MacManus is unreasonably impatient with subordinates, which suggests he's unsure of himself. This was reinforced by the way he handled the younger people who drifted into and out of his group. He seemed quite high-handed, too quick to laugh *at* other people, not *with* them. There's a difference, you know. And then, at dinner, it was obvious to me that he has his poor, simple-minded wife completely cowed.'' Tracy paused. ''I'll go out on a limb and say that he doesn't seem to be your type of person, Shane.''

''He came through when I needed him. I was flat on my face several years ago, and he helped me pick up the pieces.''

''You mean after Africa?''

''You know about that?''

''Martina told me how some woman named Erica took you for every dime you had.''

Shane nodded. ''Evan was a partner in a New York brokerage house. He thought TransWorld was an idea whose time had come, and he lined me up with some bankers who were willing to gamble. Later, when we needed a front-office type for appearances' sake, Evan was the first one I thought of. Okay, so what about Brock?''

Tracy measured out a level teaspoon of instant coffee and added boiling water to it. She stirred the cup thoughtfully. ''Oliver Brock is a horse of another color. He wants to be accepted as one of the guys, but he never wants you to forget he's something special. Even if you hadn't told me he was once a congressman, I think I'd still have guessed he's a politician. In the snatches of conversation I caught, there was none of the I-can-do-this or I-can-do-that business—simply that *this* can be done and *that* can be done. It's a subtle distinction, I know, but it suggests expertise in manipulation, which is all politics is when you get down to it.''

''What about Alfy?''

Tracy took a few sips of her coffee. ''My first impression stuck. He's *anything* but harmless. Still, I get the feeling he'd be loyal to you, whatever the situation." She put her cup down on the kitchen counter. "All right, Shane, it's your turn. Why did you want my impressions of these people?"

"Two reasons. As you know, one of the three probably will succeed me as chief executive officer, and one of them—" his calm expression didn't flicker "—wants to kill me."

Tracy stared at him. "Are you serious?"

"Deadly serious."

"Do you have any idea which of the three it is?"

"Remember that photo you found in the rocks?"

Tracy nodded.

"It was printed from a film strip I shot a few months ago for a new piece of equipment I'm developing—an electronic ID card. I got sidetracked with other things, and the negatives have been sitting in a safe in my office. Only three people have access to that safe: MacManus, Brock and Deschamps."

"What about Martina?"

Shane absentmindedly reached into his shirt pocket and came up with another cigar. He looked at it, then guiltily handed it over to Tracy, who sent it down the garbage disposer. "You tell me," he said. "What about Martina?"

"She's a variation on Alfy. She wants to be thought of as glamorous and slightly superficial, but she's really a very tough cookie. Her posturing is intended to disarm people."

"Martina saved my life in Africa. You think she's capable of killing me now?"

"I think she's capable of doing anything she considers necessary to achieve her ends, whatever they are."

"She doesn't have access to my safe."

"She has on-again, off-again access to Alfy, and *he* has access to your safe." Tracy came around the open counter and stood behind the stool upon which Shane was perched, suddenly wanting to touch him, hold him. She put her arms around his waist and rested her cheek against his shoulder. "Get out now, Shane," she said softly. "Don't wait until the first of the year."

"No way, Tracy. It's going to take until the first of the year to complete an orderly transition. Besides, if I pull the plug now, my tax burden will be higher, and the Internal Revenue Service could slap a lien on my holdings to collect the money. The way I've got this thing structured, I'm going to get out of TWS with about ten million after taxes—not all that big a return on investment when you figure I've put a good chunk of my life into it, but enough. People who stuck by me will end up as owners of a going business. It'll work out for everyone."

"Even for whoever it is who wants to kill you?"

"He won't bring it off."

"How do you know he won't?"

"I'm a survivor, Tracy. I've had a lot of practice."

"How do you stay alive if people shoot at you when you're out jogging?"

"I told you a couple of days ago that the sniper missed me on purpose. He didn't want to kill me—he wanted to scare me."

"Did he succeed?"

"Of course he did. Knowing when to be scared is what helps survivors survive. Only a fool thinks he's invulnerable."

"What makes it so different *now*, Shane? You said somebody wants you dead."

"That's right. I made sure of it."

Tracy jerked back. *"You what?"*

"I made sure of it. Until a few days ago, I was considering setting up a management committee to run things after I stepped down. I dragged my feet because I wasn't positive about the three obvious candidates for the committee. The way I figure it, somebody took potshots at me to make me realize that I wasn't indestructible; that if I wanted TWS to survive and prosper later on, I'd better get cracking and set up that management committee.'' Shane swiveled around on the bar stool and took Tracy's hands in his. ''In case you haven't noticed, I don't push any easier than you do, sheriff. But I thought it might be useful to appear as if I were bowing to pressure. Yesterday I called in my three key men and told them that as of that moment they constituted an interim management committee. I had my attorney explain that if anything happened to me, it would be up to them to see that the company was handed over to employee control. I'm sure all three realized that if I were out of the picture they could find any number of legal ways to postpone employee ownership—leaving them in the driver's seat.'' He paused. ''You with me so far?''

Tracy glared at him, her eyes flashing fire. She yanked her hands away from his. ''I'm three steps ahead of you. You set yourself up so the bad guy would show his hand. You're out of your mind, Shane! You've been reading too many cheap mysteries! Things don't work like that in real life!''

''Tracy, we're not talking about everyday real life. We're talking about the shadowland in which I've operated for years. When you live and breathe intrigue as part of your regular routine, it colors your thinking.''

Tracy climbed up on a stool alongside Shane and planted her chin in her hands. ''I don't believe this,'' she said, staring straight ahead. ''You're certifiably deranged—suicidal, even!''

''I have no intention of committing suicide. Nor do I intend to let somebody get to you.''

She gave him a quick side glance. ''So what do we do now?''

*"We?"*

"We. You and I. We seem to be in this together, Shane."

He smiled. "I was hoping you'd say that. If you don't mind, I'd like to have you stay here today, behind locked doors. The highways are closed by the blizzard, so you won't be able to get home until at least tomorrow. When you do get back to Henryville, you'll have some extra deputies on your staff. At least one of them will be with you wherever you go."

Tracy rolled her eyes. "The county commissioners will *love* that. We can barely meet our payroll now."

"Tell them not to worry. TWS will pick up the tab."

FEELING GLORIOUSLY INDOLENT, Tracy made herself another cup of instant coffee, then curled up on the couch and skimmed through the *Rocky Mountain News*. She made a mental note to phone the sheriff's office later in the morning and tell Bubba Crowley or whomever else she could reach that she was stuck in Denver and wouldn't be home for at least another day.

After a while, she put down the newspaper and went to the picture window. Earlier, the golden dome of the State Capitol had been barely visible a dozen blocks away. But now it was swallowed up by the fury of the blizzard, and all she could see was the faint, boxy outline of the high-rise across the street. It all looked so cold and grim, she gave an involuntary shudder and turned away.

She arranged kindling and logs in the red brick fireplace that took up most of the south wall dividing the living room and the bedroom. Within a few minutes she was basking in the cozy warmth of a crackling fire. She wished Shane were there. She missed him, more than she was willing to admit.

Then the phone rang.

"Don't answer it," Shane had told her before leaving for the office. "No one's supposed to know you're here."

A second ring, then a third: piercing and insistent. Tracy didn't move. The phone kept ringing. Ten rings, twelve, eighteen.

The caller *had* to be Shane. No one else would let the phone ring when it seemed so obvious there wouldn't be an answer. She went to the kitchen-dining room pass-through, in which the nearest extension was located. After waiting for one more full ring, she picked up the receiver and said, guardedly, "Yes?"

She could hear someone breathing on the other end of the line. Not the heavy, excited breathing she might associate with a deviate, but something even more menacing: a faintly gurgling, evil sound.

*All right,* she thought, *if you want to play games...* "Operator," she said crisply. "May I have your number?" She heard a little grunt, and then the connection was broken. "Have a nice day," Tracy muttered darkly, hanging up.

She went back into the living room, fingered through Shane's collection of jazz cassettes, and decided she wasn't in the mood for jazz. Her eyes fell on a pair of huge bookcases against the wall opposite the picture window. It occurred to her that Shane might have more cassettes stored in the cabinets at the base of one of the bookcases.

She plopped herself down on the floor in front of the left-hand bookcase and opened the cabinet. It was stacked full of old issues of *National Geographic* and *Sailing*. Nothing more. She tried the right-hand bookcase and found more magazines. She was about to close the door when she spotted a red, leather-bound photo album at the bottom of one of the stacks of magazines. Curious, she worked it loose and opened it.

The first thing she saw was a sheet of pale blue, silver-edged paper, the note on it written in a tiny, graceful script.

Dearest Shane:
Sorry you couldn't stay longer after the funeral, but I know you had to get back to Mexico City. Someday you and Rad will have to take a few days off and fill your sister in about life in the fast lane!

Going through Dad's things, I came upon the original of this album. I had the photos and the clippings duplicated so each of us could have a copy.

Perhaps you can come to Boston for Christmas. I understand Washington practically shuts down for the holidays. Rad said he'd try to make it if he can finish up in Cairo, and I know the children would like nothing better than to spend some time getting reacquainted with their uncles.

All my love
Mindy

Tracy began turning the stiff, gray pages of the album, seeing three very different lives pass before her eyes.

First came a score of childhood photos. A baby nestled in the arms of a darkly beautiful woman, then another baby, and a third. An older boy, perhaps ten or eleven, building a snowman while a smaller boy and a toddler look on. The same trio playing on a beach, perhaps a year or so later. A whole series of snapshots of the youngsters riding horses, clambering around a sailboat, splashing in the pounding surf.

Bit by bit, distinct personalities emerged. One of the two boys was tall, lean, dark and very serious-looking; the other was short, blond and stocky, with a devil-may-care glint to his eyes. The shorter boy had to be Shane, Tracy thought. The girl was the youngest, and she was dark and fragile-looking, but with a sparkle that said she was a charmer.

Further into the book, the clippings began. Rad had received a scholarship to Harvard, Shane an appointment to the United States Naval Academy in Annapolis. Mindy had given a violin recital, then been accepted as a student at The Juilliard School of Music. At the end of the first batch of clippings was a white card that read "In Memoriam, Tara Mahaffey Keegan."

More photos and clippings followed. Rad had been named commercial attaché at the U.S. embassy in Khartoum. Second Lieutenant Shane Keegan had been assigned to the Fleet Marine Force in the Pacific. Mindy had married a doctor. Later, Rad had been named ambassador to Egypt, and had been mentioned as a possible choice for undersecretary of state. Shane had won the Navy Cross, then had resigned his commission to join the FBI. Rad had received an honorary doctorate from Columbia. Shane, identified now only as a business consultant, had been released after several months in an African prison but had refused to talk to reporters.

There were a few personal letters tucked into the album, but Tracy passed over them. She knew she was prying into Shane's private life by looking at the album, but she had to draw the line somewhere. However, one envelope caught her attention because of the letterhead. She hesitated, then slipped the letter out. It was written on FBI stationery: a commendation given to Shane when he left the bureau.

She was about to shove the album under the stack of magazines when the rear cover dropped open and a loose clipping fluttered out. From the whiteness of the paper, the clipping looked fairly recent. It was date-lined Beirut and said that Special Ambassador Rad Keegan, who had been nominated for a Nobel Prize, had been killed by a bomb while visiting Lebanon on a peace mission.

Tracy felt the salty sting of tears in her eyes. Was this another reason that Shane wanted out of what he called "the trade"? she wondered. She sensed it was. He was reluctant to share his feelings—as if he feared that expressing them might be interpreted as weakness.

Tracy closed the album and put it away. She stared out at the snow, wishing Shane were with her. As if in response to her yearning, she heard his voice suddenly, against a humming background. "Tracy," he said, "in exactly one minute the phone will ring. Please answer it." The humming ceased.

Startled, Tracy looked around. The voice seemed to have emanated from all four walls at once. Could it have come through the stereo? Impossible. The stereo was off. She'd checked.

The phone rang, and she dashed to it. "Shane?"

"Did I frighten you?"

"Yes! How'd you do that?"

"No big deal. I rigged a voice-actuated override to an answering machine. I punch in a code and I'm automatically patched through to the stereo. Very useful little gadget. I designed it myself, and I'm even thinking of putting it on the market after I get out of the corporate rat race." He paused. "All quiet on the home front?"

She thought of the earlier call. Should she tell him about it? He'd told her not to answer the phone. No sense upsetting him. It had probably been just some nut, anyway. "All quiet."

He laughed. "Hey, what the devil did you and Martina come up with last night? She's been bugging me all morning about how she can't get in touch with you. She says the two of you have a luncheon date—"

"No way! The storm's getting worse, if anything."

"You'd be doing me a favor if you did have lunch with her, Tracy. I want to keep the lines of communication open."

"Well . . ."

"I'll send a driver for you at twelve-thirty. He and another man will be sitting a few tables away during lunch. Don't get nervous. They'll be there because I told them to be. All right?"

"All right. Wait! I just remembered—I *really* don't have a thing to wear this time. I'm certainly not venturing out into the snow in the cocktail dress I wore last night!"

"I'll have the driver bring along some clothes. By sheer coincidence, I just happen to know your size."

"I have plenty of clothes," Tracy reminded him. "Just have your man swing by the Brown Palace and pick up my suitcase."

"Sorry. The suitcase stays where it is for the time being. I want to keep the opposition off balance."

"The opposition?"

"That's how I think of it, Tracy. When the time comes to pin a name on whoever's out to get me, you'll be the first to know."

MARTINA TATARESCU had changed, as if at the witching hour a fairy godmother had waved a magic wand and turned her back into a mere mortal. The golden tresses of the night before were now a short, boyish bob of nondescript auburn, the style not all that different from Tracy's own hair. Except for pale pink lipstick and a touch of mascara and eyeliner whose effect was almost lost behind big, round-lensed sunglasses, her face was free of cosmetic touches. Oddly, Tracy thought, Martina seemed younger without makeup. She appeared to be closer to forty than the fifty Tracy had guessed earlier. Her clothes were far less exotic, too: a rough linen Cossack-style blouse belted at the waist by a jangling chain of coins, a dark gray wool skirt, a black-dyed lamb's wool hat that matched the fingertip-length coat draped over her shoulders.

"You seem surprised, my dear," Martina observed, fitting a cigarette into the end of a long, ivory holder.

"Surprised? Surprised at what?" Tracy put down her glass of mulled wine.

Martina laughed merrily. "At Tatarescu by daylight. When you walked in here a few moments ago, you did not even recognize me until I waved to you." A waiter appeared at the table, struck a match and held it for Martina to light her cigarette. When he had left, Martina took one puff, stabbed out the cigarette in an ashtray and put aside the holder. The merriment was suddenly gone. "Do not let Shane leave the company," she said in a voice that was almost too low to be heard even across the table.

"I don't make Shane's decisions for him," Tracy said, lowering her own voice. "And if I tried to, I wouldn't have much luck. He has a mind of his own."

"He respects your judgment—*sheriff*."

Tracy glanced sharply at Martina. "I wasn't aware my badge was showing. How'd you find out?"

"People who keep secrets for a living are notorious gossips among themselves. You need not be ashamed of being a sheriff. I think it is marvelous."

"I'm not ashamed. I just didn't think it was very relevant to our discussion." Tracy leaned forward. "Who told you?"

Martina shrugged. "Someone in the office—Alfy."

Tracy's heart skipped a beat. The hotel prowler had pawed through her things and had certainly seen her badge and ID. Had the man been one of Alfy's hirelings? "How did he find out?"

"He did some checking with his sources. Alfy is very protective where Shane is concerned. Shane saved his life years ago, and Alfy does not forget such things." Martina took a tentative sip of her drink. "Alfy is not a man one would care to have for an enemy."

"I hope he doesn't consider *me* an enemy."

Martina shook her head. "He just had to be sure."

"And now that he's sure?"

"The two of us are asking you to use your influence to stop Shane from going ahead with his plan to hand over the company to the employees."

"Why, for heaven's sakes? The way I understand it, the move could make Alfy a very wealthy man."

Martina fiddled for a moment with her cigarette holder, then dropped it into her purse. "Alfy Deschamps is an unusual fellow. He does not give *that*—" she snapped her fingers "—for money, and, like Shane, he has a rather old-fashioned sense of morality. Alfy would never admit it anymore than Shane would, but in his world-weary way he believes he is helping to bring peace to some of the world's troubled areas. He is afraid that if Shane leaves, the company will become a greedy colossus motivated solely by profit and loss statements."

Tracy thought about it. "Alfy would be on the management committee. He'd have as much say as Mac-Manus or Brock."

Martina gave a humorless little laugh. "Alfy does not know a *thing* about business. Those pirates would eat him alive."

"I wonder if you don't underestimate Alfy."

"I do not think so, my dear. I have known him much too long. He is a warrior, a schemer, a poet, a musician—and without a doubt the world's worst businessman. Should I ever weaken and accept his proposal of marriage, I would have to take charge of all our financial affairs."

"He's proposed?"

"He has been doing it at least twice a year since we met."

"And you've been saying no twice a year?"

"Until last night."

"You made up again?"

"We always make up, my dear. We would never fight unless we knew we would make up." Again she lowered her voice. "You *will* talk to Shane about maintaining control of the company?" As if afraid to wait for Tracy's answer, she opened her menu, ran a finger down the listings and allowed her voice to return to its normal tone. "Now, shall we order? I am absolutely famished."

"HELL, YES, I can do it," the leader of the Death's Head Demons assured his visitor. "Man, gimme the right set of wheels and I can do anything—you know?"

"Splendid," The Ragman said, peeling off five crisp one-hundred-dollar bills. "There will be another five hundred for you when I read about your results in the newspaper."

The street-gang leader reached for the bills, but The Ragman put his hand on the money. "If you are thinking of ripping me off, I suggest you think again, my young friend. I found you once, and I can easily find you again. Are you with me?"

"Man, I ain't gonna rip you off. You're okay. I can tell. You're one of us."

"Not really," The Ragman demurred. "I am merely an entrepreneur who is subcontracting rather questionable talent for a specific task. If you do your job, you will receive a total of one thousand dollars. If you do not do your job, or should you decide in any other way to double-cross me, I will return and cheerfully slit your throat. Are you with me?"

The head of the Death's Head Demons glanced across at the door, where two assistants were standing guard, heavy chains hooked around their waists. He looked as if he wanted to call out to them, but he said nothing.

The Ragman rose from his seat at the table. "We have nothing further to discuss. You have your money and you know the assignment. I shall look forward to reading about your results."

THEY'D JUST FINISHED a late supper in a restaurant in Larimer Square, the lovingly restored nineteenth-century business block at one end of Denver's Sixteenth Street Mall. The place was packed with diners waiting out the storm, but despite the crowd Shane had had no trouble obtaining a secluded table.

Tracy studied him in the candlelight and wrinkled her nose. "We look just like the Bobbsey Twins."

He laughed. "Which ones? Freddie and Flossie?"

"I was thinking more of Nan and Bert. They're older and so much more sophisticated."

"Impossible," Shane said, drinking some of his Irish whiskey and savoring it for a moment. "You don't have a gray hair in your head. There's no way we could be twins."

Tracy shrugged, enjoying herself. "Very well, take it from the top. You've got a dark brown wool turtleneck, and so have I."

"I like yours better. That is, I like what you do for it."

"May I proceed? You're wearing a tan corduroy jacket, and so am I."

"Your powers of observation are unexcelled, sheriff."

"Dark brown wool slacks, dark brown wool skirt." Tracy sighed plaintively. "There we have a minor problem."

"I know." Shane grinned. "I don't look good in skirts."

"Clown! As long as you were throwing away your money on clothes I don't need, you could have gotten me slacks."

"So I like to look at your legs."

"Then you'll need your X-ray vision, Superman. Knee-high boots are fine for foiling fiends like you."

"The boots come off."

Tracy frowned. "Everything comes off, Shane, and when it does we're the same two people underneath. You really shouldn't be spending a fortune on clothes for me. I looked at the labels when your man came up to the apartment with the boxes. I still feel funny about accepting the things you bought."

"That old bit about being a kept woman again?"

"I suppose."

"The way I look at it, it's either keep you or throw you back. I'm not about to throw you back."

"I'm serious, Shane. I'm—"

"I'm serious, too. I need you, Tracy. It just so happens we communicate, and that's rare nowadays. And it's more than—" He stopped, as if fearful of proceeding along that line, and reached for one of his ubiquitous little cigars. "Tell me, how'd it go with Martina today?"

"Fine. She was crushed when I told her my couturier at the Goodwill boutique was snowbound in Aspen and couldn't possibly get back to town until next spring, but I think she'll survive. We met at the Wellshire Inn and spent the better part of two hours in girl talk."

"What kind of girl talk?"

"This and that." Tracy studied Shane for a moment, then plunged on. "She wants me to talk you out of turning over the company to the employees."

"Oh? And what did you tell her?"

"I told her you have a mind of your own and that nothing I could say would make you do something you didn't want to do."

"Did she tell you why she wants me to call off the deal?"

"She's afraid MacManus and Brock will—how did she put it?—eat Alfy alive. Is that true? Could they dominate Alfy?"

"It would be their two votes to his one. Alfy would have to go along with them—up to a point. When it comes to survival, Alfy is in a class by himself. They could push him only so far, and that would be it."

"Maybe Martina wants to avoid that kind of confrontation."

"Maybe. But I still can't figure her stake in all this. The last I heard, she and Alfy were on the outs."

Tracy shook her head quickly. "Not anymore. They're even thinking of getting married."

"Last night they hated each other with a passion."

"That was early in the evening. I guess they got together later and decided it was more fun being miserable together than being miserable apart, what with Martina living in Paris and Alfy being based in the United States."

Shane was mildly surprised. "I didn't think Martina would ever consider living anywhere else but Europe. She always thought this country was a bit too provincial for her tastes."

"It's the other way around. Alfy is thinking of taking a job in Europe."

Shane finished unwrapping his cigar. He bit down hard on one end and his face clouded over. "Alfy's got the best job he's ever had. Why in God's name would he want to move back to Europe?"

Tracy routinely confiscated the cigar. "I told you, he's afraid of what's going to happen to TransWorld when you leave."

Shane glanced longingly at his mortally wounded cigar. "Think, Tracy. Did Martina give you any specifics?"

Tracy tried to remember how the conversation had gone when Martina had renewed her appeal for assistance. "Alfy sees no way the company can continue to be successful under employee ownership. He's afraid it will become corrupt. He doesn't want that to happen, so he's talking about selling out and moving to Europe."

Shane thought about it. "Under the terms of the trust I'm setting up, he can sell his stock only to the company if he gets out. And he certainly won't make a whole lot of money for his shares that way—not for a few years, at least."

"Martina indicated he'd do better—and so would she, in fact—if they got out early, assuming you won't change your mind. They're both convinced that MacManus intends to take TransWorld public, and if that happens employee shares will be diluted by open-market sales."

Shane was visibly angry. "No way, and MacManus knows it! We've talked about this before. A company like ours can't survive under public ownership. Being subject to government scrutiny all the time would destroy our integrity. TWS would end up being a quasi-official branch of the government, damn it!"

Tracy held up her hands. "I'm just telling you what Martina told me. She says Alfy thinks Oliver Brock is the key. He's got connections in Washington, which is why you hired him. If Brock could get a bill through Congress that would change the ground rules for multinational corporations, TWS would have to go along. If it didn't, and if it moved corporate headquarters abroad, it could lose its government contracts, which seem to be a pretty big chunk of your business."

"I wonder why Martina told you all this," Shane mused.

"No mystery about that. She's using me as a conduit."

"Or as a smokescreen."

"Meaning?"

"It's always possible she has an ulterior motive. Maybe she figures she and Alfy would have something to gain by driving a wedge between MacManus, Brock and me. Maybe I ought to add her to the list of those most likely to take a crack at me."

Tracy shook her head. "That's what I thought at first. But Martina was still in Paris when you got shot at last Monday."

"She has friends," Shane said.

SNOWPLOWS AND SAND TRUCKS had made another sweep through the lower downtown, but the wind had picked up again, sending aloft white swirls that created ever-shifting drifts in the ringed glare of the streetlamps. A few cars were inching along the street, fishtailing and skidding on the glaze of ice that lay hidden beneath the powdered snow.

"Brrrrr!" Tracy moaned, shivering. "I vote we go back inside and wait till spring."

"Cheer up," Shane said. "A crackling fire and a snifter of Napoleon brandy await you at the other end of the line. Besides, I thought you were the outdoors type."

"Oh, I am," Tracy said sweetly. "But I also believe in moderation. *This* is not moderation. It's beastly. We'll never make it to your place."

"Sure we will. We've got four-wheel drive." He put his arm around Tracy and led her toward the parking lot where he'd left the Chevrolet Blazer he'd gotten from the TransWorld motor pool. "Oh, hell!"

Tracy squinted through the stinging wind. Snow had drifted across the open lane in front of the Blazer, and another vehicle, a low-slung Corvette, apparently had tried to bull its way through the drift and had become hopelessly hung up. "So what do we do now?" she inquired, glancing at Shane.

His arm still around her, he swung her about and headed for Sixteenth Street. "The way I see it, we have three options. We can stand here and freeze to death. We can phone for a wrecker to tow that yo-yo out of the lot—but that could take days. Or we can hike uptown and try to find a taxi at one of the hotel cab stands. I'll leave the decision up to you."

Tracy laughed and kissed him on the cheek. His skin felt like ice against her lips. "Let's walk. I need to burn off some calories after that dinner."

By the time they had reached Stout Street, almost within sight of the Fairmont Hotel, Tracy was chilled to the bone and her legs were beginning to give out. "I don't think I've seen a single cab all the time we've been walking," she said.

"There'll probably be one in front of the Fairmont," Shane said, offering her his arm as they pushed their way through an extra-high drift at curbside.

"And if there isn't?"

"The office is just a block away. We'll slip up there and get the keys to another Blazer. We've got a half dozen in the garage in our building. We plan to send them down to the ranch in the next couple of weeks."

"We could always spend the night in my room at the Brown Palace," Tracy heard herself say.

"Are you propositioning me, sheriff? What about my promise?"

Tracy rested her head against his shoulder. "Just trying to be helpful, darling. Besides, your promise has expired. You said so yourself."

They were almost across the street by now, confronting yet another snowbank. Suddenly Shane swooped her up into his arms and started carrying her over the hard-packed pile.

"Hey!" Tracy cried gleefully. "What prompted this?"

"A crazed desire to hold you," he said, lowering his head and touching his lips lightly to hers. He started to straighten up, but she put her arms around his neck and pulled his head down.

"You don't get off that easy," she murmured.

Shane stopped, balanced precariously halfway up the snowbank, and hugged her tightly.

Even though her eyes were closed, Tracy was abruptly conscious of being surrounded by light, and then of a roaring noise and movement. The first thing she saw when she opened her eyes was a dark sedan practically on top of them, skidding violently amid a spray of loose, powdery snow. She felt as if she were flying through the air with Shane still holding her.

She hit the sidewalk, and Shane landed on top of her. There was an explosion of blackness, followed by oblivion.

## Chapter Seven

The angel reached out and touched her, and Tracy knew at once it was Shane. The halo was much too bright for her to make out his face, yet she *knew* it was he. She tried to sit up and lift her fingers to his cheek, but someone held her down. "Shane..."

"Take it easy, Tracy. I'm right here."

The halo hurt her eyes. She closed them and tried to remember what had happened. It was all a blur: a car skidding wildly, about to slam into the two of them. The weather had been cold, and suddenly there had been the hot flush of danger on her cheeks and she'd sprawled onto the sidewalk, hard.

"Where are we?" she asked in a weak voice.

"Denver General Hospital."

Blinking, Tracy opened her eyes again. Slowly, Shane's face and form took shape in front of a great, round lamp suspended from the ceiling. She groped for his hands. "Are you all right?"

"I'm fine, Tracy."

She tried to smile, but the effort made her face hurt. "How about me? Am I fine, too?"

"You've got a scrape on your cheek and a couple of dandy black eyes. Otherwise you seem to be all right. If you were a football player, I'd say you'd had your bell rung."

Tracy took a deep breath and succeeded in sitting up, pushing away the unseen hands that tried to restrain her. Her head ached and her vision was fuzzy. "I'll say this, Shane. There's never a dull moment with you around."

He gave a dry little laugh. "Tell me about it."

Tracy tried unsuccessfully to focus on him. "No, *you* tell me. What happened?"

"There's not a lot to tell. A car came barreling up Seventeenth Street and took the corner too fast as it turned onto Stout. It spun around on the ice a couple of times, then bounced up over the curb and almost clobbered us."

"That's not quite the whole story, lady," another voice said. Tracy twisted about and saw a police officer behind her, a clipboard under one arm. "Mr. Keegan shoved you out of the way and fell on top of you to protect you. You blacked out when you hit the sidewalk."

"It was an accident," Shane said, almost too quickly. "A couple of kids were out joyriding in a stolen car."

"On a night like this?" Tracy demanded in disbelief.

"There's no explaining what some kids do," the officer said. "They ran off as soon as the car wrapped itself around a light pole not more than three, four feet from the two of you. My guess is they're still running." He took a ballpoint pen from a zippered pocket on one sleeve of his fur-collared nylon jacket. "You feel up to it, ma'am, I'd like to get some information for my report."

Edging himself around the table on which Tracy was lying, Shane positioned himself between her and the officer. "I'm afraid she *doesn't* feel up to it. She's had a rough time."

"I've got to have a name and address for the accident report," the officer said stiffly.

"The name is Tracy Hannon. If you'll have someone call me tomorrow at this number—" Shane handed over a business card "—I'll take care of the formalities. All right?"

The policeman took the card, glanced at it, then slipped it into the holder on his clipboard. "All right, Mr. Keegan. Tomorrow." He nodded and left the room.

Tracy slid down from the examining table and stood up. Her legs were wobbly, and she had to keep both hands on the edge of the table for support. She peered at Shane out of the corners of her eyes. "Did you get a look at them?"

Shane put his hands on her shoulders to steady her. "Yes, I did, and I'll handle it. You stay out of it."

Tracy shook herself free of his hands. "I have no intention of staying out of it. I happen to be a law enforcement officer."

"You're out of your jurisdiction, Tracy, so cool it."

"This whole business started in San Isabel County, and that gives me jurisdiction!"

Shane glanced warningly at the white curtain separating the examining room from the outer hall. "Let's discuss it later, huh? You stay put. I'm going to make a phone call."

Tracy walked unsteadily across the small room and picked up her purse, then sat down quickly on the only chair there. She had a splitting headache. She opened her purse, took out her compact and flipped it open. In the mirror she saw puffy eyes ringed with a bluish-black color. Her right cheek was raw and red. Gingerly fingering it, she remembered what the policeman had said. *Mr. Keegan shoved you out of the way and fell on top of you to protect you.* How like him that was!

She was still inspecting the damage when Shane returned. "I've sent for a car," he said, "but before we leave here, the doctor wants to take one more look at you." He studied her face. "Do you think you should spend the night in the hospital?"

Tracy stood up and rested her head on his chest. Part of the ache she felt was regret for her earlier outburst. "I want to spend the night with you."

THE RAGMAN slipped off his overcoat and slung it over the back of one of the three empty chairs at the table. He sat down in another chair, directly across from the leader of the Death's Head Demons, and folded his hands in front of him. "I do not want to wait for the morning papers," he said. "I want you to tell me what happened." The Ragman already knew the story, but he wanted to hear it firsthand. He had made a career out of profiting from other's mistakes, and perhaps he could learn something more about his targets. The client had confirmed that there were *two* targets now.

The gang leader glanced sharply at one of the two young men stationed inside the door of the musty storeroom, keeping an eye on their chief. "It was Wham Wham's fault, damn it! He stole a car that didn't have no snow tires. No way you could put it through the right sort of controlled skid, you know. It just didn't end up where it was supposed to end up."

The Ragman smiled coldly. "You failed. I want my five hundred dollars back."

The head of the Death's Head Demons grunted. "Those are the breaks, Mac." His pouting lips curled in a sneering grin. "Why don't you make it easy on yourself and leave your wallet on the table? Maybe we'll let you walk out of here in one piece."

The Ragman held out his right hand, palm up. "My money."

The gang leader gave a quick little nod to his pals. They started to move slowly toward the table, but The Ragman stopped them with a single, chilling glance.

"One more time," he said, turning back to face the leader. "Give me my five hundred dollars." A pistol fitted with a silencer had appeared in his left hand. The young man reached into his pants pocket and brought out a roll of bills. He placed them on the table.

"Thank you," The Ragman said, picking up the money. "Now there is a matter of punitive damages to consider. I told you what I would do if you failed...."

TRACY PRESSED the ice pack against her throbbing forehead and watched the flames dance upon the logs in the fireplace. She and Shane had been sitting side by side on the carpet, saying little, for almost an hour. Shane had been incredibly tender since they'd returned to the apartment, and she wanted the moment to last.

For a few minutes during the ride up Capitol Hill and through the Cheesman Park district, Tracy hadn't been at all sure it was such a good idea to leave the hospital. The first icy breath of fresh air she'd gulped down had left her woozy, and she'd had to lean on Shane for support. And as the chauffeured Blazer had clawed its way up the hill, passing several other motorists stuck in the snow, her light-headedness had given way to a case of the shakes.

Shane dismissed the TransWorld driver at the front door of the apartment building, then guided Tracy through the lobby and to the elevator. At the door of the apartment, he gathered her up in his arms and carried her to the bedroom, kicking the door shut behind them.

Setting her gently on the bed, he helped her out of her coat and then pulled off her boots. He found the black-and-gold robe she'd worn earlier and laid it across the foot of the bed. They looked at each other for a moment, neither of them speaking. Finally, Tracy stood up unsteadily and unbuttoned her corduroy jacket. Shane slipped it off her, then put his arms around her waist and looked into her eyes. "They say the Caribbean is nice this time of year."

"Who are they?" she murmured.

"Anyone who's ever sailed it in December. The hurricane season is over, the skies are blue and the sea is so clear you can see the coral ten fathoms down."

"Maybe I'll check it out sometime."

"How about now—tomorrow? I'll put you on a company plane, then join you as soon as I get things worked out at this end."

She kissed him on the underside of his chin and moved back. "No way—not unless you're on the same plane." She waited for him to respond, and when he failed to, she unzipped her skirt and stepped out of it. Slowly, carefully, she eased the dark brown turtleneck over her head, wincing as the soft fabric slid across the scrape on her cheek. Next came her half-slip. Reaching behind her back with both hands, she made a face. "You're not much help at all," she complained.

Compliantly, he turned her around, unhooked her bra and pushed the straps down from her shoulders, letting the garment flutter to the floor. Hands cupped lightly against the undersides of her breasts, he lowered his head and kissed the side of her neck.

"Make love to me, Shane," she whispered, lightly tracing her fingertips against the backs of his hands.

He kissed her again on the neck and then, abruptly, reached across to the foot of the bed, picked up the robe and draped it across her shoulders. "Better get some rest, Tracy." He turned and left the room.

Tugging off her panty-hose, she put on Shane's robe and after-ski slippers and padded out into the living room.

Shane was sitting in front of the fireplace, puffing on a cigar.

Dropping down onto the carpet beside him, she curled her legs beneath her. As soon as she was settled, she plucked the cigar from between his teeth and flipped it into the crackling fire. "You said you wanted to quit," she reminded him.

"Do you believe everything I say?"

She started to shake her head but decided she wasn't ready for such a strenuous motion. "No. You promised me some Napoleon brandy, and I haven't seen a drop of it."

He grinned. "I think you might be better off with an ice pack." He got up and went into the kitchen to prepare it.

"Thank you," she said softly when he returned and handed her the ice pack.

"Compliments of the house."

She smiled. "I mean for saving my life tonight."

He sat down beside her and squeezed her hand.

Neither spoke again for several minutes. It was Tracy who broke the silence. "What are you thinking about, Shane?"

"You."

"What about me?"

"I'm thinking I'd like to whisk you the hell out of here and let my esteemed colleagues fight it out among themselves. I'm thinking of how I can keep you safe."

Tracy set aside the ice pack and laced her fingers through his. "I feel safe when I'm with you."

"Did you feel safe tonight when you almost got killed?"

Tracy shuddered at the memory. "Darling, companies change hands every day. What's so different about TWS that somebody seems willing to kill to control it?"

Shane laughed dryly. "The two great motivators: money and power. I'll admit TransWorld has chalked up some sinfully high profits. We've taken our share of risks, sure, but we've been paid handsomely. At the same time, TWS has become a decisive force in a number of Third World nations. Our people and our hardware maintain the status quo, and those who benefit from the status quo see to it that TWS benefits, too. If we wanted to, we could exploit that arrangement—hold out for special favors like trade concessions, play both ends against the middle, or what have you. That hasn't yet happened, but it could. Whoever is out to get me knows that.''

Tracy could feel his muscles tighten as if he were bracing himself to confront an unpleasant truth. ''You don't think that business tonight was an accident, do you?''

''I told the cop it was.''

''You also told me not to believe everything you say. *Was* it an accident, Shane?''

''You tell me.''

''So what do we do now? Do we run or do we fight back?''

''In the end, we'll do what's right. That's all I can say.''

''That's all I wanted to hear.'' Tracy lay back with her head on his lap. She reached up and ran her fingers down his cheeks and along the hard bands of muscle at the side of his neck. ''Love me,'' she whispered. ''Love me and make me forget all the bad things.''

Shane tenderly touched his right forefinger to the tip of her nose. ''Tracy, I've wanted you since the moment we met,'' he said softly. ''I've wanted you more than I've ever wanted any woman. I can't think of anything in the world I'd rather do right now than make love to you. But I don't think the doctor would approve.'' He lowered his head and placed his lips on the darkened swelling under each of her eyes. ''You still hurt, don't you, sweetheart?''

''I still hurt,'' she admitted, ''and you're the only one who can make me feel better.''

"Close your eyes, Tracy, and get some rest." He cradled her head against his chest.

She closed her eyes. "Then hold me. Please, just hold me."

BUBBA CROWLEY WAS SLOUCHED BACK in Tracy's swivel chair, his feet on her desk, glancing over the sports section of the *Pueblo Chieftain*, when Tracy walked into the office the next morning. "Call off the bloodhounds!" he howled, his beefy face crinkling into a sardonic smile. "The little lady's back!" The look became a stare and he straightened up. "Lordy me! What happened?"

Tracy had hoped dark glasses would conceal the black eyes, but obviously they didn't. Telling herself she didn't give a damn what Bubba thought, she whipped off the glasses and dropped them into the purse slung over her shoulder. "I had an accident."

"Whoo0-ee, I'd say you did!" Bubba cackled. "The new boyfriend get a bit rough with you, little lady?"

Tracy had decided she wasn't going to let Bubba upset her. "If you don't mind, I'd like to use my office." She cocked her thumb toward the door. "Out."

The deputy tossed aside the newspaper, got up and stretched languidly. "Whatever you say, little lady. Hell's fire, you only got a few weeks left, so you might as well enjoy them." He held out the chair for her. "Sit down and do your sheriff thing. If the boyfriend calls, what do you want me to tell him?"

Tracy found it increasingly difficult to contain her irritation. "My personal life is none of your business, Crowley!"

The deputy looked hurt. "You know, little lady, I could hardly believe my ears when somebody told me you shacked up with some dude at a motel in Pueblo Sunday night, and—"

"That's a lie!"

"—when I heard you stayed in a two-hundred-dollar-a-night suite at the Brown Palace in Denver, you could've knocked me over with a feather. No use denying it. One of the commissioners tried to call you at the motel you were supposed to be at, and they said you'd moved into the Brown. The new boyfriend shell out the money, did he?"

"Get out of here!" Tracy bristled.

Smirking because he'd just found a new weakness to exploit in his boss, Bubba ambled to the door. He glanced into the outer office and at the two men and the woman standing there, then turned to confront Tracy. "Who are those folks?"

Tracy shrugged out of her shearling-lined suede jacket and sat down at her desk. "Three new deputies I hired in Denver," she said matter-of-factly. "Try not to get in their way, will you?"

Bubba's bushy, brown eyebrows rose in crescents of astonishment. "You out of your mind?" he sputtered. "The commissioners'll nail your hide to the courthouse door! They been after you to cut the budget, and here you go taking on new people!"

Tracy smiled darkly. "These are *special* people," she said. "And you let me worry about how to pay them." She paused to allow herself more time to enjoy Bubba's perplexity. "If you'll ask them to step in, I'll introduce you."

Speechless for once, the deputy again eyed the trio in the outer office. Any invitation from him was unnecessary. The newcomers obviously had heard what Tracy had said, for they filed into her office one by one, the woman leading the way.

"This is Ingrid Pederson," Tracy announced, nodding to the trim, blond woman, who was in her mid-thirties. "To her left is Dan Rawlings, and the other gentleman is Jerry Latimer." Dan was the older of the two men, a tall and fit fiftyish. Jerry was in his late twenties, dark and sharp-featured, with the well-muscled build of a professional athlete.

Tracy unlocked the center drawer of her desk and removed a box containing several starred badges identical to the one Bubba wore. "You've already been sworn in," she said as she handed a badge to each of them. "I'll take care of ID cards later."

"Damn it!" Bubba protested. "We don't have enough cars to go around now, and you know it!"

"That's already been taken care of."

Bubba eyed the newcomers skeptically. "Any of you folks ever had any experience in law enforcement?"

Tracy settled back in her chair. "Ingrid was a police officer for nine years in New York. She walked one of the toughest beats in the Bronx until she was transferred to the police academy as an instructor." Tracy paused, smiling. "She taught unarmed combat—in case you get any ideas, Crowley."

The deputy did a bulging-eyed double take.

"Mr. Rawlings," Tracy continued, "recently retired as assistant chief of the White House Secret Service detail."

Bubba shook his head in disbelief.

"And Mr. Latimer served two hitches in Special Forces—the Green Berets—training Latin American counterinsurgency troops." Again Tracy paused. "Yes, I'd say all three of them have had some experience keeping the peace."

Bubba started to say something but changed his mind. Tromping out of the office, he slammed the door behind him.

"I trust he isn't your number-one deputy," Dan said.

Tracy shook her head quickly. "Hardly. It just so happens I'm stuck with him. This is a small county, and practically everybody is related to somebody else. Bubba Crowley is a nephew of the county chairman.''

Ingrid Pederson sat down across the desk from Tracy and dropped her badge into a side pocket of her pale blue parka. ''You're the boss, sheriff, but do you think it was wise telling him so much about us? It'll be all over the county by noon.''

Tracy checked her watch. It was just eight. ''More likely the word will go full circle by ten, with a bit of embellishment every step of the way. I'm supposed to speak at a luncheon today at Brenner's Crossing, which is on the other side of the county. I'm sure by the time I show up, the three of you will have become a full regiment.''

Dan laughed good-naturedly. ''Let's go over it one more time, Mrs. Hannon. One of us is going to be at your side every minute for the next month. Ingrid will move in with you, and Jerry and I will trade off pairing up with you wherever you go. One of us will be at the radio here in the office from eight in the morning until midnight, and whoever's free will circulate in town and keep his ears open. All right?''

Tracy frowned. ''You're stretching yourselves awfully thin.''

''We can try it for a while,'' Jerry said. ''If we need reinforcements, we can always borrow somebody from the ranch.''

''I'd rather not,'' Dan said. ''Shane indicated that the fewer people in the company who know about our assignment, the better. He didn't spell it out, but I'm sure he has his reasons.''

''That's interesting,'' Ingrid observed. ''The deputy who was just here is obviously a blabbermouth. What's the big secret?''

''The big secret,'' Dan replied patiently, ''lies in our connection with TWS. Some people are going to wonder why we suddenly showed up on the scene. Let's simply tell them we're old friends who came to help out during Mrs. Hannon's budget squeeze. Granted, it sounds farfetched, but it will have to do. Agreed?''

*The scene.* Tracy suddenly remembered the photographs she'd taken on the hillside the day the sniper fired at Shane. She'd have to get the film processed soon.

TRACY TOYED with the unappetizing mixture of creamed chicken and peas still heaped on her plate and tried her best to seem to be enjoying the proceedings. The Brenner's Crossing Kiwanis Club had wanted to give her this testimonial luncheon, and she had no wish to hurt the members' feelings. But all she could think of was Shane—Shane and the first and last big case of her brief career in law enforcement. *Damn it! Everything was so predictable until you came into my life! Predictable and boring.*

She found herself staring at Jerry Latimer, who was sitting at a table in the rear of the community hall, chatting amiably with the Kiwanians flanking him. What would these people think if they knew who Jerry really was? she wondered.

She became vaguely aware that her name was being mentioned. She looked up and saw that the master of ceremonies was standing behind the lectern, speaking to the audience. ''...a young woman who has done great credit to her office,'' he was saying. ''We all know her, we all love her. I don't know how she came up with those black eyes, but whoever did it better not show his face here in Brenner's Crossing!''

Applause and laughter.

The emcee glanced down at Tracy. ''Say, sheriff, just *how* did you come up with those shiners anyway?''

Another round of laughter.

Tracy put down her fork and stood up. She leaned over toward the microphone and smiled. "I could say I ran into a double door, but you'd never believe me."

More laughter. A man in the audience yelled out, "You got to do better'n that, Tracy! That's not very original!"

Tracy joined in the laughter. "Actually, I was in a traffic accident earlier this week in Denver. I was walking downtown during the blizzard when one of those big-city drivers decided it was safer driving on the sidewalk. Believe me—" she touched her cheekbones with her fingers "—it wasn't!"

The Kiwanians roared.

Tracy sat down. *What would they think if they knew the real story?* she wondered. *Would they still be laughing?*

One after another, club members came to the lectern to say nice things about Tracy. The emcee gave her a walnut-mounted brass plaque whose inscription praised her for a job well done. A high school girl came forward with a bouquet of red-and-white carnations.

Then Vince Emmerling, the rancher who'd been elected to succeed her as sheriff, got to his feet. "I just want to second everything that's been said here today," he announced. "Like they say in show business, this woman's going to be a tough act to follow. I'm sure glad she didn't run against me in the election!"

More laughter and applause.

"Having said all that," Emmerling went on, "let me tell you something that may make you folks want to take back all those nice going-away presents you've given her." He gave Tracy a fatherly smile. "I'm asking her here and now if she won't stay on as my undersheriff. How's about it, Tracy?"

Surprised, Tracy half rose to her feet. "I don't know what to say, Vince."

"A simple yes will do."

There were whistles and cheers from the audience. Someone yelled, jokingly, "He's just trying to get you to do all the work while he gets all the credit!"

Tracy started to say that there wasn't that much to do. She decided to use discretion. She didn't want to demean the job to which Emmerling had just been elected. "This is awfully sudden," she said. "I'll have to think about it."

"You promise you'll do that?" Emmerling asked.

"I promise."

When the luncheon meeting was breaking up, the sheriff-elect took her aside. "I was serious, Tracy. I really do want you to stay on."

Tracy smiled. "I appreciate the offer, but I think it's time for me to move on."

"You promised me you'd think about it."

"I will," she said, nodding. "But you'll be bringing in a new crew, and..."

Emmerling shook his head vigorously. "I plan to ask your deputies to stay on. You've trained 'em well, and they know their business." He chuckled. "All except Crowley, that is."

Tracy said nothing.

"That boy's trouble. So watch your back these last few weeks in office."

*I intend to,* Tracy thought. *But Bubba's the least of my worries.*

THE HELICOPTER streaked in over the canyon, nose down like a sleek mountain cat on the prowl as it followed the snow-frosted asphalt trail a few hundred feet below. The weak, midafternoon sun shone dully on the Plexiglas bubble of its cockpit, obscuring any view of the occupants.

"That's one of ours—see the black-and-gold markings?" Jerry Latimer pointed out, leaning forward in the front seat of the patrol car and twisting his neck to look up as the helicopter flew over. "TWS keeps three of them at Stapleton Airfield to fly courier runs to the ranch."

Tracy eased up on the gas and tried to catch another glimpse of the helicopter in her rearview mirror. Could it be Shane already? she wondered. The last time she'd talked to him on the phone he didn't think he'd be able to get down to the ranch until Saturday morning, if then.

The mirror gave her a fleeting glimpse of the helicopter swinging off from its route above the canyon road and heading due south toward the Donnelly place. On impulse Tracy picked up the microphone from the dashboard. "K double A six-oh-six to base."

"Go ahead, sheriff," she heard Dan Rawlings reply.

"We're on our way in from Brenner's Crossing. Any messages?"

"A few," Dan said crisply. "Nothing urgent."

"Any word from our mutual friend?" she persisted.

"What's your ETA, sheriff?"

"Ten minutes—no more. We're coming in on the canyon road just west of Henryville."

"We'll talk when you get in."

Tracy replaced the microphone in its holder. "Mr. Rawlings certainly isn't very communicative."

Her companion seemed amused. "People who've spent a lifetime in this line of work tend to become pretty close-mouthed."

"Yes, but we're on the same side," Tracy pointed out.

"Sure, but you never know who might be listening in and which side *they're* on. It doesn't matter. We're almost there."

Passing the old mill, Tracy glanced up at the ridge road. It was deserted. She wondered what she might have missed in her first search of the area, how much more she might have turned up if she'd had Dan or Jerry or Ingrid with her. Too late now. The blizzard had obliterated any clues that might have remained.

Their route into town took them by the photo shop. Tracy double-parked and sent Jerry in with the film she wanted developed, waited for him, then drove on to the courthouse. As she pulled into her reserved slot at the curb, she noticed that Crowley's patrol car was gone. She picked up the microphone. "K double A six-oh-six to base. Any idea of Unit Three's location?"

"He hasn't checked in for a while. Want me to try to raise him?"

"Negative." Tracy turned to Jerry. "Why don't you go on inside. I want to call Crowley."

"Sorry, but I'm not going to let you out of my sight. Boss's orders."

"I'll be right here in the car. You can keep watch from the courthouse steps."

Jerry started to protest further, then changed his mind. He glanced at the courthouse. The steps leading down to the sheriff's office were no more than fifty feet away. "Give him my regards," he said, getting out of the patrol car.

Tracy thumbed down the Transmit button. "K double A six-oh-six to Unit Three."

No answer.

She tried again. And then a third time.

"Whatcha need, little lady?" the reply crackled forth.

"What's your location, Unit Three?"

"Five, maybe six miles east of Henryville, trying to get this here radar unit to work."

"I want you in my office in ten minutes, Unit Three. Move it! K double A six-oh-six out."

As she started to hang up the the microphone, she noticed that one of the indicator lights on the citizens band side of her radio was blinking red. She reached over and punched in the channel.

"...looks like it might be a bad one!" a man's voice chattered excitedly. "It went down out of sight across the river, but I can see the flames from here."

"Unable to copy," Tracy radioed back. "Please repeat."

"I said, we got a helicopter crash out here. Can you get word to whatever sort of fire department you got?"

Tracy's heart began to pound. "Give me an exact location!"

"It's about six, seven miles west of town, just across the state highway. I'm driving this drilling rig up from Alamosa, taking a shortcut to Pueblo, when I—"

Tracy dropped the microphone, slammed the gearshift into reverse and screeched backward onto the street in a wide, sweeping turn as Jerry sprinted toward the car in a futile attempt to rejoin her. Switching on her emergency lights, she raced out of the square, siren screaming. She switched back to the sheriff's office frequency. "K double A six-oh-six to base! Any word from the ranch about a helicopter crash?"

It took a few seconds for Dan to respond. "I'm on the phone now, sheriff. I want you to get back here and pick up your deputy." His tone was stern, insistent.

"I don't have time! Call the volunteer fire department and get some equipment rolling!"

"It's already taken care of, sheriff. Listen to me—"

Tracy switched off the radio.

She was traveling too fast when she swung onto the gravel road leading from the state highway to the ranch, and the Ford's rear end skidded across the tire-rutted snow, almost ending up in a ditch. She wrestled the car under control and drove the final mile at a reduced speed, the lights and siren still going.

The same guard she'd encountered five days before was on duty. He was out of his Blazer and walking toward the chain-link gate, his short-barreled shotgun slung over his shoulder, before Tracy had even braked her car to a halt.

She rolled down her window. "Open the gate!" she shouted at him. "There's been an accident and I'm coming in!"

"It's being taken care of, sheriff," he called out.

"I said, I want in!"

"Sorry, sheriff."

Angry, Tracy turned the car around and headed toward the state highway. Beyond the first bend in the gravel road, she slammed on the brakes. Federal reservation or not, the guard had no right to refuse her entry! The main gate obviously was the quickest way into the area of the crash, and she intended to use that gate!

She twisted around in her seat and unlocked the heavy clamp holding the 12-gauge riot gun in the metal scabbard behind the seat. She'd never held the shotgun before, and the coldness of the barrel against her bare fingers gave her a fleeting case of the jitters. Quickly she worked the pump action back and forth, ejecting all six shells from the weapon, then laid the shotgun across her lap. She threw the shells into the glove compartment, out of sight.

Carefully turning around on the narrow road, she headed toward the gate and stopped, only inches from the chain link.

"Can you take a message?" Tracy yelled out the open window at the guard, who'd returned to his truck.

He got out of the truck, slung his weapon over his shoulder, barrel down, and started for the gate. He was less than ten feet away when Tracy raised her own weapon and trained it on him. "Stop right there!" she commanded.

The guard halted in his tracks, his right hand tightening on the leather sling of his shotgun. He said nothing, but

Tracy sensed he would be quick to react at the slightest opening. "Very slowly take that shotgun off your shoulder," Tracy instructed him. "Don't touch anything but the sling."

Grim-faced, the man did as he was told.

"Now throw the gun over there—" She flicked the muzzle of the riot gun toward a towering snowdrift across the road from where he stood. "Be quick about it!"

"You're making a big mistake, sheriff," he grumbled.

"You'll be making an even bigger one if you don't do as you're told."

The guard hesitated, as if to assess his chances of defying her. Perhaps it was the tone of Tracy's voice that made him decide to follow instructions. He tossed the shotgun into the snowdrift, where it was immediately swallowed up.

"Now open the gate and stand aside."

"You're going to have federal agents all over you by the time you get back to your office," he informed her. "I wouldn't want to be in your shoes. You're asking for trouble."

"Are you going to open the gate for me, or do I just ram it down?" Tracy demanded, touching her toe to the gas pedal and revving the engine. "I'm coming in, one way or another."

Frowning, the guard stepped up to the gate, drew back the bolt and swung aside the heavy steel barrier.

Tracy lowered her unloaded riot gun and placed it across her lap. She slammed the gearshift lever into low, and the patrol car shot forward through the opening and onto the ranch. Glancing into the rearview mirror, Tracy could see the guard scurry to the Blazer, throw open the door and grab the microphone from the dashboard. She saw, too, that another patrol car was approaching the gate from the road leading off the state highway, and she guessed that one or more of the bodyguards Shane had assigned to her were in the car.

She crested a hill, and ahead lay the narrow, tree-walled valley in which the main ranch house was located. The valley had changed dramatically in the six months since she'd last seen it. The ranch house, which had been a small, squarish log structure flanked on one side by a decrepit barn and corral and on the other by a work shed and metal-roofed storage buildings, had been enlarged. Four long wings had been added, leaving the original house as the hub of a sprawling, cross-shaped building. The corral was gone, replaced by two huge warehouse-type buildings facing each other across a concrete apron that had been cleared of snow. On the opposite side of the main building was a parking area and service garage with room for at least eight vehicles. In the distance, beyond the main compound, was another concrete pad that also had been cleared of snow; painted across the pad was a bright yellow circle.

Tracy took in the changes at a glance, but her main attention was riveted on a rocky area on the banks of the river, fifty yards from the outlying pad. Framed by a thick stand of pines that blocked the view from the river and the highway, orange flames and black smoke were rising from the wreckage of a helicopter that had landed on its side, its rotors crumpled.

"Oh, God!" she gasped, tromping down on the gas pedal, the rear end of the Ford fishtailing as the car careened around the snow-packed curves. At the foot of the hill, the road branched, one prong of the fork leading to the main compound and parking area, the other to the helicopter pad. As Tracy's patrol car came out onto the flat of the valley, she could see another black Blazer race toward the fork from the direction of the ranch house. Other trucks were already at the crash site.

Tracy got to the fork seconds ahead of the Blazer, which, she guessed, had set out to intercept her. She turned more sharply than she had intended and went into a skid, sending up a shower of loose snow and gravel that spattered against the windshield of the oncoming truck. As she pulled up alongside the vehicles at the helicopter pad, two men dressed in black parkas and jeans, each carrying a shotgun, appeared on either side of the patrol car. Tracy brushed her gun off her lap and started to open the door.

"You're off limits, lady," said the man who stood blocking her door. "Turn your car around and get out of here—now."

Tracy pushed at the door, but the guard held it shut.

"Get out of my way!" Tracy cried in frustration.

"It's all right, Mitch!" she heard someone shout. She looked back and saw Dan Rawlings get out of an unmarked car that had pulled in behind her.

As the guard stepped aside, Tracy leaped out of the Ford and then sprinted toward a cluster of men gathered around a blanket-draped mound alongside the truck closest to the wreckage. Beyond, three other men were using heavy-duty fire extinguishers on the flames. Tracy shouldered her way into the group just in time to see a middle-aged woman wearing a blue smock adjust the blanket over the mound and rise wearily to her feet from a kneeling position.

"He's dead," the woman said.

## Chapter Eight

Strong hands grasped Tracy's upper arms and shook her. "Get hold of yourself," said a gentle but firm voice that came from a form without a face. "It's all right, it's all right..."

Blinking through glassy eyes, Tracy squirmed about to stare at the blanket-draped mound. "Shane!" she screamed.

"Tracy, listen to me! It's not Shane! Do you understand? It's *not* Shane!"

She pulled free to look at whoever was holding her, shaking her. It took her several seconds to recognize Dan Rawlings. "It's...it's not?" she asked in a hollow voice.

Dan shook his head and released his grip on her. "He's in Denver. I talked to him on the phone just before the crash."

Tracy glanced again at the body. "Who...who's that?"

"The pilot."

"Was he alone?"

"As far as we know. We've got to knock down those flames before we can get into the wreckage and find out for sure."

Tracy looked away from the body and rubbed her temples with her fingertips. "I'm sorry," she murmured. "I shouldn't have gone to pieces. It's not . . . not very professional, I know.''

Dan smiled sympathetically. "You're human, Tracy. Nobody can be a decent law enforcement officer without first of all being human. Hey, look out!" He threw her to the ground as a massive fireball whooshed up from the wreckage and exploded with an ear-hammering thump, scattering bits of fiery debris.

"The reserve tank!" someone shouted.

Then there was silence, and the flames around the wreckage retreated and died, leaving in their place isolated black wisps of smoke. Two of the firefighters moved in closer, laying a protective carpet of fluffy white chemical foam ahead of them.

Dan scrambled to his feet and pulled Tracy up. "You okay?"

She nodded.

"All right, let's take a look," he suggested, starting to follow the firefighters.

"Dan! Wait!" A man whom Tracy had never seen before came running up from the line of trucks parked closest to the wreckage. "I've got Denver on the radio. There *was* somebody else on the chopper—a woman from the Paris office."

Tracy stared at the man. "Martina Tatarescu?"

"Yeah. She was coming down for the weekend." Grimly he surveyed the smoldering wreckage. "She must still be in there."

"Oh, God!" Tracy groaned, pushing forward onto the scorched rocks and kicking aside chunks of metal as she searched for signs of life. The thin soles of her shoes were becoming painfully hot, and tiny flying embers were stinging her legs and burning holes in her stockings. Why, she wondered crazily, had she chosen to wear a dress today of all days?

"There's nobody alive in there," Dan said. He was close behind her, conducting his own examination.

"How can you be so sure?" Tracy demanded, heaving aside a length of crumpled rotor. Her hands scrabbled at the rocks where the blade had been, just outside the fuselage.

Another man was waving at them from the side of a huge boulder twenty yards distant. "Over here!" he shouted.

Tracy was the first to arrive at the boulder, with Dan hard at her heels. She saw Martina sprawled on her back on the ground, her fists held up to her face, her knuckles white. Martina was trembling violently. Tracy dropped to her knees and cradled the woman's head in her arms. "Don't try to move," she said soothingly.

Martina went limp for a moment, and her eyes closed. Her blue quilted jumpsuit was torn and seared, and there was a tiny trickle of blood that started in one corner of her mouth, ran down her chin and disappeared under her dark blue scarf. Tracy became aware that Martina was speaking to her in a voice that was hoarse and gasping. "So this . . . your . . . quiet little corner of the world . . . eh?"

"Be still," Tracy told her. "We'll get a doctor."

The middle-aged woman Tracy had seen earlier by the blanket-covered mound, knelt beside her and began to examine Martina. "I'm the medical officer," she said tersely. "Please—give me some room."

Martina's eyes opened and her hands reached out for Tracy's. "Stay," she pleaded. "Please . . . stay here."

The doctor glanced from Martina to Tracy, then back to Martina. "All right. Can you move your legs?"

Martina nodded weakly and, as if to prove she was telling the truth, brought up her knees and twisted them from side to side. The medical officer unzipped Martina's jumpsuit to her waistline and probed carefully at her neck, shoulders, ribs. Martina winced a few times but said nothing.

"Tell me what happened," the doctor instructed her.

"It was…very sudden," Martina said, again closing her eyes. "We were no more than five or six meters above the ground when the helicopter—what is the word?—lurched. It fell on its side…hit the ground…began burning." She paused. "I tried…to get the pilot out…fire was too hot. I started crawling…away from the fire. The next thing I knew…somebody was shouting."

"Did you hear anything or see anything just before the crash?" Dan asked. Tracy saw that the former Secret Service man was standing directly behind her.

Martina opened her eyes, stared at him, then closed her eyes again. "I do not…feel well. So very cold."

"We've got to get this woman to the dispensary at once," the doctor decreed, standing up. "I'd appreciate it if one of you would go to those emergency trucks and get a stretcher."

Tracy started to leave, but Dan grabbed her arm. "Doctor," he said, looking squarely at the medical officer, "please see to the stretcher yourself."

The woman started to protest, but thought better of it when she saw the determination etched on Dan's face. "I'll only be a minute," she said grudgingly. She headed toward the line of trucks, giving a wide berth to the smoldering wreckage.

Dan dropped to his knees beside Martina, who reopened her eyes and glanced warily at the men standing nearby, watching her. "Get them away!" she whispered.

Dan turned and waved off the spectators, then hunkered down again. "Make it fast," he said.

Martina nodded, and when she spoke again her voice was strong, although she was clearly in pain. "There were three shots—I will swear to it. The first hit a rotor blade. I know this because I heard a clanging noise overhead and the helicopter started shaking violently. Almost immediately there was a second shot. That bullet came through the windscreen as we spun around out of control. I saw the hole take shape inches from my face—almost like one of those slow-motion scenes in the movies when they want to dramatize the violence. I think that was when the pilot was hit, because he slumped over the controls and the helicopter began to fall. I am sure I heard a third shot. There was a sharp, screeching sound just behind the cockpit—the sound of metal piercing metal—and then we caught fire, even before we hit the ground.''

"You're sure of all this?'' Dan asked.

"Being sure of things is a requirement of my profession,'' Martina said haughtily.

"You didn't see who was doing the shooting?''

"Everything happened too fast. There might have been flashes among the trees. I cannot be certain, though.''

Dan glanced over his shoulder. The medical officer was returning with two men carrying a stretcher. "What trees?''

"On the hillside, the one leading up to what looks like a big forest. Not the side the river is on. The other side.''

"That's enough talk for now,'' the doctor announced, curtly motioning Tracy and Dan aside as she attempted to regain control of the situation. "I want to get the patient out of here.''

"Go with her,'' Dan told Tracy out of the corner of his mouth as Martina was loaded onto the stretcher. "I'll be back for you later. Under no circumstances are you to leave the dispensary until I come for you. Understood?''

"Where are you going?''

"I'm taking Jerry and I'm going to scout around.''

"Just the two of you?''

Dan nodded. "We both know Shane wants to play this close to the vest. Obviously, Martina Tatarescu does, too. If someone in the company is involved, the less talk the better."

"I'm going with you," Tracy said determinedly.

"You're going to the dispensary."

"You seem to be forgetting something," Tracy retorted. "You're only a deputy. I'm the sheriff."

"That may be," Dan conceded, "but Shane's the boss."

"He's not *my* boss!"

Dan thought about it. Tracy imagined he was marshaling his arguments, so she decided to keep him off balance. "Those trees up there," she said, nodding her head in the direction of the hillside, "are not part of the ranch. TransWorld may control what happens down here but not up there. That's forest land and it's within San Isabel County, and San Isabel County happens to be *my* jurisdiction. In short, Mr. Rawlings, I'm going with you. And don't tell me I'd only be in the way. I don't like chauvinism."

Dan looked at her, at the smoke-smudged, green wool suit she was wearing, the loden coat hanging loosely over her shoulders. He noted her shoes and burned stockings. "You're hardly dressed to go tramping through the forest," he pointed out.

"I've got a parka and quilted coveralls in the trunk. Hiking boots, too. It'll take me less than a minute to put them on."

Dan took a deep breath. "Are you carrying a weapon?"

"You know very well I'm not."

That was the opening he sought. "You realize we'd be so busy keeping an eye on you that our search would be compromised?"

Tracy didn't hesitate. "I've got a shotgun in the car—a Winchester. I'll get it if it will make you feel any better."

"Do you know how to use it?" Dan called after her.

"I can manage."

BUT FOR THE BITTER COLD and the uncertain footing, conditions were ideal for tracking. The blizzard had left a virginal layer of white upon which even the slightest trail stood out clearly. Here and there the powdery snow was broken by prints of a deer or a snowshoe rabbit. But there was no evidence that a human had traveled the slope.

"If there *was* a shooter, he had to have been higher up," Jerry said, surveying the slope from the edge of a grove. He, Dan and Tracy were crouched behind the brittle, brown skeleton of a clump of scrub oak, catching their breath after the hundred-yard climb from the site of the crash. It had been a rigorous trek through deep powder and the underlying crust of earlier snowfalls. Fifty yards up the slope loomed the edge of the forest, the towering pines silent sentinels whose ominousness grew with the lengthening shadows.

"We don't have much time," Dan said. "It's already three o'clock, so there are only a few more hours of daylight." He looked at Tracy. "All right, sheriff, this is your turf. You know of any trails in there through the trees?"

"Lots of them. But they'd be drifted over at this time of year."

"They're marked?"

"Yes, the Forest Service is very good about that. Why?"

Dan shrugged. "It's possible our man was on skis, or maybe he had a snowmobile waiting for him on one of those trails. If so, he's well ahead of us—but at least we can track him to wherever he left his vehicle. You never know what might turn up. What's the nearest road?"

"The canyon highway. But he'd have to get across the river, and that doesn't seem very likely in this kind of weather. The ice hasn't had enough time to get thick, and anyone would be taking his life in his hands by venturing out onto it."

"Any bridges nearby? Any places where he could ford the river quickly? I'm thinking of someplace with a campground or a picnic area on the other side of the river, where it wouldn't attract attention to leave a car parked."

Tracy knew of two such locations. She described them.

Dan brought out a Forest Service map, unfolded it across his knees and checked the coordinates of the campgrounds. Then he borrowed Tracy's walkie-talkie. "K double A six-oh-six."

"Go ahead," Ingrid Pederson responded.

"Ingrid, I'm going to give you a couple of map coordinates. Get ranch security on the horn and have them cover those coordinates. Tell them to check anybody who doesn't look right to them—especially anyone in possession of a rifle. If our people get any static, they have authorization to flash their tin."

"Affirmative."

"What do you mean by 'tin'?" Tracy asked when Dan handed her back the walkie-talkie.

"All our security people carry commissions as deputy federal marshals," he explained, slipping his revolver from his holster and examining the cylinder. "Tin is shop slang for badge." The former Secret Service agent stood up and put away the pistol. "This is as far as you go. Jerry and I will take it from here."

"Let's not start that again. I'm going with you."

"No way," Jerry said.

Her cheeks reddening with frustration, Tracy spun around and confronted the younger man. "Look, don't you start in on me, too! I'm going, and there's nothing you can do about it!''

''I think she means it,'' Dan observed.

''Shane's not going to like it,'' Jerry pointed out.

Tracy cradled the short-barreled riot gun in the crook of her right arm and drew herself erect. ''We're wasting time,'' she said, setting out for the edge of the forest.

''Hold it!'' Dan stepped quickly in front of her. ''If we're going to do this, we're going to do it properly. Tracy, you take the center. Jerry will go to the right about fifty yards, and I'll go to the left fifty yards. We'll work our way into the trees and then head for the river, watching for tracks.''

''How far into the trees?'' Jerry asked.

''Five or ten yards—no more. The shooter needed a clear field of fire as well as cover, so let that be your guide. Tracy, if you hear any gunfire you get on that walkie-talkie for some backup. And if you see anything that doesn't look right to you, call out. If one of us doesn't answer you in ten seconds, fire a single shot. If anyone jumps you, I want you to use that scattergun on him. All right?''

Tracy nodded.

''You *do* know how to use it?'' the older man prodded her.

''I told you I did.''

''All right, let's go. You first, Jerry. We'll cover you.''

*He's just like Shane,* Tracy mused as she watched Jerry angle his way up the snowy slope, moving at a dogtrot, slowing from time to time to bull his way through a drift. *He has no idea what's ahead, and yet he doesn't hesitate to forge on.* That was exactly how Shane had acted, setting himself up for a killer. And it was probably the way Alfy Deschamps would handle things, too. And Dan Rawlings, Ingrid Pederson and all the others who worked for Shane. Shane would expect a certain kind of fearlessness on their part. What would he think of her, Tracy wondered, if he knew how scared she was, standing there in the snow and staring up into the unknown?

Jerry reached the top of the slope, paused just outside the edge of the forest, then brought out a pistol from a pocket in his parka. He turned, waved and disappeared into the trees.

"You next, Tracy," Dan said.

Tracy glanced at him. Maybe he was right. Maybe she should stay behind. She wouldn't be much help. She'd never fired the riot gun. Could she do it if her life depended on it? What if *other* lives depended on it? All she could do was put herself to the test and find out. Without a word, she started up the slope.

"Don't forget, now," Dan reminded her. "If anybody jumps you, I expect you to use that weapon."

She nodded absently.

"You've got the safety on?"

Tracy looked at the Winchester. The safety: was it that little crossbolt switch in front of the trigger guard? She wasn't sure, but she wasn't about to admit it. "Of course," she said curtly, taking up the shotgun with her left hand and holding it out at arm's length. "See for yourself."

Dan smiled patiently, without bothering to check. "All right, sheriff, you pass inspection. Now get cracking."

Instead of angling up the mountainside as Jerry had done, Tracy worked her way straight to the line of trees at the edge of the forest, pausing occasionally to catch her breath. Twice her feet slipped out from under her on rocks buried under the powdery snow, and twice she came down unceremoniously on her rear end, almost losing the shotgun. She refused to look back at Dan, fearing he might interpret the slightest glance as a silent appeal for help. She could carry her own weight, and he'd better realize it!

Pushing on, she tried not to think about what might lie ahead. Time enough for that later. And then she was at the treeline. She turned, waved at Dan and stepped into the semidarkness of the dense forest. Without quite realizing what she was doing, she brought back the walnut pump handle of the shotgun and slid it forward—as if a voice that was hers, but *not* hers, was ordering her to play it safe and be certain there was a shell in the chamber.

It was only then that she remembered she'd unloaded the riot gun before she forced her way past the guard at the gate. She'd hidden the shells in the glove compartment so he wouldn't see them. She'd been so shaken up by the crash, she'd forgotten about the shells until now. *Do I go running to Dan and say I made a silly mistake? Do I wait for him to laugh at me, and then trudge down the mountainside to let him and Jerry handle things, let the men do men's work? Not a chance!*

She rammed forward the slide action, once again cradled the shotgun in the crook of her right arm, and set out through the edge of the forest, working her way parallel to the front line of trees, just far enough from the open slope to keep the crash site in view.

They weren't going to find anyone, she told herself. Whoever had done the shooting was long gone. They might pick up a trail, but that was all. Surely their quarry had his escape route well established before he'd taken aim at the incoming helicopter. What was it Shane had said? *We're dealing with a professional.*

She studied the ground in front and on either side as she moved along at a steady pace. There were occasional drifts where gusts of wind had blustered through the edge of the forest, but for the most part the ground was covered with a fairly even layer of snow, undisturbed by human tracks.

Her pulse quickened when, suddenly, she spotted footprints in the snow leading in the same direction in which she was headed. But less than a minute later, as she approached a clearing, she caught a glimpse of Dan about fifty yards in front of her, and she realized the footprints were his.

Looking to her right, she had an almost unobstructed view of the helicopter pad. This, she knew, was the most logical area for the assassin to take up his position—and yet there was no sign of any tracks except Dan's crossing the ground.

*The ground...*

She stopped and gazed up at the lodgepole pines that nearly cut off her view of the sky. On this side of the clearing, the tree trunks were so close together they were almost touching. The branches high up *were* touching, in fact. Was it so terribly far fetched to assume that a reasonably agile person could climb a tree farther back inside the forest and, throwing a rope from tree to tree, work his way to the very edge of the forest without leaving tracks? The killer had already demonstrated mountaineering skills.

Well, why not?

Tracy glanced around to see if Jerry was anywhere nearby. She couldn't tell. The forest was much too thick. She considered calling out but decided not to. It would be a mistake to let their quarry know their position.

Abruptly she spun to her left and trudged into the trees and up the slope, ten, fifteen, twenty yards. If her theory was correct, it didn't seem likely the killer would have started his overhead approach any farther back. He'd want to make his exit in a hurry, and it would be tedious going from tree to tree. No, twenty yards had to be the outer limit.

She worked her way south for several minutes, paralleling her original path, and then, finding nothing, turned and doubled back north. From time to time she paused to see if she could spot either Dan or Jerry. She didn't have anything to report, but it was reassuring to have them close by. They knew their business. How well would *she* be able to handle herself? she wondered.

Fifteen minutes later her toes were going numb inside her hiking boots, and her leg muscles ached from slipping and sliding across the difficult terrain. Then something caught her eye: an angular kind of darkness against the deepening shadows of the inner forest. Forgetting her weariness, Tracy moved from tree to tree, trying to maintain protective cover as she closed in on whatever it was she'd seen. Again she thought about calling out, and again she discarded the idea. She'd investigate first.

When she was within five yards of her objective, she pointed the stubby barrel of the Winchester straight ahead, the gloved finger of her right hand curled around the useless trigger, the fingers of her left hand clutching the slide action. And then her hunch became cold, hard reality. There on the ground, under a hastily constructed camouflage of broken tree limbs, was a dark blue snowmobile.

Tracy examined the sleek, low-slung vehicle that sat under the tangle of branches. The trampled snow on the upslope side of a nearby tree told part of the story. Someone had climbed down from the tree, tried to start the snowmobile, failed, then abandoned the machine. The footprints that led uphill, paralleling and woven into the tread and runner tracks of the vehicle, told another part of the story. Someone had come down the hill on the snowmobile, gone up in the trees and, his work done, been left afoot. And if the killer was afoot, he couldn't be too far away.

*Now* it was time to call for reinforcements.

She propped the shotgun against the tree and cupped her hands to her mouth. "Dan! Jerry! I've got something!" She patted the lump under her jacket, where her radio was clipped to the belt of her jeans. Damn! The radio wouldn't do any good. Dan didn't have a matching unit, or he wouldn't have had to borrow hers to call Ingrid. All she could do was direct Ingrid to send in additional searchers from the ranch, and by the time they found her, the assassin would be long gone.

"Dan! Jerry! Can you hear me?"

Still no response.

Crouching down, Tracy lifted the branches from the snowmobile. She had no idea what was wrong with the machine. Her lack of knowledge of things mechanical was rivaled only by her ignorance of firearms.

The key was still in the ignition. On an impulse, she turned the key. There was a distinct click, but that was all. She unscrewed the gas cap and sniffed. Plenty of fuel. Could it be the battery? The wiring? Possibly the fuel line? What did it matter? She wouldn't know how to fix anything. Except . . .

She'd once seen a ski patrolman at Crested Butte start a recalcitrant snowmobile by rocking the aft end, literally bouncing the machine up and down on its tractorlike treads. But that sort of action couldn't possibly work for her. The snowmobile was heavy, and she doubted she had the strength to lift it. Still, maybe she could jar it enough to make *something* happen. It was worth a try.

Planting her feet firmly in the snow, she grabbed the sides of the open cockpit and began alternatingly pushing and pulling. The snowmobile barely moved. She tried harder, and almost succeeded in getting the treads on her side up out of the snow. But she lost her grip on the cold metal and the machine bounced down, creaking and groaning.

She leaned inside it and once again turned the key. *Click.* She straightened up and cupped her hands to her mouth. "Dan! Jerry! Answer me!"

What was it Dan had told her to do? Fire a single shot in the air if she didn't get an answer within ten seconds! Only one thing was wrong with that bit of advice: it assumed she had sense enough to travel with a loaded weapon.

She couldn't wait. Every minute counted. Dan and Jerry would be bound to double back, and they could follow her tracks to the snowmobile. Then they could do what she was about to do—set out along the path churned up by the vehicle.

She snatched up the shotgun and had taken only a few steps when she stopped and looked over her shoulder. It would be so much simpler if the snowmobile were working. Then she'd stand a chance of catching up with the assassin. Tracy had absolutely no idea what she might do if and when she accomplished that, but she had no choice. She'd cross that bridge when she came to it. She decided to give the snowmobile one more try. Using the stock of the Winchester as a lever, she succeeded in raising the machine off its tracks on one side, then let it slam down into the snow. She repeated this maneuver several times. After five minutes she was gasping for breath, and the gunmetal-gray cockpit began to take on the appearance of an evil, leering mouth that mocked her silently.

One more time, she thought. Just one more time...

She eased herself into the cockpit, pulled out the choke, twisted the handgrip throttle as far as she could, then turned it back halfway and tried the key. The tiny gasoline engine gave a belching cough and sputtered into life, firing unevenly at first until it smoothed out into a steady, throaty roar.

*The power of positive thinking!* Tracy congratulated herself. She let the engine warm up for a few minutes before she dared release the clutch. When she did, the snowmobile lurched forward, its twin studded treads crunching into the snow. She let up on the throttle long enough to steer the vehicle onto the trail on which it had come down the slope. Gradually she increased its speed. The ski-like runners at the front of the machine chattered as they slapped at the rock-and-ice-covered blanket of snow. The trail rose steeply, then leveled off after another thirty yards and wound through the trees.

One set of snowmobile tracks. One set of footprints. All she had to do was follow them wherever they led. And then— Tracy suddenly realized that she'd left the riot gun behind, but she decided against going back for it. Even if it had been loaded, it would probably have been useless to her. Somehow, she still felt safer without any sort of weapon.

The assassin had followed a marked trail as he came through the forest. Every once in a while, Tracy noticed Forest Service signs—carved, yellow letters against dark wood shingles—and she tried to remember where this particular trail led. Was it to the other side of the front range? Possibly. That would put the start of the trail in Huerfano County, miles from the two campgrounds Dan Rawlings had told Ingrid to have covered. If the killer could get across the range to wherever he had left his car, he could make good his escape.

She eased off on the throttle and let the snowmobile grind to a halt. She had to check in and tell Ingrid to contact the Huerfano County sheriff's office in Walsenburg so they could cover the other end of the trail.

"K double A six-oh-six."

Releasing the Transmit button, she stared in frustration at the radio handset. It was out of commission, probably as a result of the bouncing around it had taken on her climb up the mountain. Why hadn't she taken it in for repair as Shane had suggested?

Now the trail was climbing again in steep switchbacks, and she slowed the snowmobile and stayed well inside the turns to avoid going over the side and tangling with the trees. The killer could be anywhere up ahead, she knew. He could be just over the mountain, or even just beyond the next switchback. And he'd have the advantage because he'd hear her coming and he was armed.

Suddenly the darkening sky could be seen clearly overhead, and Tracy knew she was almost at the top of the pass. She speeded up, wanting instinctively to narrow the distance between her and the fleeing quarry, yet closing her mind to the inevitable consequences of the encounter that would follow. All she could hope to do was surprise him, delay him somehow until Dan and Jerry could catch up with her.

As she came up on the summit of the pass, the walkie-talkie slipped out from between her legs and tumbled to the metal floor of the cockpit. She leaned down to retrieve it, and at that instant something struck the windshield. The Plexiglas splintered outward from a tiny hole inches from where her head had been. Two seconds later she heard a sharp cracking sound and realized someone was shooting at her.

Without raising her body, she yanked at the steering handles and hung on tight as the snowmobile careered off the trail amid a shower of snow. The machine lingered for a terrifying second or two, half on and half off the trail, before pitching forward and tumbling end-over-end down the mountainside. Tracy was thrown out of the cockpit on the first roll. She somersaulted for what seemed forever, then slid to a jarring halt on her hands and knees just short of an ugly outcropping of icy gray rock.

She heard the snowmobile crash into the trees lower on the slope with a clatter and wrenching of metal. Silence followed. Dazed, she shook her head. *I'm alive,* she reassured herself. *I'm alive, but there's someone up there who obviously wants to kill me. What do I do now? What would Shane do?*

She struggled groggily to her feet, then immediately dropped to her knees and scrambled behind the outcropping of rock. Another shot had kicked up a puff of powder and splintery rock less than a foot from her head.

*What would Shane do?*

"K double A six-oh-six!" she shouted into a nonexistent radio from behind the rock. "He's got me pinned down near the summit! Get some men to work their way up either side of the trail! Do you copy? Good! See you soon! Ten-four!"

Three more shots echoed across the slope, the slugs thudding into the rock at the top of the outcropping.

She had him worried now, Tracy tried to persuade herself. He thought she was alone, but now he wasn't so sure. What could she do to worry him even more?

Tracy looked around and spotted some loose chunks of ice at the base of the outcropping. The chunks had apparently been broken free by the gunshots. She reached over and hefted one of the pieces of ice, but it was too heavy for her purpose. She selected a smaller chunk and, grasping it shotput fashion, sent it scuttling up across the trail and into the trees beyond, where it landed with a solid thump.

Almost immediately there were two more shots—not in her direction this time, but aimed approximately at where the glob of ice had fallen. Tracy wondered crazily if he would run out of bullets before she ran out of ice.

She picked up another piece and hurled it up the slope on her side of the trail. It landed without making a sound, so she tried again. The third chunk of ice bounced off a rock and succeeded in prompting one more shot from the hidden assassin.

As the echo of the shot reverberated along the mountainside and died, Tracy sat down, her back to the outcropping. She wrapped her arms around her drawn-up knees for warmth and waited.

That was all she could do now, she realized. Wait.

THE RAGMAN squinted through the telescopic sight of his rifle. He had seen a hand, a foot, a brief flash of a red parka, and he had fired and missed. Perhaps it was for the best, he consoled himself. He would only have wounded the woman, and that was not what he wanted. He wanted Tracy Hannon dead. She'd been nothing but trouble. As for the evidence she had collected, it would be meaningless, because she would not be alive to testify as to where and how she had acquired it.

He waited. In time she would make a move. Tracy Hannon was impetuous. Moreover, she was angry—for hadn't he just slain her lover? The Ragman smiled as he reran a mental film strip of the helicopter crash. Tracy Hannon's anger and impetuosity would compel her to seek vengeance, and she could not seek vengeance while hiding behind a rock. She would come out, her gun blazing in the best tradition of the Old West, and he would have a clear shot. Anger and impetuosity would be her death.

The Ragman heard a noise to one side of the trail. He spun around, rifle at his hip, and froze. He could see nothing, but he could hear her yell. What was she saying? *Ten-four?* He looked down again at the outcropping behind which his target hid. Could she possibly have a two-way radio?

The Ragman studied the sky. It would be dark before long. He did not know this forest, and, presumably, Tracy Hannon did.

He listened for voices, for the sounds of feet crunching through the snow and of other snowmobiles that might be joining the pursuit.

Nothing.

He squeezed off two more shots at the outcropping, then started trotting up the trail. He could not risk waiting her out any longer.

Tracy Hannon would die another day.

## Chapter Nine

Shane stopped pacing long enough to pound his fist on the old-fashioned oak desk. "I don't care what you say!" he thundered, glowering at Tracy. "They're through—both of them! I told them to put you on ice and they didn't do it! When somebody works for me, he follows orders or he gets out!"

Tracy felt her own rage build. Not just rage, but a release of all the stomach-knotting tensions of the long afternoon. She slammed down her heavy mug of hot chocolate, spilling some of the liquid, and cast aside the wool blanket draped over her shoulders. "Don't bully me, Shane Keegan!" she fired back, staring daggers at him. "Dan and Jerry are my deputies! You *can't* fire them!"

"I pay their wages!" Shane sputtered, thrusting a cigar between his teeth. "I sure as hell can dump them, *sheriff!*"

"You do and I walk, too!"

"Fine! Send me a postcard when you get where you're going!" He struck a kitchen match against the seat of his jeans and lighted his cigar, puffing at it furiously.

"You're insufferable, Shane—absolutely insufferable! It's easy to see why your ex-wife left you!"

She was vaguely aware that Alfy Deschamps was standing behind her, clanging a spoon against the mug she'd thumped down on the desk. "Time!" Alfy called out good-naturedly. "End of Round One. Everybody back to his own corner."

"Oh, for God's sake shut up, Alfy!" Shane growled.

"Sorry, *mon ami*," Alfy persisted, stepping between Shane and Tracy as if he were a referee separating two prizefighters. "I think the two of you have said just about enough, eh? You keep this up, it is apt to get nasty. I hate to see two people ruin a good thing by saying a lot of things they do not mean—"

"I'm just getting started!" Tracy interrupted him, shoving aside his outstretched arm and glaring at Shane. "If this baboon thinks he's going to push me around, he's got another think coming! He's angry at me, so he takes it out on two of his most loyal employees! That's despicable!"

"Break it up!" Alfy roared, pulling Tracy back by the shoulders as she lunged forward at Shane.

"You stay out of this," Tracy warned Alfy out of the side of her mouth, clenching her fists at her sides and not taking her eyes off Shane. "Lay another hand on me and..."

Alfy sighed and rolled his eyes. "Ah, such is the fate of the peacemaker. Did I ever tell you about the time in Chad when I tried to stop a quarrel between two of my brother Legionnaires? No? Well..."

Shane and Alfy had already arrived at the ranch by helicopter when Tracy, Dan and Jerry—weary and frostbitten—had shown up to report on what had happened in the forest. The assassin had not been found, and they assumed he'd had a truck or some other vehicle parked at a campground on the far side of the mountain pass.

Shane had bundled Tracy off to the dispensary while Alfy looked in on Martina, and he'd had little to say until the three of them were closeted in his office in the hub of the complex. Only then did he cut loose, loudly denouncing Dan and Jerry for allowing Tracy to be exposed to danger. He refused to listen when Tracy told him it wasn't their doing, but hers.

"...as it turned out," Alfy was saying, "these two Legionnaires enjoyed each other's company more than they did mine. Ever since, I have tried to avoid interfering in friends' disputes. Still, it grieves me when two nice people go at it so fiercely, each of them too proud to back down."

"I told you to shut up!" Shane snapped. Suddenly the lines of fury on his face dissolved and he came close to smiling, a bit sheepishly. "Sorry," he said, lowering his voice and placing a hand on his friend's shoulder.

"Do not apologize to me, Shane. Apologize to the lady. I think you have broken her heart, eh?"

Tracy snorted. "If you think I'm some shrinking violet who's putty in the hands of every obnoxious, self-centered clod who..." All at once, she was both laughing and crying, burying her face against Shane's chest.

"Actually," Alfy said, "the peacemaker role isn't all bad."

Tracy tilted back her head and looked tentatively at Shane. "Are we through yelling at each other?"

Shane dug a handkerchief from his hip pocket and blotted at her still-swollen cheeks. "I'm through. How about you?"

"It depends. Are you still ticked off at Dan and Jerry?"

"You're damn right I am!" Shane replied, his temper starting to boil again. "They had their orders!"

"Believe me, darling, they both tried to stop me," Tracy said evenly. "I gave them a bad time. I told them I was going with them no matter what they said."

"You could have been killed, Tracy."

"I just didn't let myself think about it. I was upset because our mystery man had killed the helicopter pilot and injured Martina.'' She paused, eyes downcast. ''I'm sorry.''

Shane drew her toward him. ''I'll think about forgiving you,'' he said, calming down again.

''And I will think about getting out of here,'' Alfy said, heading for the door. ''You people no longer need a peacemaker.''

''No, stay,'' Shane said quickly. He kissed Tracy on the cheek, then turned to his friend. ''Tell me, Alfy, how do you size up the situation?''

''You know what I think, *mon ami*. We talked about it on the way down here.'' His face darkened in a fierce scowl, and it occurred to Tracy that Alfy was anything but the keyboard-tinkling dandy now. In his brown leather jacket, black turtleneck and jeans, he could easily pass for a street tough from the big city. ''Somebody at the office knew you were supposed to be on that chopper. They put out the word, and that was that.''

Tracy peered worriedly at Shane. ''You were going to fly down on the helicopter that crashed?''

''I had a last-minute change of plans,'' Shane said. ''On my way out of the office, I had an urgent phone call from Africa. Another problem had come up, and it looked like I was going to be tied up most of the afternoon. I told Martina to go along without me and that I'd join her later.''

Alfy settled into one of the oak side chairs and laced his fingers behind his head. ''All right, who knew you were planning to make that trip?''

''Nobody—until noon. I didn't know myself until then. It had been a wild morning and I wasn't sure I could get clear.''

''Who did you tell when you changed your plans?''

''I mentioned it to you and MacManus—Brock, too, I think. And my secretary. She had to cancel a couple of appointments. And the two pilots on duty in the flight of-fice at the airport knew."

Tracy asked a question that had been troubling her. "What about Martina?" She glanced at Alfy, but he didn't seem to take offense at the suggestion implicit in her in-quiry.

"It doesn't figure," Shane said. "Martina wouldn't call in a hit if she was sitting next to the target. Too risky. She'd have no way of telling how hard the chopper would come down. She's gutsy, sure, but she's not crazy. No, it wasn't her."

Alfy pursed his lips thoughtfully. "So we narrow it down to six suspects, eh?"

"Not necessarily. Somebody might have told some-body else—innocently. You know how those things work, Alfy."

The Belgian shook his head. "This was no seat-of-the-pants operation, *mon ami*. The people who are trying to waste you do not depend on the off chance that some-body will tell somebody else. They work on hard intelli-gence. That leaves MacManus, Brock, the secretary, the pilots and yours truly. One of us hired the gun. It is as simple as that."

"So which one was it?" Tracy asked.

"If I knew the answer, I would not be sitting here bid-ing my time," Alfy said languidly, leaning back in his chair until its front legs were off the floor. "I would resolve the situation, eh?"

"Scratch Mrs. Hoyt," Shane said. His cigar had gone out and he paused to relight it. "She's been with me for years. Behind that blue-haired, unflappable facade of su-perefficiency, she's as loyal as any secretary can be."

Tracy routinely took the cigar from Shane and snuffed it out in an ashtray. Since when had he started accepting people on faith? she wondered. She'd have to meet Mrs. Hoyt.

"Are you really sure of her?" Alfy asked.

"Don't you trust my instincts anymore? Sure, I'm sure. Besides, I've had staff security run a close surveillance on her ever since this trouble started. She's as clean as a whistle. The same goes for the pilots."

"You have a wire on them, too?"

"What do you think?"

Tracy sighed. She should have known. Why didn't Alfy ask the inevitable question: were he, MacManus and Brock also being watched? She suspected they were. The "trade" certainly brought out the distrustful side of a person's nature.

"That leaves three," she heard herself say.

"That leaves three," the Belgian repeated, staring up sleepily at the soundproof ceiling. "Or, to put it another way, that leaves three trusted associates with motive, opportunity and the innate capacity to do violence, eh?"

Tracy felt uncomfortable with the direction of Alfy's remarks. She wished he'd lighten up. "Where were *you* at noon today, Monsieur Deschamps?" she demanded with mock sternness.

"Scheming, naturally," Alfy replied without hesitation, a thin smile on his lips. "Strange you should ask—"

"Alfy spends almost every waking hour scheming," Shane cut in. "That's what I pay him for, and he's good at it."

"I was joking," Tracy said quickly. "I didn't mean to suggest that I actually suspect him."

"Then you disappoint me, my charming sheriff," Alfy sighed. "You *should* suspect not only me but everyone. Ah, but you would quickly discover the essential truth of that if only you were in the trade. Suspicion is an integral part of our business. Healthy suspicion is what has kept both Shane and me alive this long."

SHANE CAME TO HER in the night, when the ranch house was quiet beneath the stark glare of the floodlights ringing the perimeter of the complex. He'd just showered, and he was barefoot, wearing a navy blue wool robe. A damp white towel was slung around his neck. He rapped at her door softly, and when she opened it he grinned at her and said, "Just checking. I wanted to make sure you were all right."

"I'm fine." Tracy smiled back, standing framed in the open doorway, one hand on the inside knob, the other at her side, her woman's body all but lost in the abundant folds of the oversized, blue-and-white striped flannel pajamas that had been left for her at the foot of her bed in the guest room.

"My room's right across the hall," Shane nodded in the direction of the door that stood open across the way. "I heard you moving about and I got worried."

"I was trying not to make any noise."

"Can't you sleep?"

Tracy shook her head. "I should have gone home. I've always had trouble getting to sleep in new surroundings."

He frowned. "You're better off here tonight. Besides, I want the doctor to have another look at you in the morning."

"That's not necessary, Shane."

"Maybe it's too cold in your room. I can turn up the heat."

"No, really. I'm fine."

He put his hands on her upper arms, just below her shoulders. "You *are* cold. You're trembling."

"Delayed reaction, I guess. Every time I close my eyes I see bullets coming at me. I know it's crazy. You can't actually *see* bullets coming at you. But I do."

Shane touched her cheeks lightly with his fingertips. His touch seemed to draw out the worst of the hurt. "It's not crazy. I've been there." He laughed. "Maybe we ought to walk over to the kitchen and see if we can find some steaks for those shiners of yours."

*"Steaks?"*

"You've still got two of the most perfect black eyes I've ever seen. Raw steak is supposed to make the swelling go down."

Tracy cocked her head in bemused skepticism. "This is the first time I ever heard *that*!"

"Seriously. Didn't you ever read the comic strips when you were little? Remember *Moon Mullins*? Somebody was always giving Moon a black eye, and the first thing he'd do was put a slab of beefsteak over it. Worked every time."

"Darling, that was before steak went up to five dollars or more a pound."

"Long before. Tracy, I—" He looked up and down the hall, then took her by the hand. "Come on. I don't want to stand out here making a fool out of myself." He reached past her and closed her door, then led her into his room. The lights were off and flames were crackling in a huge stone fireplace, sending shadows dancing around the pine-paneled walls. After he closed and locked his door, he went over to the hearth and stood there, his back to her. "I want to say something."

Tracy curled up in a soft leather easy chair on one side of the fireplace. The fire felt good, but his nearness felt even better. "I've never known you to be at a loss for words," she murmured, tucking her legs beneath her and burrowing her hands into the sleeve cuffs of her borrowed pajamas.

"As a rule, I'm not," he admitted. "I can usually out-cuss, outshout, outmaneuver and generally intimidate anybody I come up against. I'm not exactly what you'd call a wimp."

"It *never* occurred to me that you were."

"And then I met you . . ."

"And then you met me."

"I met you and I started coming apart at the seams. I didn't sleep at all that night I made a move on you in Pueblo. I lay awake until dawn, thinking what an ass I'd been, how you'd probably never want to look at me again. You were the one woman I've wanted all my life, and I treated you like the target of a corporate takeover. I figured I'd make it up to you in Denver, so I had you moved to the Brown Palace. What a mistake *that* was! Then I almost got you killed the next day when we went out to dinner. And today, when you were chasing off after that trigger-happy maniac, I was climbing the walls, worrying myself sick about you." He paused. "I love you, Tracy."

She knew he hadn't wanted to look at her as he spoke for fear she'd see as well as hear what he considered weakness. His emotional toughness was a barrier designed to keep himself from exposing his human side. In the trade, to be human was to be weak, and to be weak was to be dead.

"Shane?"

"Uh-huh?"

"Shane, shut up, will you?"

He grunted. "All right, no more confessions."

"Just turn around. Turn around and look at me."

He sat down on the hearth, his back to the fire, leaning forward, arms crossed, elbows on his knees. The back-lighting effect of the flames made him look somehow vulnerable, like a gambler who'd staked everything on one turn of the cards.

"Shane, you don't have to tell me how it is. I know. I know because I went through the same sort of hell today when I thought you were on that helicopter. But now you're here and I'm here, and that's all behind us and I don't even want to talk about it. It's just the two of us, and there's no room for bad memories." She cocked a finger at him. "Come over here." He got up, knelt at her feet and put his head in her lap. "I love you, too, Shane," she said, stroking the back of his neck.

He pressed his face against her midriff and nuzzled her, then began to undo the buttons on her pajama top. At the second button he paused. "Don't stop," she whispered.

He gave a throaty little laugh that was partially muffled against her cool, smooth flesh. "Got to," he said. "The Geneva Convention has very strict rules about mistreatment of prisoners—particularly the wounded."

"We're not at war, darling. Not anymore. The Geneva Convention doesn't apply."

"If you say so."

"And I don't consider myself your prisoner. I could walk out of here anytime I want." She squeezed him, then leaned forward and kissed the top of his head. "And as for being wounded—"

"Got you there."

"—I'll grant you I need tender, loving care."

"One hundred cc's of TLC coming up."

Tracy laughed. "Starting now, with an emphasis on the loving." She kissed him behind the right ear. "Shane?"

"Uh-huh?"

"Take me to bed—please."

He raised his head and looked at her. "We'd better wait a few days, sweetheart. With all those bumps and bruises, I don't want to risk hurting you."

Gently she pushed him back and stood up, pulling him to his feet. "You could never hurt me—not that way." She finished unbuttoning her pajama top and tossed it onto the chair. "You're a fraud, Shane. You're not anywhere near as tough as you make yourself out to be."

He hugged her. "Don't let that get around. You'll ruin my reputation."

Tracy fumbled for the knot on the drawstring of her pajama bottoms. She untied it, shoved down the pants and kicked them free of her ankles. "You have my solemn pledge of silence—for a price," she said, undoing the belt on his robe and pressing her body against his, her arms around his waist. "Let's get under the covers," she murmured into his ear.

He led her across to the double bed and she slid in between the sheets. Slipping out of his robe, he let it fall at his feet, his hard-muscled body glistening in the flickering light of the fire. He climbed in beside her and drew her close, his breath warm against her cheek. "Are you sure?" he asked.

She was aching with the need for him. "I've never been more sure of anything in my life."

AFTER HE HAD FALLEN ASLEEP, Tracy twisted around until her head was at the foot of the double bed and her feet were tucked snugly under the pillow. Propping herself up on her elbows, she gazed dreamily at the logs still sputtering with little tongues of flame behind the fireplace screen. It was chilly in the room now that the fire was dying down, and the puffy comforter felt luxuriously warm and light against the smooth, bare flesh of her back and thighs. Staring into the flames, she let her mind wander randomly over the events of the past week. It had been the worst week of her life, and also the most wonderful. Everything that had happened had led inexorably to this moment, and she wished that the moment would never end.

After a while she felt Shane stir, felt her pillow move, felt his beard-roughened cheek against one ankle. His fingers slipped under the comforter and touched the backs of her knees, and her desire for him renewed itself in a delicious tingling that started at her toes and worked its way up.

"You awake?" Shane asked softly.

"Uh-huh."

He pushed aside the comforter and brushed his lips against the back of each of her knees. She tried not to squirm, tried not to let him know how she delighted in his touch. They'd made love twice, and what would he think if he knew she still hadn't had enough of him?

"What're you doing at that end?" he inquired, one hand sliding up along the side of her thigh and coming to rest on the small of her back.

"Thinking deep philosophical thoughts. I minored in philosophy in college, you know."

"The mind boggles." He burrowed under the comforter and came up with his shoulder touching hers at the foot of the bed.

"Some minds boggle more easily than others, darling," Tracy said, tugging at the comforter until a portion of it was again warming her backside.

"I preferred math myself."

She patted his head teasingly. "I used to hate people who were good in math. They made me feel inadequate."

"Do *I* make you feel inadequate?"

Tracy turned to look at him, hoping that in the waning light of the fire he would see not the ugly discoloration that ringed her eyes but only the warmth and love she felt for him. "What do you think?"

Shane grinned. "You'd have been crazy about math if you'd given it a chance. Math is precise, it follows established rules, and it's orderly. Two and two always add up to four, pi is—"

"Would it cut you to the quick if I yawned?"

"I thought so." He shifted onto his side, rested his head on his right arm and gazed at her. "I bore you."

"Not really. It's just that your little lecture on math hardly makes very fascinating pillow talk." She snuggled down deeper under the comforter and folded her arms under her head, her face inches from his. "I love you," she whispered. "I don't need math to prove it."

He drew closer to her, his nose against her cheek, his body pressing hers, and for a long time she said nothing more. She lay perfectly still under the comforter, his breath warm on her ear, his heart beating against hers, slowly, powerfully. He was such a strong person, she thought, yet he had weaknesses, the kind that strong people made a special effort to hide: an underlying sentimentality, an almost archaic sense of rightness, an unyielding determination bordering on sheer stubbornness. Well, they *were* weaknesses, weren't they?

"Shane?" she said at last.

"Huh?"

"Confession time again. I'm sorry I screamed at you."

"The way I remember it, we screamed at each other."

"I know, but *you* had good reason. I did a dumb thing."

"I know."

She giggled. "You needn't be so quick to agree."

"I can't help it. I'm something of an expert on doing dumb things. I speak from firsthand experience."

"You would have done just what I did, wouldn't you?"

"I suppose."

She put her right arm around his neck. "Shane, let's never ever fight again. Agreed?"

"No deal."

"Why not?"

"Making up is too much fun...."

THE ICE GRAY OF A NEW DAY shone bleakly through the window overlooking the workshop area when Tracy awoke to find Shane gone. She vaguely remembered a stirring in the bedroom when it was still dark, remembered him whispering to her from across the room that he had something to do, remembered pulling up the covers and wishing he'd come to bed and make love to her.

Gingerly rubbing the sleep from her eyes, Tracy focused on the digital clock that sat on the rough-hewn oak dresser at the side of the bed. It was after eight. Shane must have been gone for hours, she realized. But where?

A comment he'd made the night before pricked at her memory: "I'm something of an expert on doing dumb things."

She sat upright. "Oh, my God," she said aloud. "He's gone up into the mountains—I just know it!" Throwing aside the covers, she got out of bed, put on Shane's robe and scurried to the window, her bare feet flinching at the slick cold of the pegged plank floor.

And then everything was all right again—everything that mattered. There was Shane, getting out of his open M.G., and Alfy was with him. Shane was wearing the same gray sweatshirt and cutoff jeans he'd worn the day they'd met, and his black parka was unzipped and hanging loosely from his shoulders. Alfy had more sense, Tracy noted approvingly. He was wearing a long wolf-fur jacket and a gray muffler that he'd draped up over his head and ears and wrapped securely around his neck, one tasseled end flung debonairly over his shoulder.

The two men stood by the sports car, their breath misty clouds of white, and talked for several minutes as Tracy watched unseen, unwilling to let Shane out of her sight.

Just before Shane reached over to fasten down the tonneau cover on the passenger side, Alfy bent across the open seat and plucked up two small submachine guns. He tucked the two weapons under one arm, the way a commuter might handle a folded copy of his morning newspaper, and headed for the workshop.

Tracy stepped away from the window. When would it end, this business of always having to look over one's shoulder, knowing that sooner or later the result would be to kill or be killed?

Gathering up her borrowed pajamas, she darted for the hallway door and peeked out to assure herself that no one was in sight; then she scampered across the hall to the guest room. Locking the door behind her, she stripped off the robe and got under the shower in the adjoining bathroom.

Wrapped in a bath towel, she returned to the bedroom a few minutes later to find Martina sitting on a chair by the door, wearing a full-length quilted black robe. She looked pale and yet vibrant.

"Good morning," Martina greeted her. "Did you sleep well?"

Tracy glanced at the bed. The covers had been turned down the night before, but they remained unruffled. Martina had noticed, of course; Martina didn't miss anything. "Quite well," Tracy said easily. She looked at the hallway door, which she distinctly remembered locking. "I didn't hear you come in."

Martina smiled innocently. "I knocked, but no answer. I wanted to be sure you were all right, so I let myself in."

"You let yourself in?"

Martina dangled a ring of tiny, wirelike rods in front of her, then dropped the ring into a pocket in her robe. "Alfy has shared some of his darker secrets with me."

Tracy tried to conceal her irritation. She disliked being spied upon, being reminded that her privacy was violable at any time at the whim of another person. To her way of thinking, privacy was synonymous with dignity, and dignity was precious. But when she opened her mouth to protest the intrusion, the words on the tip of her tongue seemed stuffy and standoffish. She told herself she didn't want to hurt Martina—that, selfishly, she needed her. "Do you think you ought to be up and about yet?" she asked. "You took quite a bouncing around yesterday."

"If you want to know the truth, my dear, I have taken quite a bouncing around all my life. However, I am still in one piece, more or less. That must tell you something."

With a shrug, Tracy turned away from her visitor and examined her clothes. The wool suit she'd worn to the luncheon the day before was a rumpled mess that smelled of smoke. Her black pumps were ruined. She'd have to wear the quilted coveralls, at least until she could go home and change.

"You are more than welcome to some of my clothes," Martina offered brightly. "I had an extra bag sent ahead yesterday. I must have had some sort of premonition something would happen."

"I'll manage, thank you."

Martina started to get up. "Really, I insist. Let me—"

"I said that I'll manage." The words came out in a tone of icy finality, and as soon as she'd spoken them, Tracy was sorry. "It's very kind of you, Martina," she said, her voice softening, "but I'm going home and I'll change there." She dropped the bath towel and started to climb into the coveralls.

Martina settled back in her chair. "May I ask you something?"

"Of course."

"Were you able to make your point with Shane?"

Tracy zipped up the coveralls. "My point?"

"What we talked about the other day—the possibility of his retaining control of TransWorld Systems."

Tracy tried to appear noncommittal. "I mentioned it to him."

"And?"

"Shane's going to do what he believes is right. That's all I can tell you, Martina."

"What do *you* believe is right, my dear?"

What should she tell her? Tracy wondered. Should she tell Martina that the right thing was to have everybody go away and leave them alone? No, that wouldn't do any good. All Martina cared about was herself and Alfy and her own little world. Still, why should Tracy fault her? She understood where Martina was coming from, because she'd been there herself; in fact, she was there right now, as she asked herself what could possibly happen next.

"I don't know," Tracy admitted. "I thought I did, but now I'm not so sure...."

SHANE WAVED JERRY LATIMER AWAY and walked with Tracy to the patrol car. He held the door open for her, oblivious to the cheek-stinging wind that howled down the mountainside, sending up fitful little swirls of snow and ice crystals around the parking area. He'd changed into gray wool slacks and a dark blue sweater, and he was freshly shaved and scrubbed, looking for all the world like a contented suburbanite about to start his weekend with a quiet stroll. "I won't be long," he was saying. "That business in Africa just won't keep."

Tracy looked up at the gray clouds scudding across the wintry sky. She knew that another snowstorm was in the making. "You're not going to fly out in this, are you?"

He shook his head. "No way. But it's still fairly clear in Pueblo. I'll drive over there and have one of our pilots pick me up. If Denver gets socked in, we'll scoot down to Albuquerque and I'll catch a commercial flight east. I've got to be in Washington tomorrow morning and in Senegal by noon on Monday.''

"Would it make any difference if I asked you not to go?"

"Everything you say makes a difference, Tracy. But why?"

She shook her head slowly. "I don't know—I just have bad vibes." She put a hand on his arm. "Shane, where did you disappear to this morning?"

His eyes avoided hers. "I ran a few miles to work out the kinks."

"With Alfy?"

"Alfy just came along for the ride. He hates to run. Says it plays hell with his mental equilibrium."

"So what did he do while you were out there on the ridge road getting your lungs frostbitten?"

"He sat in the car under a couple of lap robes and baby-sat a flask of cognac."

"With a machine gun on his lap?"

Shane didn't bat an eyelash. "Alfy's a Boy Scout at heart. He believes in being prepared for any eventuality."

"I saw him take *two* machine guns out of the car."

"Did you?"

"Shane, you're the most infuriating person I've ever met! Somebody's out to kill you and you know it. The last thing in the world you should have done was go running this morning. You keep lecturing me to be careful, and yet you dash around the countryside like an idiot, just daring that killer to take another shot at you. We can't go on like this!"

He gave her a quick kiss on the forehead. "Another month, and we'll be home free. You'll be an ex-sheriff and I'll be an ex-chairman of the board. And you know what it means when you string two X's together." He pulled her to him and kissed her again, long and demanding.

"You're not only infuriating," she murmured when she finally came up for air, "you're impossible."

"So what? You can always try to make me over."

"I wouldn't dream of even trying." She brushed his cold cheek with her lips as she slipped past him and got into the patrol car. "I wouldn't know where to begin. Besides—" she made a face at him "—maybe I love you the way you are."

AT FIRST the client thought it was a robbery. A dark figure came out of the shadows in the parking garage and pressed something against his back just as he was getting into the car. "Don't turn around," the figure said.

"What do you want?"

"Conversation." A little laugh, deep, dark, humorless. "No, not just conversation, but a meaningful dialogue."

The client's shoulders sagged. He was both relieved and annoyed. "I told you we must never again meet in person. It is much too dangerous."

The Ragman nudged him to get behind the wheel and slid into the back seat. "You have told me many things. You told me, for example, that the target would be aboard that helicopter. Such was not the case."

"There was a last-minute change of plans. By the time I found out, it was too late to call you back."

"Because you have not been completely truthful with me, I have had to risk my life unnecessarily." The Ragman leaned forward until he was so close that his breath was warm against the client's neck. "The cost of doing business has just gone up. I want an additional fifty thousand dollars deposited in my account Monday morning."

The other man hesitated. "All right. But that has to be the end of it. I am not made of money."

The Ragman was amused at this. "You underrate your potential. You will be worth many millions when this is over."

"It is over now. I shall take care of it myself."

"You do not have the nerve to look your associate in the eye and pull the trigger. That is why you hired me."

"I said, you are no longer needed. I have made some very elaborate arrangements for Keegan." That was not quite true. Someone else had made the arrangements, but he himself would reap the benefits.

The Ragman sniffed. "Very well, we shall just see how well these elaborate arrangements serve you. What about the woman?"

"The woman is yours. You believe her to be a threat, so do whatever you like with her—if you think you can carry it off."

The Ragman chose to ignore the insult. "You can order flowers for Tracy Hannon—on your way to the bank."

## Chapter Ten

The following Thursday, the day before Shane was due home, Tracy was to be guest of honor at yet another farewell luncheon, this one given by the Henryville Rotary Club. In deference to the occasion, she'd foregone her customary jeans and flannel shirt, opting for the gray suit and green sweater she'd worn to Denver. She was just about to leave the office when Dan came in. She hadn't seen him since Tuesday afternoon, and neither Ingrid nor Jerry knew where he'd gone, only that he'd said he had business to take care of. From the way he was dressed, Tracy sensed it was serious business. A tan, gabardine overcoat hung open loosely from his squared shoulders, partly showing a dark suit, white shirt and striped tie. A leather portfolio was tucked under one arm. He glanced around the office as if there was something about it he didn't quite trust. "Got a minute?"

"I'm on my way to a meeting at the hotel," Tracy said.

"Fine. I'll walk along with you."

"Be my guest. Jerry's coming, too. He says he's not letting me out of his sight, not after what happened last week."

Dan stepped aside to let Tracy pass into the outer office. "Tell Jerry to bring up the rear," he said softly. "You and I have to have a talk."

He waited until they were outside to explain his absence. "I went up to Denver and dropped in on an old friend who works for Mountain Bell. Shane had already taken care of monitoring calls from the executive suite. I took it a step further. I asked my friend at the phone company to check on long-distance calls made from pay phones in the building at certain critical times. It was just a shot in the dark."

Tracy stopped walking and stared at him. "And?"

"One call in particular caught my attention. I don't know who made it, but the timing was right. It was a call to a motel in Walsenburg at 12:15 last Friday. So I did some more checking. The only long-distance call logged in the motel between 11:00 a.m. and 2:00 p.m. Friday was to a fellow named Raul Fernandez who'd checked in the night before. He was driving a pickup carrying a blue snowmobile."

Tracy's mouth dropped open. "Oh, my God!"

Dan nodded. "Fernandez checked out of the motel a few minutes after he got his call. One of the maids paid special attention to him because he's a very good-looking fellow and he reminded her of the singer Julio Iglesias. Anyway, she said his luggage included a couple of leather cases, the kind hunters use for rifles. The timing would have been tight, but he probably could have driven out to one of the campgrounds, parked the truck and scooted over the pass on the snowmobile before the chopper came in for a landing. Chances are he already had his ropes rigged in the trees—even though we never found any."

Tracy knew what she had to do. "I'd better get over to the courthouse and see about a warrant."

"No way, Tracy."

"What do you mean, no way?" she demanded, suddenly annoyed by his nonchalant manner. "Fernandez is a killer!"

The former Secret Service agent shook his head patiently. "A smart lawyer would have him waltzing out of the courtroom in nothing flat. We don't have a shred of hard evidence that would stand up at a preliminary hearing."

"Oh, come on, Dan! There's that phone call from Denver, and the people who saw him at the motel and—"

"And nothing. Say we lucked out and had Fernandez picked up—which is unlikely, since he's obviously a pro and doesn't want to be found. What have we got? We've got a young man out for a good time on his snowmobile in a national forest. We can't even place him in the forest. We know only that he had a blue snowmobile and that he might have gone to the forest after leaving the motel."

"What about the rifles? The hunting season is over."

"You aren't listening, Tracy," Dan chided her. "I didn't say he was seen with any rifles. I said a maid saw him with two cases that *could have* been used to carry rifles. As for the phone call, we can't prove a thing by it. We have no idea what was said."

Tracy wasn't about to give up. "It may not be hard evidence, but it's enough to suggest what happened."

"The law doesn't recognize suggestions, Tracy. You know that as well as I do. I've got enough to bring in the FBI, but the bureau would start by touching base with the United States Attorney's Office, given TWS's status as a quasi-governmental operation. And I've got a hunch Shane doesn't want any more interference from the feds than he already has."

"Shane doesn't have anything to say about it," Tracy declared grimly. "A human being was murdered the other day, and that makes it a criminal case."

"Correction: a human being was *killed*. Murder is a legal determination. There's no evidence the pilot was murdered."

Tracy found it hard to believe what she was hearing. "Martina told us what happened. Three shots were fired at the helicopter, and one of the shots hit the pilot."

Dan smiled thinly. "The National Transportation Safety Board sent an investigator down to the ranch last weekend. Martina told him a gust of wind knocked the chopper out of control as it was coming in for a landing."

"That's not true!"

"That's what Martina told him."

"Why, for God's sake?"

"Because Shane told her to."

"This is preposterous!" Tracy seethed, glaring at Dan.

Dan shrugged. "It's the way Shane wants to handle it."

"Damn it, it's not going to hold up! All anyone has to do is look at the wreckage and see the bullet holes. And what about the autopsy on the pilot? I haven't seen the pathologist's report, but there's no way he can get around listing a gunshot wound as a contributing factor."

Dan put an arm around Tracy's shoulder and started her off toward the hotel. "Both the wreckage and the autopsy have been taken care of."

"That's tampering with evidence!"

"Call it what you will, Tracy. Shane intends to keep everything in the family."

*Some family!* Tracy thought.

On her way back to the office after the luncheon, she stopped off at the photo shop to pick up her film. She and Jerry leafed through the prints but saw nothing revealing. "Just trash," Tracy remarked. "Wastepaper, old cans and bottles, everything under the sun. People are so messy!"

Jerry squinted at one of the prints. "Everything's very sharp, though. Look, you can almost make out the words on that torn ski-lift ticket."

"Big deal." Tracy sighed, wondering if the commissioners would reimburse her for the four-dollar cost of the film development.

SHE COULDN'T BRING HERSELF to mention her conversation with Dan when Shane called late that evening from Dakar, Senegal. She was still at the office, trying to catch up on her work, but finding it difficult to concentrate. Shane was uppermost in her thoughts. She was angry at him, even to the minute she picked up the phone to take the overseas call. He was completely off base by making her virtually a co-conspirator in—what was the legal term she'd looked up in the county attorney's office?—misprision of a felony. She wanted to give him a piece of her mind, but the angry words wouldn't come, even though she'd rehearsed them in her mind. Hearing his voice again made everything seem right.

"They're calling my flight soon, so I've got to talk fast," he began. "First off, I need a favor. Things are taking longer here than I expected. It doesn't look like I'll be back for the Christmas party Saturday—"

"Is anything wrong?" Tracy broke in, an edge to her voice.

"Nothing I can't handle," Shane assured her quickly.

"You're not in any danger, are you?"

He laughed. "Whatever gave you that idea? It's just that I've run into a bunch of paper-shufflers who seem determined to give me a bad time. The point is, I'm going to be tied up for a few more days. Suppose you could fill in for me at the party—make excuses for the missing host and all that?"

"Shane, I *can't*! I hardly know your people. I don't have any connection with the company. I—"

"Have you checked your mail lately? At home, I mean?"

"I've been on the go all day. I haven't been home since seven o'clock this morning."

"When you get there, take a look. You should have a letter from the United Bank of Denver, transferring one hundred shares of TransWorld treasury stock to your name. That gives you a connection with the company. I owe you an even one thousand dollars for that job you did for TWS in Denver—remember? I'm paying you in stock instead of cash. As a stockholder, you owe it to the company to help keep up corporate morale. The Christmas party comes under the general heading of morale."

"But why me, Shane?"

"Because I asked you. Isn't that reason enough?"

"You've got to do better than that!"

"Okay, I'll give it to you straight. I know I can depend on you to cover for me. I trust you. That's saying a good deal."

Tracy hesitated. "What do you mean 'cover' for you?"

"Only three people know where I am at the moment—you, my lawyer and Alfy. I want to keep everybody else guessing."

"What am I supposed to tell them?"

"Anything but the truth. Tell them you've talked to me, and that I'm in South America. Say I had to rush off on family business. They know me. They're used to my doing screwy things. I don't care what you say. Just don't let them know I'm in Africa."

"Darling, I'm afraid I don't lie very convincingly."

He chuckled. "It's for a good cause, sweetheart."

"You trust Alfy, too, don't you? Let him play host."

"He may have to leave suddenly."

"Why?"

Shane ignored the question. "Will you do it, Tracy? It would mean a great deal to me."

Tracy sighed. She didn't understand, but Shane obviously had no intention of telling her just what he was up to. "All right, I'll lie for you. Why, I don't know. But I'll do it."

"I knew I could count on you! I've got to run, sweetheart—got a plane to catch."

"Hey, wait! You said you had two things you wanted to talk to me about!"

"The second thing really isn't a subject of discussion. It's a simple statement of fact, Tracy."

"And just what is this simple statement of fact?"

"I love you. . . ."

THE PARTY WAS IN FULL SWING when the MacManuses and Oliver Brock, all of them bundled up in heavy parkas and ski togs, arrived at the ranch to learn that Shane wouldn't be there. It had started snowing again that afternoon, grounding the company helicopters, and the three of them had flown by jet to Pueblo and driven over to Henryville in a rented car. Martina and a large group of TWS executives, department managers and their wives had come down from Denver earlier in the day.

"With Shane, you have to expect the unexpected," Brock said, shrugging out of his parka in the hallway and accepting a mug of hot buttered rum from Mrs. Fitzpatrick, the plump and smiling woman who served as ranch housekeeper. He stepped back to look at Tracy, who was wearing black slacks and a bulky, white wool sweater with a cowl neck. "For example, he never said a word about this little lady being chief custodian of law and order in San Isabel County."

Tracy smiled absently. Her attention was riveted on the bright blue parka Brock had hung on the hall rack. A torn ski-lift ticket dangled from the zipper tab of the parka.

Alfy was somewhere in the building. Maybe she ought to talk to him about her suspicions.

"Our hostess is a woman of many dimensions," Martina said, putting her arm around Tracy's waist and maneuvering the group toward the warmth of the huge fireplace in the main hall where the other guests had gathered. "She also has a master's degree in education and is a shareholder in TransWorld. Shane has been trying to get her to come to work for us, you know."

Tracy glanced at Martina, wondering where she'd picked up *that* particular piece of information.

"Really?" Pamela MacManus clapped her hands together in obvious delight. "It would be wonderful if you did join us. I told Evan just the other day that TWS people sometimes seem so cold and standoffish. The company needs a woman's touch."

MacManus frowned. "The trade doesn't seem to attract the gentle-natured, outgoing sort."

*Thanks,* Tracy thought, amused at the suggestion that she had the qualifications to succeed in this corporate den of tigers.

"But that's not to say we couldn't use a softer image," Brock put in. "One of our operations people testified a few weeks ago before a House subcommittee in Washington, and an old colleague of mine told me it was like pulling teeth to get him to answer the simplest question. Talk about stonewalling!"

"What would you be doing for the company, Mrs. Hannon?" MacManus asked. Tracy was sure she detected a note of jealousy in his voice. Was he afraid she'd be a threat to him?

"I haven't yet decided if I *want* to work for TWS," Tracy said. "Shane hasn't actually offered me a job. Besides, I'm not the cloak-and-dagger type."

"Welcome to the club!" Brock said, putting his empty mug on the mantle and signaling Mrs. Fitzpatrick to bring another round of drinks. "We pussycats need all the support we can get."

Martina giggled. "Sorry, Oliver, but I just cannot think of you as a pussycat. You are every bit as ruthless as the rest of us, and you know it."

Brock laughed. "Yes, but there's a difference, my dear. There's physical ruthlessness and then there's intellectual ruthlessness." He patted the ample midsection beneath his red-and-white ski sweater. "My forte is hardly the physical—not with forty-seven years of good living under my belt."

"You really should get more exercise, Oliver," Mac-Manus said. "Obesity is an insidious killer, you know."

"The world is full of insidious killers." Brock glanced at the lavish buffet Mrs. Fitzpatrick was placing on a table in the center of the room. The table was fairly groaning with ham, turkey, a huge round of roast beef and an artful assortment of side dishes. "Just go down the list: the food we eat, the liquor we drink, the air we breathe—"

*Not to mention hired assassins who lurk on mountainsides and prowl through hotel rooms,* Tracy thought. Out of the corner of her eye she saw Alfy carry drinks to a couple in a far corner of the room. She started toward him, but MacManus caught her arm.

"Please," he said. "Stay and visit. I should like to get better acquainted with you, Mrs. Hannon."

She looked across the room. Alfy had disappeared. Oh, well, she'd catch him later. She turned back to Brock. "You ski, don't you?" she ventured, trying to sound only mildly interested.

Brock gave her a clowning sort of frown. "Surely you joke? I've never put on a pair of skis in my life."

"He just dresses the part," Martina said with a laugh.

"When I'm in this arctic paradise of yours, I borrow from the MacManus haberdashery," Brock replied with a good-natured shrug. "I don't want people thinking I'm too serious about this nonsense."

While the others were eating, Tracy tried to find Alfy, but learned he'd left after receiving a phone call. She'd do her own detective work. After telling Mrs. Fitzpatrick that she had something to do in the office and would return shortly, she put on her after-ski coat and went out to her patrol car. Ingrid followed her.

"Anything I can take care of?" the former policewoman asked.

"No. I just want to check something out."

It took ten minutes for them to drive to the office and another five minutes for Tracy to find the photos she and Jerry had looked at. She leafed through the three-by-five prints, but the images were too small.

There was one other possibility. She picked up the phone and called Chester Bagby, owner of the photo shop. He was home watching television, but he agreed to meet her at the store.

Ten minutes later Tracy showed him the black-and-white print she wanted blown up—"just as big as you can."

"I wish you'd told me over the phone," Bagby grumbled. "I could have saved you a trip. I'm fresh out of developer. The supply house in Denver was supposed to ship me some this past week, but the big blizzard held up deliveries. Probably won't have any more in until Monday or Tuesday."

Ingrid saw the disappointment in Tracy's face. "If you tell me what you're doing, maybe I can help."

Why not? Tracy thought. Ingrid would know eventually. Taking her aside so that Bagby couldn't hear, she explained the situation.

"Simple," Ingrid asked. "Ask this man to set his en-larger, and we'll make a tracing on plain paper. You can get regular prints next week when the developer comes in."

Twenty minutes later the two women were back at the ranch. And three minutes after that, Tracy's hunch evaporated.

She had compared the torn ski-lift ticket on Brock's jacket with the tracing of the lift ticket she'd captured on film. Both were from the Vail ski area. But there the similarity ended. The torn edges didn't even come close to matching.

THE CLIENT had been watching her closely, wondering what was going through her mind. Tracy Hannon was warm and vivacious as she circulated through the living room greeting the guests and making them feel welcome. But every time she got near the main hallway, she seemed tense and preoccupied, as if she hadn't quite made up her mind about something. She'd disappeared once during the evening but then had come back to the party.

He carried a drink over to where Tracy was standing, talking to the head of one of the TWS communications divisions. At an appropriate lull in the conversation he congratulated her on how well she was handling herself.

"The trade attracts more than its share of scoundrels," he observed. "How pleasant it is to encounter someone with social graces."

Tracy smiled. "Thank you, but I have to confess my party manners are a bit rusty. I haven't done much entertaining the past few years."

The client smiled back at her. "I take it the job keeps you rather busy."

"Not really."

"But when TransWorld expands its operations, I'm sure your department will have its hands full. The company is just getting its operation set up here, and look at all the trouble we've caused already.'' He laughed, as if to be sure Tracy accepted the comment as a joke. But it was not a joke. He wanted Tracy to talk about her present caseload, and this was only an opening.

"TWS really hasn't been that much trouble,'' Tracy said. She glanced in the direction of the kitchen, where the housekeeper was preparing coffee. "If you'll excuse me, I've got to see if I can help Mrs. Fitzpatrick.'' She nodded and walked away.

The Ragman was right, the client thought as he watched her go. She knew something. And if she knew something, she was a danger to both of them. They *had* to deal with her.

But first things first. Shane Keegan was the main priority. When Shane's death was confirmed, that would be the time to zero in on Tracy Hannon. Only a matter of days...

IT WAS just after seven the following Tuesday night when Shane phoned from Madrid. "You're on your way home?'' Tracy asked. She didn't add the words "I hope.'' She didn't have to. Her tone said it for her.

"Not yet. I've got some people to talk to here, and then it's back to Dakar and into the interior for a heart-to-heart discussion with our client.''

Tracy felt a prickling at the back of her neck. "Trouble?''

"They're trying to pull a fast one. It's a deal Brock worked out in Washington. If we went ahead with it, we'd find ourselves in the middle of a revolution. I won't sit still for it.''

"Sounds like it was Brock who pulled the fast one.'' She wondered if she should mention the business of the ski-lift ticket. She decided not to. The torn tickets weren't even the same color. She'd checked to be sure.

Shane's voice became sharper. "For the time being, I'll give Oliver the benefit of the doubt. It's possible he didn't know what these yo-yos were up to."

"Are you in any danger?"

"Of course not. This is strictly a business problem that has to be ironed out. Our client is the interior ministry of Kagera, a former French colony that was given its independence several years ago. We've already delivered fourteen million dollars in hardware, and our technicians are in place. Now the ministry intends to use our hardware and personnel to carry out a coup with the army to get rid of the president and his pals. I don't like it, Tracy. The whole idea of TWS is to help maintain order. Once we start playing sides—or allow ourselves to be used by someone who is playing sides—we lose our integrity, and once we lose our integrity we have nothing."

"Tell me truthfully, Shane. You *do* suspect Brock betrayed you, don't you?"

"It's not a matter of betrayal, Tracy. It's a matter of self-interest. Maybe Brock knew what was coming off, maybe he didn't. Maybe he saw a way to advance one of his pet projects. Hell, maybe one of his buddies in Washington got to him and sold him a bill of goods. I don't know. I do know I have to get our people out of there and do something about our hardware."

"Does it really matter, Shane? In a few weeks you'll be free and clear of the whole business—the trade, as you call it."

"It matters—believe me. I sent seventeen people in there, and I'm going to get them out if it's the last thing I do."

She'd just hung up the phone when Martina came to the house, a bottle of Dom Perignon cradled in one arm. "'They also serve who stand and wait,'" Martina quoted, stepping into the foyer. "Shakespeare, no?"

"Milton," Tracy said absently.

"Ah, my dear, I can never keep those English writers straight." Handing over the bottle of champagne, she shrugged out of her beaver jacket and flung it carelessly across the back of the nearest chair. She was wearing an oversize blouse belted with a silver chain, tight black designer jeans and silver leather boots. "I thought I might join you for a bit of mutual commiseration. Are you alone?"

Tracy glanced out the front window and saw a Blazer from the ranch parked behind her patrol car. The Blazer's engine was running, sending up a cloud of thick white exhaust against the blackness of the night. Martina hadn't seen fit to invite her driver to come inside with her, Tracy realized. "Not really," she said. "One of my deputies is upstairs."

"Male or female?" Martina asked with a smile.

"Her name is Ingrid," Tracy replied patiently.

Martina dropped onto the couch. "My dear, you must not let the champagne get warm. Do you have any tulip glasses? Dom Perignon is at its best when served in tulip glasses, you know."

"I have some wineglasses." Tracy was becoming annoyed. She was in no mood for idle chatter.

"They will have to do, I suppose. Let me wrestle with it while you fetch the glasses." She got up and took the bottle from Tracy. For the first time that evening, Tracy got a close look at her face. Martina had been crying.

When she returned from the kitchen with the glasses, Martina had the bottle open.

"What did you mean by mutual commiseration?" Tracy asked as Martina filled the glasses, then settled back down on the couch.

"Our men have flown the coop. We are incomplete beings." She raised her glass. "To the success of their mission."

Tracy stared at her. "What mission?"

"Surely Shane has told you?"

"I talked to him a little while ago. He was in Madrid. He'll be going back to Africa for a while—that's all I know."

Martina sighed. "Obviously he did not wish to worry you."

"Worry me?"

"He is meeting Alfy in Senegal. Shane recruited some mercenaries in Madrid, and they are going into that little country that is giving them so much trouble and they plan to bring out the TransWorld technicians. It should be quite a confrontation—a dozen or so men against an army of thousands."

Tracy's knuckles went white as she squeezed the wineglass, and she set it down before she broke it. When she spoke, she almost choked on the words. "I . . . I thought it was purely a business negotiation."

Martina drained her glass and refilled it. "There are times, my dear, when a business negotiation can be concluded only at the point of a gun. This is such a time. Shane's back is to the wall. The clients show no inclination to release TransWorld from its contract. In essence, they are holding our people as hostages against the performance of the contract. Shane refuses to accept that. He intends to personally rescue his people and bring out as much of the company's equipment as he can. Barring that, Alfy tells me, he plans to destroy it on the spot.

"My God, Martina! That's almost an act of war!"

Martina's pink lips curved slightly in a knowing smile. "No, it is what the military calls a preemptive strike. If there is a revolution in Kagera, a great many more people will die. Already there has been much bloodshed in that place—some of it Shane's.'' Martina took another sip of champagne. ''Kagera is where Shane was imprisoned years ago, where the two of us met when I was with the United Nations. Shane still has enemies there.''

Tracy began pacing the floor. ''He was set up, wasn't he? Brock saw a way to kill him off and take over the company—didn't he? Brock knew how Shane would react. He knew Shane would risk his life to save his people, to protect his integrity.''

Martina nodded. ''That is what Alfy thinks. Brock was in Washington when Alfy got word to meet Shane in Dakar. It is a good thing for Brock, too. Alfy would have wrung his neck.''

''Isn't there anything we can do, Martina? Can't we talk to somebody in Washington? If the State Department knew...''

Martina seemed amused by Tracy's naïveté. ''I think it is safe to assume that certain people in high places want the revolution to proceed, and that was why it was handled through Brock instead of Shane. These people would not be at all disposed to do anything to call attention to the situation.''

''But if Shane and Alfy should...should get killed, how would they explain it?'' *Killed.* The word was a white-hot knife slashing across Tracy's chest.

''Have you ever been in a revolution, my dear? No, of course not. Well, I have. All sorts of people run around with guns, and you never really know who is who. Washington would have no trouble explaining away two deaths. Governments are very good with words, you know. They can make you believe just about anything.'' She reached for the champagne bottle. ''Drink up. I seem to be ahead of you.''

''What are we going to do, Martina?''

Martina shrugged. " 'They also serve who stand and wait.' There is nothing we can do.''

THE RAGMAN felt cheated. He had been hired to deal with Shane Keegan, and now the client had given the assignment to someone else. Still, a merchant of death could not expect to compete with an entire army, could he?

With the Keegan death a foregone conclusion, he could devote more time and ingenuity to Tracy Hannon. The woman had embarrassed him by slipping through his fingers on three separate occasions. He would wait until the client had played out his African gambit, and then he would strike. The result would be a masterpiece of poetic simplicity, one that would be talked about for years to come.

He leaned over the washbasin and carefully inserted the contact lenses that changed his eyes from dark brown to blue. He had already dyed his hair a sandy brown, and ordinarily that would have been enough. He had taken plenty of chances so far. He would take no more.

And after Tracy Hannon, he would do one more job and then leave this terrible, snowswept country, to return to the land of beaches and swaying palms.

His last job would be the client himself.

FOR TRACY, the rest of the week was a blur. Christmas was only ten days away, and the season inevitably meant an upswing in complaints for the usually understaffed sheriff's department to handle. There were occasional loud parties to quiet, drunk drivers to transport home after confiscating their car keys, now and then a young shoplifter to turn over to outraged parents.

Bubba Crowley was no help. He'd called in sick all week.

While she was finishing up some paperwork in her office late Thursday afternoon, Tracy heard Ingrid say, "Yes, sir, she's here. I'll get her on the line."

Tracy snatched up her extension phone. "Shane?"

"No, Mrs. Hannon, this is Greg Vinson, Mr. Keegan's attorney. Can you speak freely?"

Tracy covered the mouthpiece. "Hang up, Ingrid!" she called out. "I've got it!" She reached out, pushed shut the door of the inner office and leaned against the edge of her desk. "Have you heard from him, Mr. Vinson?"

"Not directly, Mrs. Hannon, but I do have some news for you. Mr. Keegan will be—how did he put it?—'out of pocket' for several days, so he left instructions for me to ask you if you'd accept a position as personnel director at TransWorld Systems. The job pays sixty thousand a year to start, and Mr. Keegan would like you to come aboard the first week in January to spend some time with your predecessor, who's taking over as our Far Eastern representative."

Sixty thousand dollars was three times as much as Tracy had been paid to teach in Los Angeles. Even so, her heart sank. "I'll have to think about it," she said.

"One other thing, Mrs. Hannon. I don't mean to alarm you, but Mr. Keegan also has executed a will designating you and me as co-administrators of his estate. If he should die, the two of us would have to see to it that his plans for TWS are carried out."

"What are you telling me?" Tracy asked in a shaken voice.

"I'm simply advising you of your position, Mrs. Hannon. There are some papers that must be signed and recorded, which I'll get to you tomorrow. In the meantime, I think you should prepare yourself to join in the active management of the company. Mr. Keegan thinks you're quite capable...."

After hanging up, Tracy stared at the phone. The next time it rang, she prayed it would be Shane calling to say that he was on his way home.

There was a buzz on the extension and she picked up the receiver. Ingrid said, "Vince Emmerling called. He wants you to come to dinner tonight. He said the two of you had something to talk about."

Tracy remembered that Emmerling had asked her to stay on as undersheriff. "Ingrid, would you call him back for me? Tell him I'm tied up, but perhaps we can get together next week."

Sunday morning, with Jerry in tow, Tracy stopped by the office. Ingrid was off duty, and Dan Rawlings was at the radio console. When Tracy asked how things were going, Dan handed over the clipboard showing the morning assignments. Bubba had called in sick again. The other deputies had to double up.

Tracy was disgusted. "Get him on the phone," she instructed Dan. "Tell him to be here at seven tomorrow morning, ready to work, or else have the funeral home send me a certified copy of his death certificate. I've had it with him!"

"No more Ms. Nice Gal?" Dan grinned.

"No more Ms. Nice Gal," Tracy muttered, stomping out of the office with Jerry at her heels.

Bubba Crowley showed up the following morning, shambling and bleary eyed. He wore a dirty parka over his rumpled uniform. "The doctor says I shouldn't be out of bed yet," he groused.

"Which doctor is that? Hollings or the new man who opened that clinic at Brenner's Crossing?" Tracy reached for the phone.

"I been going to this sawbones in Pueblo, little lady."

"Name and number?"

"He doesn't have a phone yet. He, ah——"

"A physician without a telephone? Oh, come on, Crowley!"

"Actually, he's what you call a wholistic practitioner."

Tracy eyed him pitilessly. "What does this holistic practitioner say is wrong with you?"

Crowley seemed relieved that Tracy had stopped pressing him for a name. "I got this here infection I picked up on the job and—"

"It's terminal, of course," Tracy interrupted him.

"Terminal?" Crowley stared at her blankly.

"Terminal—meaning a limit or an end or, in the medical sense, a condition that cannot be reversed. 'Term' is the prefix for 'terminate,' a synonym for the verb 'fire.' Consider yourself terminated, Crowley."

He drew himself erect. "Hey, you hold on! You can't fire me. My uncle ain't going to like it!"

"You're breaking my heart."

"I kid you not, little lady. You got to go on living in this here town. Besides, Vince Emmerling is taking over in a couple of weeks and he'll see that I'm put back to work."

"Oh? I've got news for you. Vince doesn't have any use for you, either. Now give Mr. Rawlings your equipment and get out of my sight!"

"Just a damn minute! I—"

"Dan!" Her temporary deputy stepped into the doorway. "Dan, Mr. Crowley is going to give you his gun, his badge and his keys. Give him a receipt and show him the way out."

Crowley's chunky cheeks turned redder than usual. "You're making a big mistake!"

"No way," Tracy said confidently, shaking her head. "I'm *correcting* a big mistake. I should have done this long ago."

After Crowley had left the building, Dan came to Tracy's door and grinned. "Feel better now, sheriff?"

She looked up at him, guiltily. "I've never fired anyone before. Does it always make you feel this good?"

"Not as a rule. But Bubba is the exception to the rule."

That night there was a special report on the television news about a political upheaval in subSaharan Africa. The report made only a passing reference to a country called Kagera, where an internal power struggle was in progress, but it was enough to bring Tracy bolt upright on the couch, hanging on to every word. She found it hard to sleep that night.

The next morning Vince called again with another invitation to supper. She couldn't decline this time. He was much too nice a man. She promised to see him that night.

Midway through the news reports later in the day, there was more on the Kagera revolt. Loyalist troops were locked in a fierce battle with rebel forces near the capital. The State Department had recommended evacuation of American oil-drilling crews, along with an unspecified number of technical consultants. Then the jungle scenes gave way to a beer commercial.

The phone rang and Tracy jumped to her feet. Ingrid got there first, said hello, listened, handed the receiver to Tracy.

"Mrs. Hannon?" The voice was strained and trembling.

"Yes?"

"This is Laura Emmerling. I'm afraid—" there was a choking sound "—we'll have to put off our dinner. I'm at Parkview Episcopal Hospital in Pueblo. Vince is in intensive care."

Tracy felt a numbness in her throat. "What happened?"

"The doctor thinks it was a heart attack. We got him here just in time. A few minutes later..." Her voice trailed off.

"Is there anything I can do—anything at all?"

"There's not anything anybody can do now except pray."

It wasn't until the following morning that Jerry Latimer told her what had happened. Bubba Crowley had gone over to see the sheriff-elect. They'd quarreled, and an hour later Emmerling had collapsed with chest pains and was rushed to the hospital.

"If Crowley ever walks in here again, I'll kill him with my bare hands!" Tracy fumed. "Don't let him get near me!"

"Let me handle it, sheriff." Jerry's tone made it clear he intended to do just that.

He was already in the office when Tracy and Ingrid walked in on Thursday morning. He looked up from his *Rocky Mountain News* and grinned. "There's a sign at the city limits that gives the population of Henryville," he said. "What's the figure?"

"Six thousand, four hundred and nine," Tracy replied. She remembered it well. It had been the same for years, ever since she'd come to town. The number was burned in her memory.

"Better get somebody to change it to six thousand, four hundred and eight. Bubba has decided to relocate in California. In fact, he moved out this morning."

Tracy smiled. "You helped him make up his mind?"

"It was the least I could do, sheriff."

That night, the news on television reported an abrupt end of the Kagera rebellion. For some unexplained reason, the rebels' munitions dump, which contained equipment whose value could only be speculated, blew sky high,

scattering debris over the western outskirts of the belea-
guered capital.

Tracy's phone rang at one the next morning.

"Tracy?"

"Shane!"

"I'm coming home. Leave a light in the window."

# Chapter Eleven

Tracy had never been happier. She and Shane had loved and laughed, gone places and done things, shared secrets and held hands, as if each needed assurance that the other was real and not an illusion.

He'd returned to her on Christmas Eve, brightly wrapped boxes under each arm, just as he'd come to her hotel in Denver. This time he didn't wait outside. When she opened the door, he pushed on past her, stacked his parcels in the hall, then spun around and planted a brief kiss on her lips. "Merry Christmas! Ho-ho-ho!"

Tracy stood in the open doorway, shaking her head. "Bah humbug!" she muttered through lips quivering with suppressed laughter. "Is that all I get after your big disappearing act?"

"You want more?" He reached into a pocket of his trench coat, slipped out a roll of Lifesavers and discreetly thumbed one free.

"You don't buy me off with candy," she scolded. Her eyes fixed on his, she wrinkled her nose as she sniffed at him. "The truth will out! You've been smoking those wretched little cigars again, haven't you?"

Shane popped a Lifesaver into his mouth. "You're supposed to read me my rights before you start making wild accusations."

"*What* rights? Condemned men have no rights." She held out her right hand. "Give me the evidence and I might be willing to entertain a plea bargain."

Shane sighed, dug into an inside pocket and surrendered an open package of cigars. Tracy took it with her left hand but kept her right hand extended. "Keep going," she said. He brought out an unopened package and handed it over. She looked at it, then at him. He sighed again and came up a with third package, which he dropped into her waiting hand.

"So help me, that's the lot," he said.

Without taking her eyes off him, Tracy placed the cigars on the hall table. "I don't know," she said skeptically. "What in the world am I going to do with you?"

He raised her hands to his lips and kissed her fingertips. "Is the condemned man allowed a last statement?"

"I'm all ears."

"I love you, sheriff."

She could play the game no longer. Tears of joy glistened in her eyes as she moved into his arms, her open mouth on his, her fingers digging possessively into his shoulders. She lifted one foot and kicked the front door shut.

"This has been the longest two weeks of my life," she said finally, tilting back her head and looking into his eyes. "I want to know *everything*. Is Alfy all right? Did you get all your people out? What about—"

He touched a finger to her lips to silence her. "Everybody came home in good shape. But let's talk about it later." He kissed her again on the mouth, lightly this time. "In fact," he murmured, "let's not talk at all for a while."

"WHY DON'T YOU PACK a bag and we'll get out of here for a few days?" Shane suggested as they sat at her kitchen table drinking coffee, early on Christmas morning.

Tracy took a deep breath and let it out in a wistful sigh. "I can't go anywhere yet. I still have a job to do."

"Please, Tracy? I've given Ingrid the week off. Dan and Jerry can hold down the fort."

"All right," she said.

A short time later she came downstairs wearing the clothes he'd bought for her in Denver: the tan corduroy jacket, brown turtleneck and skirt and brown boots. "The last time I had this outfit on, I ended up with two black eyes," she reminded him. "What do you suppose will happen this time?"

He shrugged. "Who knows? Maybe three black eyes."

"Shane?"

He looked at her.

"Shane, Vince has asked me to fill in for him until he gets back on his feet. It'll be a month at least, maybe even two months. The county needs me."

"I need you, too, Tracy. So does TWS."

"Shane, I . . ." The words wouldn't come. They were words that would only get in the way.

He smiled at her. It wasn't his little-boy smile, but a smile that said he understood what was troubling her. "You feel you have an obligation, don't you?"

She nodded.

"We'll keep our extra people on the job until Emmerling is ready to take over. Okay?"

"Okay," she said. She started for the phone in the dining room. "Before we go, I want to talk to my folks in Florida. It's Christmas, and they'll be calling here later. They'll be worried if they don't get an answer."

"Later, sweetheart." He picked up the suitcases standing by the door. "Trust me, huh? I promise you can talk to them later."

"Shane—" She didn't finish. Trust him, he'd told her. And she did. Completely.

That was at seven o'clock in the morning. Five hours later the TransWorld Systems Learjet that had been standing by at Pueblo Municipal Airport was touching down at Lakeland, Florida. And it wasn't until the copilot opened the cabin door and lowered the ladder that Tracy realized where they were.

"You're insane!" she bubbled delightedly to Shane. "We can't just go barging in on them..."

"Sure we can. You're their only child and I'm your very good friend. Besides, you sent them a telegram."

*"I did?"*

"Sure you did. You said you were bringing a surprise."

Shane hit it off immediately with Richard and Verna Wells. Tracy's father, a retired insurance broker, had served in the Navy during the Korean War and had made it a point to follow the service careers of Naval Academy graduates who'd distinguished themselves. "Weren't you the Keegan who—"

"You have a lovely place here," Shane said self-consciously, staring out the window at the orange grove behind the house.

The older man laughed. "I can take a hint, my boy. You don't want to talk about it, and I can't blame you. But you did your country proud."

"I did what I was paid to do," Shane said. Absently, he reached for an inside pocket of his jacket.

Tracy, sitting cross-legged on the floor at his feet, held out her right hand. With a plaintive sigh, Shane turned over his cigars.

Richard Wells chuckled. "That's not a good sign. She's telling us she has you trained."

*Never,* Tracy thought. *I wouldn't stand a chance. And I wouldn't want to, anyway.*

The next day they flew to Boston to visit Shane's sister, Mindy, who met them at the airport with her physician husband and their nine-year-old twins. Tracy found herself wholly captivated by Mindy, a dark-eyed and delicately featured beauty.

The two women hugged, and then Mindy looked gravely at Shane. "I've changed my mind," she announced. "I'm going to stay in Boston and get acquainted with Tracy."

"You can get acquainted tonight, Min," Shane said in an equally firm tone. "Tomorrow morning you and Carlos and the kids are going to be on a plane for Jamaica."

"But I don't *want* to go to Jamaica!"

"You'll love it. It'll do you good to get away from this rotten climate for a week." He glanced at his brother-in-law for support. "You're a doctor, Carlito. Tell your bride about the therapeutic effects of warm sun, sandy beach and swaying palms."

Carlos threw up his hands. "I try. Believe me, I try. She is one stubborn woman."

"Can't you and Tracy go with us?" Mindy asked.

"Another time—I promise. Don't worry, you won't be lonely. There are some people I want you to meet in Jamaica. Their name is Wells. You'll like them."

Tracy stared at Shane. He gave her a look that said, in coolly eloquent silence, *later*.

Later came when the two of them were seated on the floor in front of the fire in Mindy and Carlos's living room. It was well past midnight, and the rest of the family had gone to bed.

Tracy peered over her shoulder to make sure they were alone. She then raised the question that had been on her mind all afternoon. "What's this about Jamaica?"

Shane didn't bat an eyelash. "Actually, it's a friend's place in the Virgin Islands."

"You've lost me."

"Your folks and my sister and her family think they're going to Jamaica as my guests. Actually, they'll be vacationing in the Virgin Islands. I let them think it would be

Jamaica because I didn't want them telling anyone where they'd be."

"Why not?"

Shane reached into an inside jacket pocket and brought out cigars and matches that had escaped Tracy's earlier searches. Automatically she plucked them out of his hand and pitched them into the fire, where the matches puffed up in a little ball of yellow flame.

"Insurance," Shane said, glumly watching the matchbook turn black and disintegrate. "In five days, I sign over my company to its employees. You know what happens if I'm not around to sign those papers then—we've talked about it before." He placed his hands on her shoulders. "Tracy, I can take care of the two of us. But there are other people at risk because of their relationship to us. I intend to see that they're safe until any danger is past." He stared at the fire. "I can't save the world, but I can look after my own. I promise you."

Tracy put her hands over his. The tendons on the backs of his hands were rigid. "And nothing's going to happen to *you*?"

"I'm a survivor, Tracy. I thought you knew that."

"All I know is someone's trying to kill you, and he'll keep on trying until he succeeds or until you stop him."

"That's exactly what's going to happen."

Tracy looked at him dumbly.

"I'm going to stop him," he said.

THE NEXT MORNING, after loading Mindy and her family aboard a plane for Miami, Shane followed the signs to the turnpike and headed west in their rented Trans Am.

"Where now?" Tracy inquired, not really expecting him to tell her. At times he could be maddeningly uncommunicative.

"Here and there," he said. He turned off the highway and wound through the back streets of Brookline, keeping a vigilant watch on the rearview mirror.

Thirty minutes later they'd exchanged the Trans Am for a Ford station wagon at a Hertz office in downtown Boston.

"I take it we're still headed here and there," Tracy said as they headed back onto the turnpike.

"We've been here. We're going there." He winked at her. "There's Fenway Park, where the Red Sox play. You like baseball?"

"It's all right, I suppose."

"Great game, baseball. Ahead on your left is Boston University, and over there you can get a glimpse of Harvard."

"Your brother went to Harvard, didn't he?"

Shane just nodded but said nothing more for several minutes. When they came in sight of the Waltham exit, he said, "I used to play baseball."

"I know. Football, too."

"You know what I like about baseball and football?"

"What?"

"They're orderly."

"Now I *know* you're out of your mind, Shane. Athletes, especially football players, go out on the field and some of them practically get maimed for life. You call that orderly?"

"Sure," he said, warming to the subject. "Organized sports are played by rules. You have to do certain things and not do certain things, or you get kicked out of the game. It's too bad life can't be like that...."

That afternoon, they checked into a white clapboard, Revolution-era inn in Framingham. Shane remembered it from his childhood and assured Tracy that nothing had changed over the years. In an age of plastic and chrome, the inn was an anachronism: a refuge containing silver-blue wainscoting and solid brickwork, oak floors and hooked rugs, burnished pewter and canopied beds.

"It's quite lovely," Tracy said wistfully as they sipped hot toddies in the lamplighted tavern. "But we *do* have to get home. I owe it to the county to finish out my last few days in office."

"Relax," Shane said, reaching for one of his ever-available cigars. "What'll they do? Fire you?"

The next day, after a late lunch that followed a leisurely drive through the snow-splotched New England countryside, she tried again. "I've got a million things to do, Shane. For one thing, I've got to get the house fixed up if I'm ever going to sell it."

"Ingrid can see to it. I called her this morning. She's gone down to Henryville again and she's really enjoying herself."

"I've got to do something about Festus."

"Festus?"

"My horse." Tracy's cheeks crinkled in a guilty smile. "Actually, I'm deathly afraid of that beast, but the county sheriffs have always ridden horses in parades. People would have taken a dim view if I'd broken with tradition."

Shane took an envelope from his jacket pocket and scribbled a note to himself. "Maybe we could put him out at the ranch. I was thinking about buying some horses. That would give our visitors something to do besides learning to get along with one another."

Tracy made one last attempt. "I'm out of office as of Monday, and I've simply got to get my books in order."

"Jerry Latimer has a degree in accounting—among his many other talents. I'm sure the commissioners will be more than satisfied." He glanced down at the luncheon check, then reached for his billfold. "Your obligations are being met. Trust me."

The following day, Tracy tried another tack. When they went to their room after breakfast, she started packing.

Shane at once began gathering up his own things. "I've been stalling because I've wanted to keep you out of harm's way as long as possible," he announced. "But you've got a mind of your own, and I respect that. I'll have the Learjet pick us up in Worcester. Fair enough?"

"Fair enough," she said, kissing him on the cheek, loving him more than ever.

And so they went home. To their appointment with The Ragman.

IT HAD SNOWED again the night before New Year's Eve, and the bedroom windows were dusted with dry flakes that piled up in the bottom corners of the frosted panes and clung there before collapsing of their own weight and swirling away on the wind. Outside, the sullen gray of the dawn reluctantly began to give way to shafts of sunlight poking through gunmetal clouds.

Eyes only half open, Tracy lay on her side in bed, the down comforter tucked up under her chin. She looked across at the window, seeing only the sunlight and not the gray, only the promise and not the past. One day to go, she thought. One more day and she and Shane could become normal people living normal lives, free from worry that someone wanted to kill them.

Without turning, she reached behind her to touch him, to take courage in his nearness.

He wasn't there.

"Shane?" she murmured, sitting up and running her fingers through her sleep-mussed hair.

No answer.

She swung her legs over the side of the bed and thrust her feet into furry white slippers. Her robe had fallen to the floor, and she retrieved it and put it on. As she straightened up, she glanced out the window at the street in front

of the house. There was a clear spot on the asphalt pave-
ment where Shane had parked his M.G. the night before.

*Oh, good God!* Tracy thought, knowing instinctively
where he'd gone. *The man is out of his mind!*

She hurried downstairs and, clutching the robe around
her, stepped out onto the porch, where the thermometer
informed her it was five degrees below zero. Shivering in
the numbing cold, she waved at the Blazer parked across
the street, its exhaust a billow of cottony white against the
early morning gray. Jerry Latimer climbed down from the
cab and trotted over to the porch.

"How long ago did he leave?" she demanded.

"About an hour, Tracy."

"Did anyone go with him?"

Jerry shook his head. "I wanted to call Dan, but Shane
told me not to disturb him. He said he could take care of
himself." Jerry sounded as if he was reciting the facts and
wasn't at all happy about the situation.

"You might as well come in and warm up. I'm going to
get dressed."

She ran upstairs and put on a heavy sweater, wool slacks
and fur-lined boots. She refused to let herself think about
what sort of trouble Shane might find himself in.

She was downstairs in three minutes, bundled up in her
loden coat and searching for her mittens. Jerry was in the
kitchen, warming his hands over the stove.

"I'll be right back," Tracy announced, winding a long,
green-and-blue plaid muffler around her neck and fishing
in her purse for her car keys as she headed for the front
door.

"I'm going with you," Jerry said, following her out of
the house. "It's pretty slick on the road. We'd better take
the Blazer. We might need a four-wheel drive."

Tracy said nothing as they headed out of town with Jerry
at the wheel. He turned onto the gravel road beyond the
mill, the truck's heavy-treaded tires occasionally spinning

in the fresh snow as the Blazer rumbled up the hill to the ridge road.

Shane was just returning from his run, his feet pounding along the frozen dirt road, his arms swinging, his breath a swirl of white before his face.

Tracy threw open the door of the Blazer and jumped out almost before Jerry had brought the vehicle to a sluing halt. She planted herself in Shane's path, alongside the ankle-deep tracks he'd made when he'd headed out. Breathing hard, Shane kept running, closing the distance between them in pile-driving strides. When it seemed he surely would crash into her, he swerved, slowing for the merest fraction of a second to brush a frosty kiss across her left cheek.

Tracy wheeled about and tried to grab his arm, but was unable to get a grip on him. "You come back here this instant, Shane!" she shouted.

He kept on running.

"Shane!"

Without turning to look back at her, he raised his right hand in a clenched-fist salute.

"Idiot!" she growled, following him at a fast walk, the Blazer close at her heels.

She caught up with him at the grove where he'd parked the M.G. He already had his thermos out and was pouring coffee for her. "I don't know about this stuff," he said, handing her the cup. "I didn't want to make noise and wake you, so I stopped at the Kachina and had them fill the thermos. Looks kind of weak."

Tracy eyed him darkly. "If you're so damned considerate, you might at least have left a suicide note."

Shane reached under the tonneau cover of the M.G. and brought out one of his packets of cigars. "Nobody's lurking around with a rifle, Tracy. I borrowed your binoculars and checked the hillside before I set out. A few deer tracks—period."

Tracy took the cigars and dropped them into her coat pocket. "I suppose you also checked out the M.G.?"

He motioned to the area around the sports car. "No need. You can see for yourself. One set of footprints in the snow, and they're mine. And one set of tire tracks—mine, too."

"I still don't like it. You've got only one more day until you sign over the company. Why take a chance with our lives?"

"*Our* lives?"

"What happens to you happens to me."

Shane took a long pull at his thermos. "I came up here today because I wanted to run, and I wanted to do it here. I have a sentimental attachment to this road. I don't like some faceless son of a bitch with a rifle telling me what I can and cannot do. I'm not going to be pushed around."

Tracy studied his face. She'd come to know his strengths and weaknesses. She knew he could be every bit as stubborn as she, stubborn to the point of obstinacy when precious principle was involved. But this time his stubbornness was marked by a fatalism that made her tremble.

He mistook her reaction. Setting down his thermos on the front fender of the M.G., he pulled her into his arms and held her tight. "You're freezing, sweetheart. Let's go into town and find some breakfast, huh?"

Tracy glanced warily at the open M.G. "I don't want to sound like a nag, but can't you buy a hardtop for that thing?"

Shane laughed. "That's TransWorld property. When the company goes, it goes. Maybe somebody else can work out the last few bugs in the electronics. Come on." He steered her toward the Blazer. "If you're cold, let's see if we can trade off with Jerry."

Jerry was already out of the truck, studying the hillside. "Before we head in, I want to take a look around," he said in a low voice, as if afraid his words would carry.

Shane frowned. "Did I miss something?"

Jerry shook his head. "I just have a spooky feeling." He ducked into the cab of the Blazer and brought out a shotgun. "The two of you sit. I won't be long." His shotgun cradled in his right arm, he set out west on the ridge road, hugging the line of trees, scrutinizing the slopes on either side of the road.

Tracy could tell that Shane was uncomfortable with the idea of staying behind while someone else took the chances. She put her hand on his arm, but said nothing.

Shane helped her into the truck and climbed in beside her. Peeling off her mittens, Tracy rubbed her hands in the warm air pouring out of the heater. "How do you manage it?"

"Manage what?"

"Going on day after day, week after week, always a target, always wondering if some lunatic is lining up his sights on you. I'm a nervous wreck."

He shrugged. "It goes with the territory, Tracy. I knew what I was getting into when I left government service ten years ago. I was sticking my neck out, financially and personally, in what was then pretty much a virgin field. I convinced myself that the greater the risks, the greater the rewards. When you hire out to solve someone else's problems, you automatically acquire a few of your own." He put an arm around her shoulder. "Don't sweat it. As of tomorrow, it's a moot question. The minute I sign over TransWorld, nobody has any reason to want to kill me."

"After tomorrow what will we be doing—the two of us? We really haven't talked much about it."

"I don't know. Maybe fly to Galveston and pick up the boat and head out into the Gulf—do the Caribbean and hit all those picture-postcard islands. Did you ever sail?"

Tracy shook her head.

"You'd love it. In good weather, there's just enough work to keep you in shape, and there's all sorts of time for watching sunsets, contemplating your navel, and plain old daydreaming."

"It sounds wonderful, but it also sounds like running away from real life. Besides, I've got to find a job."

"You've got a job—personnel director at Trans-World."

She smiled. "It wouldn't be much fun without you."

"So maybe I *won't* go sailing." Leaning forward, he used the sleeve of his sweatshirt to wipe the condensation from the inside of the windshield. "I wonder what's keeping Jerry. Maybe I should take a look." He switched off the ignition, opened the door and stepped down into the snow. "Stay here where it's warm."

"Don't be so bossy," Tracy said resolutely, following him out of the truck. "I'm going with you."

They were scarcely twenty feet from the two parked vehicles when they saw Jerry striding toward them along the road.

"No problem," he assured them, glancing strangely at Shane. "I found a couple of guys camping west of here. I checked them out. They seem harmless enough."

"They're probably escapees from the state hospital in Pueblo," Tracy observed. "Nobody in his right mind would be up here camping out in this kind of weather."

"To each his own," Shane said with a shrug. He dug into a pocket in his cutoffs and came up with a set of keys, which he tossed to Jerry. "You mind driving the M.G.? The sheriff's on strike until I get a top for it."

Jerry chuckled. "Sure. I've always wanted to take it for a spin. It growls like it's got a caged lion under the hood."

"You should have asked. It's been sitting out there in the maintenance yard at the ranch, waiting for somebody to give it a workout." Draping his parka over his shoulders, he led Tracy toward the Blazer. "The sheriff and I will go home in heated comfort. You can freeze your buns off."

When they were seated again in the truck, Tracy half-turned and put her hand on his shoulder. "What's the matter, darling?"

He glanced at her. "Everything's fine."

"I saw that look Jerry gave you."

Shane turned the key in the ignition, and the engine rumbled to life. "Just out of curiosity, I want to have a look at those campers." He reached inside his sweatshirt and brought out a heavy, snub-nosed revolver holstered there. He checked the cylinder, then dropped the pistol into the right-hand side pocket of his parka.

"Look," Tracy said, "if you're worried, let's radio for backup. We don't have to go charging in there—"

"It's probably nothing."

Tracy twisted around and saw Jerry sink down into the driver's seat of the M.G. They had traveled only a short distance from the parked sports car. "Even so," she said, "I—" Her words were lost in a blinding flash of orange and yellow flame as the M.G. disintegrated before her eyes.

In the ear-ringing silence that followed the explosion, Tracy instinctively grabbed at Shane, her rigid fingers digging into his right shoulder, wild thoughts tumbling through her brain. *It's him . . . oh, God, it's him! No, it can't be! He's here and I'm with him, touching him! He's here, not there in the middle of that boiling cloud of flame and smoke.* "Shane!" she screamed.

He snatched up the microphone. "TWS One to K double A six-oh-six. Do you copy?" His voice was calm, deadly cold.

"K double A six-oh-six," Dan Rawlings said. "That's affirmative, TWS One."

"K double A six-oh-six. Trouble on the ridge road. Latimer's been taken out by a car bomb. Get some men from the ranch and have them work their way up the road from the west. Nobody gets out of the area.''

"Affirmative, TWS One. Stand by.'' The radio speaker in the Blazer was silent for a half-minute, then, "They're rolling, TWS One. Anything special to look for?''

"Possibly a couple of campers, but there may be others. I don't know for sure. The bomb was a remote-controlled device, so they'll have some sort of transmitter with them.''

"Your location, TWS One?''

"Two hundred yards west of the point where the main access road crests at the ridge, behind the mill. It might be a good idea to send me some backup.''

"Pederson just came in. I'll have her work the radio and I'll join you. Stay on this channel, TWS One.''

Tracy was still twisted in her seat, looking out the rear window of the Blazer, sickened by the sight of the broken bits of wreckage. She was aware Shane was squeezing her right hand and talking to her, but his words didn't register.

Shane reached up with his left hand and gently turned her head until she was looking at him. "Tracy, listen to me. I want—''

She buried her face in his shoulder and began sobbing. This time both his hands pressed against her cheeks and eased her head upright. "Snap out of it, Tracy! You've got a job to do. Are you listening to me?''

She looked straight into his eyes and nodded silently.

"I know how you feel about guns,'' he said, his tone crisp, "but let me ask you this: have you ever fired one before?''

She shook her head.

"All right, sweetheart,'' Shane said, reaching down with his right hand and bringing out his revolver. "I'm going to give you a crash course.'' He pressed the fingers of her right hand around the grip of the revolver. "Take this and go duck down behind those rocks over there. Stay put. If anyone gives you trouble, point the gun at him and squeeze the trigger. Are you with me?''

"But I . . . I don't . . ."

"Damn it, Tracy, don't give me any buts!" Shane said fiercely. "We'll argue morality later. Nobody's going to hurt you again. Now come on..." He threw open the door on his side of the Blazer and yanked her out after him. Leading her to the rocks, he pointed to where he wanted her to position herself, and then he stepped aside and let go of her hand. "Keep your eyes and ears open. If you have to shoot, hold the butt with both hands and look squarely at your target." He thumbed down a lever on the side of the pistol. "The safety's off, so be careful." He gave her a pecking kiss on the cheek.

"Where are you going?"

"Down the road, the way Jerry went. I'm leaving the truck here, but I'll take the keys. The truck's too good a target."

"No!" Tracy grabbed his arm, but he pushed her hands away and shoved her back between the rocks.

"Remember, keep your head down," he instructed her.

"Wait for Dan!" she pleaded. "You don't even have a gun."

"Do as I say!"

"No! I'm going with you!"

Glowering fiercely, he stabbed a rigid forefinger at her. "I swear to God, Hannon, if you don't stay put—"

His angry expression was a splash of ice water against her shock-dulled consciousness. "You'll *what*?" she asked defiantly.

He turned and set off on a run. Then he was gone, darting through the trees, his open parka flapping loosely around the tops of his cut-off jeans.

Tracy slumped against the rocks. *Damn him! He's going off after some killers with nothing but his bare hands, and there's not a thing I can do to stop him. He's not just proving something to me, he's proving something to himself as well.*

She slipped down into the opening in the rocks and crouched, both hands clutched around the grip of the revolver, trying not to think about Jerry. If it hadn't been Jerry in the M.G., it would have been she and Shane. She was glad it hadn't been them, and the thought made her feel guilty. *Why did anyone have to die?*

Raising herself until she could barely see over the jagged tops of the rocks in front of her, Tracy surveyed the road, east and west. All she could see was the empty road and bleak, snowswept slope, a picture-postcard image of a winter-locked wilderness. Security men from the ranch would be coming up the foot trail from the west, she knew. Dan would be on the scene any minute. There was no way the killers could escape. No way at all.

*Please, Shane,* she prayed, *be careful.*

She ventured another peek over the rocks. The road was still deserted in either direction. Just as she was about to duck down again, she saw Dan's dark blue Ford zoom up onto the ridge road from the gravel access road. He made a skidding turn to the west, and Tracy leaped out from between the rocks and ran to the road.

"Shane's gone after them!" she shouted as Dan stopped and rolled down his window.

"He knows what he's doing, Tracy," Dan assured her, glancing impassively at the still-smoldering wreckage of the M.G. "How long has he been gone?"

"Since right after he talked to you on the radio—ten minutes, no more. He gave me this gun—" she held up the pistol "—and told me to stay behind those rocks. I'm getting worried."

"Get back over there and I'll have a look," Dan said, starting to pull away from where Tracy was standing.

"Dan, he's unarmed..."

Dan grabbed for his radio microphone. "I'll get someone to block the access road at the highway. Keep an eye out, Tracy."

Less than a minute later, before she could settle back down behind the rocks, she heard popping noises off in the distance. She took another look.

Nothing.

No, there *was* something. A car was moving along the ridge from the west. She caught a glimpse of it through the trees, and then it came around the bend in full view. It was Dan's Ford, traveling at high speed, spewing up snow and loose rocks as it roared eastward.

Straightening up, Tracy slipped out from behind the rocks and hurried toward the road. Maybe someone had been hurt. Maybe it was Shane. Maybe they were taking him to the ranch dispensary. She had to find out, had to be with him.

She quickened her pace and reached the side of the road while the Ford was still fifty yards away. Looking at the oncoming car, she realized something was wrong. The windshield was a silvered cobweb of cracked glass, and the vehicle was yawing wildly from one side of the road to the other.

Tracy stepped back, and the Ford dipped down into and then up out of the shallow borrow pit on the downhill side of the roadway. As it thundered past her, nearly sideswiping the parked Blazer, Tracy had a fleeting glimpse of the two figures in the front seat. Both were wearing brightly colored ski masks, and she could see the blue barrel of a rifle jutting out of the window in the passenger side.

Instinctively she jumped farther back, away from the cold wash of air left in the wake of the car. She stumbled on a rock hidden under the snow and toppled over onto the frozen ground just as the crack of a rifle shot erupted from the car window. She felt more than heard a bullet whistle past her head.

Without thinking about what she was doing, Tracy sat up and raised the pistol. She planted the heels of her boots securely against the rock over which she'd stumbled and rested both hands on one knee, her left hand closed around the right. Taking aim at the left rear tire of the fleeing sedan, she began squeezing off shots, one after another, the recoil sending jolting shock waves through her wrists.

As the Ford began its turn onto the access road a hundred yards to the east, Tracy could hear a dull *thump* as the left rear tire blew out, sending the vehicle into a violent skid that spun it around and slammed its rear end into a towering snowdrift. The driver gunned the engine and rocked the Ford back and forth between low gear and reverse, trying desperately to force the sedan onto the packed tracks of the road.

Scrambling to her feet, Tracy started running toward the car, crouching low, keeping a wary watch for the rifle barrel to appear out of the passenger window. She could smell the transmission fluid overheating, and burning rubber as the rear tires clawed at the now-exposed gravel, sending the car lurching a few inches forward, then a few inches backward.

She heard another shot and felt a slug tear through the loose folds of her jacket, just above her right hip. Throwing herself face-down onto the road, she rolled over quickly and dropped into the borrow pit. She kept moving, crawling now, the pistol clutched tightly in her right hand. She couldn't see the Ford from her refuge in the ditch, but she could hear the whine of its engine.

When she was almost abreast of the car and still hidden from view of its occupants, she peeked over the top of the ditch. One of the two men, the passenger, was outside the Ford, pushing at it from behind as the driver continued rocking the rear wheels. The passenger was a small man, and he looked almost childlike in his garish ski mask and white coveralls. His rifle was nowhere in sight.

Tracy jumped to her feet and held the pistol out in front of her with both hands. "Both of you—away from the car!" she shouted. "And get those hands up!"

The Ford's engine roared again, and this time the vehicle managed to move forward a full two feet before locking up. The sudden surge forward caught the man outside by surprise, and he slipped and fell behind the car. A second later the driver shifted into reverse and sent the Ford slamming backward, crushing his partner's legs under the rear wheels.

Hearing the man's scream but not realizing what was happening, Tracy dropped down into the borrow pit and rested her pistol on the edge of the pit, ready to fire again. The body of the passenger, now crammed into the depression made by the spinning wheels, was enough to supply the added traction necessary to bring the car out of the drift. As Tracy watched in horror, the Ford lurched ahead, hesitated a second—as if the driver had just become aware of what had happened—and then spun around, facing downhill, at a right angle to the drift from whose clutches it had just escaped.

Again the car came to a stop. Tracy wondered if the driver was going to jump out and try to help his companion. His intentions were far less charitable. He leaned over in the seat, and she could hear the angry chattering of a submachine gun. The awful truth sank in. He was killing his own accomplice.

Her heart pounding furiously, Tracy rose from the borrow pit. She had to stop the execution. She was too late. The car was moving again, downhill, weaving and fishtailing, crazily off-balance with its flat tire.

Holding the pistol in both hands, Tracy took careful aim at the rear window and squeezed the trigger. She braced herself for a repeat of the now-familiar roar of the gun.

This time there was only a heavy click.

She tried again.

Another click.

Still holding the pistol, she ran after the Ford. She could see two cars converge on the spot where the access road led off from the state highway. One of the cars was coming from the direction of town. It was a patrol car, and its roof lights were flashing and its siren wailing. The other car, coming from the direction of the ranch, was a light blue Volvo.

The patrol car and the Volvo blocked the intersection with a V of metal, the front bumpers angled at the access road and the oncoming Ford. The drivers jumped out and crouched behind their doors, shotguns at the ready.

The driver of the fleeing Ford jammed on his brakes and skidded to a halt thirty yards from the roadblock. He, too, got out of his car and immediately opened up with his submachine gun, stitching a horizontal pattern of holes across the windshields and windows of the vehicles before him. Then he turned and ran up the road, toward Tracy.

Tracy stopped and raised her pistol. ''Drop it!'' she screamed at the top of her lungs, training the muzzle of her empty revolver on the ski-masked figure who was headed straight at her.

He kept coming, the barrel of his weapon swinging up and to the right until it was pointed directly at her.

Then a single shot rang out. Tracy sank to her knees on the snow-packed road and dropped the gun....

# Chapter Twelve

The Ragman felt nothing. He was beyond pain, drifting silently through a tunnel of memories: his childhood on the streets of Miami's Little Havana...being beaten within an inch of his life after having been caught picking the wrong pocket...the iron clang of the detention center doors...the education he'd received there, the friends he'd made—no, not friends, for he had no friends, just associates—his first love, and his first killing, which were one and the same...the pleasant realization that there was money to be made from murder, a lot of money.

He began to hear voices, snatches of conversation.

"...lodged in the spine. Can't move him..."

"...talk to him?"

"...let you know...specialist...Denver..."

The Ragman knew his eyes were open. He could see light and vague shapes. The shapes were moving slowly.

"...do what you can...need to talk to him..."

He tried to focus, to make out the faces. Was that...yes, it was the woman! She was the one who had been his undoing. If only he hadn't become obsessed with killing her. That damnable woman! He tried to push himself up.

"...think he's trying to move..."

"...impossible...paralyzed..."

He had made one mistake after another, he knew. And he had made one mistake too many. Instead of trying to kill her on the road, he should have seized her as a hostage. Then he might have been able to force them to give him a plane and a pilot. The man would have agreed. The man loved the woman. Any fool could tell. . . .

"HE'S DYING," Shane said as he and Tracy stood outside the ranch dispensary talking to Alfy. "He's dying and he hasn't told us a thing. The bureau will run a fingerprint check, but it'll be too late. We still won't know who hired him."

Alfy slipped off his leather jacket and draped it over his shoulders, cape fashion. He was wearing jeans and a black knit sweater and he needed a shave. Shane's call had found him in bed, and he'd raced out to the airport and flown down to the ranch on one of the company's helicopters. "Give me a quick recap, eh?"

Shane told him the story, and when he had finished, Alfy made a hissing noise through clenched teeth. "The same M.G. we took that morning you went out running?"

"The same M.G. I know it had to be a remote detonation because no one got near the car when it was parked on the hillside. Our friend probably sneaked onto the ranch—or was let in—and planted the bomb while the car was in the maintenance yard."

Alfy glanced admiringly at Tracy. "It took the lady to stop him, eh?"

Tracy shook her head quickly. "I just delayed him. The people who came in on the canyon road actually shot him."

"The other fellow is dead?"

Shane nodded. "The getaway car ran over him, and our friend in there finished him off with his Uzi to keep him from talking."

"Nice people. Okay, *mon ami*, I will go in and see what I can get out of him." He patted an angular bulge under his sweater, and Tracy looked at him questioningly. He smiled. "No, sheriff, it is not a gun." He pulled up his sweater to show her the compact tape recorder fastened to his belt. "I may be a monster, but even I have my limits."

THE HAZE was clearing, his senses sharpening. He could hear things, little things: the gurgle of the liquid in the tubes that were stuck into his arm; the hum of a furnace blower somewhere in the building. He could feel things: a deep hurt in his back and legs; tentacles of pain that squeezed at his chest and his throat. He could see a dark-complexioned man standing over him, his unshaven face impassive.

"Go to hell," The Ragman said weakly.

His visitor smiled. "I probably shall. Save a place for me, eh? You will get there long before I do."

The Ragman closed his eyes and slept for what seemed to him a thousand years.

When he opened his eyes again, only minutes later, his visitor was still there.

"It is a shame," the man said. "I grieve for you. But, alas, I am the only one who will grieve."

The Ragman coughed, and the pain increased. "What do you mean?"

"I mean that you will die soon, and no one will know you are gone. You will rot in a potter's grave, with a simple John Doe on your headstone. A terrible irony for one so accomplished in his field, eh? I know I would not want my passing to go unnoticed. It would be as if I had never lived."

"Go to hell," The Ragman said again, closing his eyes.

He slept another thousand years, dreaming of the client and of the job that had gone wrong. And when he awakened, the man was still at his side.

"Time is fast running out," he said. "And so is your chance for immortality. Tell me, what is your name?"

"Luis Calderón," The Ragman said. "My name is Luis..."

IT WAS LATE AFTERNOON when Alfy came into the living room, poured himself a brandy, and settled down on the couch opposite Tracy and Shane. He placed his tape recorder on the coffee table. "The assassin is dead," he said wearily. "The specialist arrived from Denver, but there was nothing more he could do."

"Did you get anything out of him?" Shane asked.

"His every word is preserved on tape."

Tracy took a deep breath. "Did he tell you who hired him?"

The Belgian didn't seem to hear her. "His name is Luis Calderón, alias The Ragman, also alias Raul Fernandez. Our paths have crossed a dozen or more times in the past, although neither of us knew it. The Ragman is, or was, a professional killer. He worked through a middleman named Dimitri, who has his headquarters in Atlanta, Georgia. I am sure the FBI will be interested in Dimitri's operation. As best as I can determine, Dimitri arranged at least twenty assignments for The Ragman. You, *mon ami*—" he nodded to Shane "—were to be number twenty-one."

Tracy stood up. "But who at TransWorld paid him to kill Shane?" she demanded.

Alfy sighed. "I had to take it step by step. I had to appeal to his ego to start him talking and then gently guide him. I had to build up to the most important question of all, as far as the three of us are concerned. He would talk for a while, then drift off, then talk some more. Finally—" The Belgian shrugged.

Tracy and Shane waited.

"—he told me of meeting his last client on a ski lift at Vail, and of negotiating the price and terms of the agreement."

"Who was the client?" Shane asked.

"I do not know. He died with the name forming on his lips."

"I think I know," Tracy said. "I hope I can prove it."

IT WAS NEW YEAR'S DAY, a Sunday, and the man-made canyon of concrete, steel and glass that is Denver's Seventeenth Street was all but deserted in the frosty gloom of midmorning. Thirty stories below, the wind danced a drunken jig from one corner to the next, building rippled little drifts of snow and toying with them impatiently before knocking them down. There were few cars on the street this holiday morning and still fewer pedestrians on the sidewalk.

Tracy turned away from the floor-to-ceiling window from which she'd been looking down at the street and saw that Shane, who was sitting at one end of the long conference table, had closed the folder in front of him and was about to light a cigar. She went over to him, took the matchbook from his hands, tore off one of the matches and lighted it. "Go ahead—poison yourself," she muttered as he leaned forward, steadied her hand with his and lighted the cigar. "See if I care."

Shane eyed the cigar, then crumpled it and dropped the tattered remains into the black steel ashtray next to the file folder. "Psychological warfare, huh?" He smiled as he said it.

Tracy sat down next to him. "Just sharpening my skills at subtle intimidation. Did you bring the letter?"

He reached into the pocket of his shirt and handed over a folded envelope.

"Now let me have that photo."

He took out his billfold and gave her the ID photo she'd found in the rocks above the ridge road. He watched her slip the photo into a glassine envelope. Both envelopes went into her own folder. "I don't suppose you care to confide in me, sheriff?"

"*Ex*-sheriff," Tracy corrected him. "And no, I'll handle it my way. This is Hannon's first and last big case, and she's going to get all the mileage she can out of it!"

Shane shrugged. "Okay, you're calling the shots. Incidentally, I talked to Vince Emmerling on the phone last night. He's more than happy to let Ingrid handle things in your absence. He likes Ingrid. She reminds him of his favorite niece."

"You shouldn't have bothered him, Shane."

"He was glad to hear from me—especially when I told him TWS was making a two-hundred-and-fifty-thousand-dollar grant to the sheriff's department for new equipment and extra personnel. When that think tank conference center gets going, there'll be a whole bunch of new people settling down in Henryville, and your successor is going to need more manpower. Deep thinkers tend to get a bit rowdy when they start bending their elbows."

"Oh? What if the new management of TransWorld decides to drop the think tank?"

Ignoring the question, Shane unstrapped his wrist-watch and placed it on top of the file folder. "Ten o'clock," he said. "It's time."

As if on cue, the door leading to the reception area opened, and Alfy stepped into the conference room, accompanied by a tall, gaunt man about Shane's age. The tall man was lugging a bulging, well-worn, brown briefcase.

"Tracy, this is Greg Vinson, my attorney," Shane said by way of introduction. He didn't get up.

Vinson shook hands with Tracy, then took a seat across from her. Alfy sat down next to him. "We've talked on the phone, Mrs. Hannon," Vinson said.

"I remember."

The attorney looked at Shane. "You want to fill me in before the others get here, or do you want to surprise me again?" His mildly reproving tone was tempered with patience.

Shane laughed. "I just work here. This is Tracy's show."

Vinson sighed a who-am-I-to-ask sort of sigh and proceeded to light a cigar. Shane glanced at him, licking his lips.

"Our friends will be right along, boss," Alfy said. "My man in the garage buzzed me when they got into the elevator."

"They're together?"

Alfy nodded. "Brock took a cab out to Cherry Hills at eight this morning and had breakfast with our esteemed president. Then they got into MacManus's Cadillac and rode downtown together." The Belgian cocked an eyebrow at Shane. "You think it was a good idea to give them a chance to get their stories straight?"

"It doesn't matter," Shane said. He checked his watch. "Ten-oh-three. We might as well get the formalities over. Greg, I don't want to call anyone else in on this, so would you take the minutes?"

"I can do it," Tracy said, taking a legal pad from her folder. "My shorthand's rusty, but passable."

"A minor point of order," Vinson cut in. "If this is to be a formal meeting, Mrs. Hannon has to be duly elected secretary."

"So moved," Alfy said.

Shane looked at Vinson. "Do I hear a second?"

"Seconded."

"The majority shareholder hereby elects you, Tracy," Shane said.

At that moment Evan MacManus and Oliver Brock entered the conference room. Both nodded to Shane without speaking and took their places on either side of the conference table, MacManus next to Tracy, Brock alongside Alfy. Both men were well dressed and appeared very poised.

"Tracy has just been elected secretary," Shane announced.

Brock's bushy eyebrows rose. "What happened to Mrs. Hoyt?"

"I gave her the day off. Now, let's get down to business. We'll dispense with reading of the minutes. Everybody knows what we talked about last time: corporate reorganization. And that's one of the reasons we're here today. But first—" his fingers began tapping the folder in front of him "—I want to find out why you tried to do a number on me with that African deal." He looked at his executive vice president. "Oliver?"

Brock glanced down at his folded hands. "Nobody tried to do a number on you, Shane. The contract made a lot of sense. We would have been in the catbird seat if the revolution had succeeded. I planned to talk to you about it, but something always came up and it slipped my mind."

"We're not in business to play king-maker. It's happened before, Oliver. That deal in South America—you tried to sandbag the company on that one, too. I let it pass, figuring you'd simply made a mistake in the contract. Kagera was your second mistake. Sorry, Mr. Congressman, you're only allowed one mistake." He looked at Greg Vinson. "There's a clause in his contract that covers this. He can resign, or I can fire him. He has his choice."

Brock stood up. "You're off base, Shane. I think I'll talk to my own lawyer before I do anything."

"Sit down, Oliver. We're not finished."

Brock started for the door. Alfy was suddenly on his feet, blocking his way. "I think you better do as the man says, eh?"

Brock sat down.

"It seems we have a vacancy in the corporate structure," Shane observed. "Before we proceed, we might want to fill that vacancy."

Tracy caught his eye. "We might also want to wait," she said. "We might have more than one vacancy."

Shane settled back in his chair and laced his fingers across his chest. "You've got the floor."

Tracy stood up and directed her gaze at each of the men, one by one. "I'm sure you've all read the morning papers. You know what happened yesterday at the ranch. I see no need to rehash *that* part of it." She paused, choosing her words carefully. "But only one of you knows the whole story—and that, of course, would be the one who hired Luis Calderón. If Mr. Calderón's employer would care to make himself known, he can save himself the humiliation of having a county sheriff unmask him." She winked at Shane. "Pardon me—*ex*-sheriff."

No one spoke.

"All right." She looked at Alfy. "Would you bring it in, please?"

Alfy left the room and returned a moment later with a red duffel bag. He set it on Tracy's empty chair, then returned to his seat.

Tracy picked up her folder. "Luis Calderón and his employer met on a ski lift at Vail. The man didn't want Calderón to be able to identify him, so he wore goggles and a wool hat pulled down over his ears. He was naive. Calderón was quite good at tracing people.

"To make a long story short, a deal was struck—not to kill Shane, but to shake him up so badly that he'd get out of TransWorld and leave control to a management committee. With Shane out of the way, one prospective member of the management committee figured he could get away with murder." Again she paused and looked around at the five men. "If I'm going too fast for you, just tell me."

"You're doing fine, Tracy," Shane said.

Tracy opened the folder and glanced inside. "I searched the crime scene. I found two items of evidence—a fragment of a Vail ski-lift ticket and an identification photo of Shane." She held up the item for the others to see. "Ski-lift tickets are funny. Some people leave them dangling from their parkas like airplane baggage tags. Real status symbols, I suppose—something to show they've been around." She smiled. "I've been known to do the same thing myself."

She opened the duffel bag. "At any rate, I found another Vail lift ticket at a most unusual place—at the ranch house during the Christmas party." She reached into the bag, brought out a bright blue parka and placed it on the conference table. A lift tag was still attached to the zipper. "This is the parka worn that night by Oliver Brock."

The former congressman jumped to his feet, his face red with rage. "I've never been on a ski lift in my life!" he protested.

"I never said you had," Tracy said evenly. "You don't believe in exercise, as I recall. No, you borrowed the parka—" she looked squarely at the president of TransWorld Services "—from Evan MacManus. That night at the party you mentioned you hadn't come prepared for a Colorado winter. Remember?"

MacManus looked at the other men as if to appeal for support. "So the parka's mine. But even at a glance I can see that those torn tickets don't come close to matching."

Tracy nodded. "True, Mr. MacManus. But lift tickets are stamped with a date. The ticket on your jacket and the torn one bore the same date. Same date, same ski lift. Mr.

MacManus, you rode that lift the day you contracted with The Ragman!''

"That's ridiculous! Thousands of people were out skiing that weekend!''

"*What* weekend, Mr. MacManus? You haven't even taken a look at the date on the ticket yet!''

MacManus turned to Vinson. "You used to be a prosecutor, Greg. Do you want to tell this woman how weak a case she's got? She won't believe me.''

"No," Tracy said, "I don't believe you, Mr. MacManus. I don't believe *anything* you say. But I do believe *this*!'' From the folder she took out the glassine envelope containing Shane's ID photo. "This has your fingerprints on it.'' She reached back into the folder and brought out the envelope Shane had given her, holding it up so they all could see the letterhead. "And I do believe *this*! It's a notarized statement from the FBI lab, confirming that the prints are yours.'' She took another envelope from the folder and slapped it down on the table. The envelope bore the Mountain Bell letterhead. "And *this*! A list of calls from certain pay phones near the TransWorld building. The list doesn't mean much by itself, but it does when you add sworn affidavits from witnesses who saw you talk on those phones at specific times.''

Alfy leaned forward in his chair and placed his tape recorder on the table. "If you want more, there's always this statement from Calderón. Would you like to hear it, Evan?''

MacManus's shoulders sagged, and he slumped forward, his forehead pressed against the knuckles of his fists. At first Tracy thought he was having a heart attack. "I didn't want him killed—believe me," he said in a choking voice. "It was just something that got out of hand. I couldn't control The Ragman.''

Shane got up slowly, his jaw set, a look of sadness in his eyes. "Alfy, stay with him. Greg, it's a federal case, so call in the bureau. Tell them to see that ex-Sheriff Tracy Hannon gets credit for the collar.'' He left the room.

Tracy gathered up her things, wondering if it would be wise to intrude upon him at this moment. She'd half-imagined he'd blow up midway through her presentation and the session would have turned into a shouting match, maybe worse. But he'd remained deliberately cool. He had to be hurting inside, knowing how two trusted associates had turned against him.

Well, he still had friends, and he'd better believe it.

She left the conference room, went to his office and closed the door behind her. Shane was standing at the window, staring out at the low-hanging clouds over the mountains. She put her arms around him and rested her head against his back.

They stood that way for a long time, neither speaking. How long it was, she didn't know or care. Being with him, holding him—that was all that mattered.

After a while, he said, ''I see now what you wanted with that old FBI commendation letter. Nice bluff, but you didn't tell me you'd found a lift ticket on the rocks.''

''I didn't,'' she said. ''But I *did* get a photo of it.''

He smiled. ''And the letter from Mountain Bell?''

''A notice that the phone company would garnishee Bubba Crowley's salary if he didn't pay an overdue bill.''

''What about the photo? There were no prints on it, sheriff.''

''Bluff—pure bluff.''

''Nice. Remind me never to play poker with you and Alfy.''

She laughed. ''You like the way he fooled MacManus with the suggestion that Calderón had identified him by name?''

''I couldn't have done better, sheriff.''

"Ex-sheriff, if you please." She reached for his hands and realized he was holding an unlighted cigar. She plucked the cigar from his fingers and broke it in half.

"I love you," he said softly, watching her flip the ruined cigar into a wastebasket.

"Because I help you break your bad habits?"

"Because you're a good habit, Tracy." He turned and took her into his arms. "You're the best habit I'll ever have."

# JULIE ELLIS

**author of the bestselling**
*Rich Is Best* **rivals the likes of**
**Judith Krantz and Belva Plain with**

# THE ONLY SIN

It sweeps through the glamorous cities of Paris, London, New York and Hollywood. It captures life at the turn of the century and moves to the present day. *The Only Sin* is the triumphant story of Lilli Landau's rise to power, wealth and international fame in the sensational fast-paced world of cosmetics.

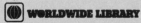